ALLIGATOR DANCE

SOUTHWEST LIFE AND LETTERS

A series designed to publish outstanding new fiction and nonfiction about Texas and the American Southwest and to present classic works of the region in handsome new editions.

GENERAL EDITORS: Kathryn Lang, Southern Methodist University Press; Tom Pilkington, Tarleton State University.

Alligator Dance

Stories by
Janet Peery

Southern Methodist University Press

DALLAS

Copyright © 1993 by Janet Peery
All rights reserved
Printed in the United States of America

FIRST EDITION, 1993

Requests for permission to reproduce material from this work should be sent to:
Rights and Permissions
Southern Methodist University Press
Box 415
Dallas, Texas 75275

The stories in this collection appeared first in the following publications: "South Padre" and "Daughter of the Moon" in *American Short Fiction;* "Alligator Dance" in *Quarterly West;* "The Waco Wego" in *Southwest Review;* "Mountains, Road, the Tops of Trees" in *The Chattahoochee Review;* "Nosotros" and "Whitewing" in *Shenandoah;* "Huevos" (as "Back Road to Brownsville") in *New Virginia Review;* "What the Thunder Said" in *Black Warrior Review;* and "Job's Daughters" in *Kansas Quarterly.*

Library of Congress Cataloging-in-Publication Data

Peery, Janet.
    Alligator dance : stories / by Janet Peery. — 1st ed.
        p.   cm.
    ISBN 0-87074-353-8.—ISBN 0-87074-366-x (pbk.)
    I. Title.
PS3566.E284A79   1993
813'.54—dc20   93-18694

For my parents,
Walter Albert and Joyce Davis Sawhill,
for the old, good steps they taught by heart;
for Joanna, Gretchen, and Bridget,
through whose spirited variations I have learned joy;
and for all the teachers—strangers, friends, or kin—
whose lives and work have helped me
study grace.

But where shall wisdom be found? and where is the place of understanding? Man knoweth not the price thereof; neither is it found in the land of the living.

—Job 28:12–13

CONTENTS

SOUTH PADRE

JUST below the northern line of Oklahoma lies a pleasant region, once part of an inland sea, where bluestem pastures rise from small draws of cottonwood and willow to cover cutbank hills of soil the color of a rusted plow blade. Wind blows strong across the land, flattening the grasses as though hurrying to other places with more for it to catch on. A quiet region, it encourages no scenery-hounds or gawkers, lets travelers keep their breath for more magnificent sights, but rewards those patient in its seasons with sand plums and red sumac, bees, wild grapes and clover, deer, and the sense that every now and then time holds still long enough to fix into memory. Jesse Folcher's farm—three hundred acres on the banks of a shallow sand-bed creek called Broken Moses—lay at its heart.

In April of his sixty-second year, Jesse stood at the edge of a field shot green with seedling wheat, looked across the furrows, and didn't see what he had always seen before—fat cattle, a bursting granary, the promise of another year. He saw instead the end of his own life, as near to him and suddenly as startling as the flush of blackbirds from the hedgerow at the field's boundary. He drove into town and sold off eighty acres, then bought an Airstream trailer. When November came, he left the farm in the care of his oldest son, and with his wife beside him in the Ford Fairlane, he headed down the highway toward the Texas Gulf, away from prairie winter. "Spring fever," Ida Grace said. "Early."

Snowbird, he called himself, and he smiled. He pressed the accelerator and set the cruise control. Aside from the time he'd spent on Saipan with the signal aircraft warning detachment, buzzed by overflights of Bettys and Zeroes (he didn't think that counted; everyone was enlisting), this trip was the most daring thing he had ever tried. He felt he had escaped.

"Hot," Ida Grace said on the second day of the drive, looking out at the scrubby hills around Austin, then, skeptically, "Cactus." She bundled the afghan she'd been knitting into a lawn-and-leaf bag and pushed it over the seat back.

Jesse nodded. "That over there is huisache."

He was surprised that the name of the shrub came to him. He remembered it from the science book he'd used when he taught school in Enid, before his father had died and he himself had gone back to work the farm.

"Not very pretty, is it?" Ida Grace leaned forward to slip her sweater from her shoulders. She folded it, then leaned back and closed her eyes. "It doesn't look right, somehow."

Sunlight streamed across her face and through her hair, still light brown at a time when her friends had gone gray. She wore it curled, round as a fluffy helmet, though Jesse longed for the fuller waves of their courtship. She was tall and spare, and she sat with her knees drawn up, feet laced into thick-soled, putty-colored shoes planted parallel on the floor. Nurse's shoes, he thought, remembering how they had met—she'd been the traveling nurse for their rural school district, and he'd taken a student to her health room.

As the car and trailer rounded a curve, her knees beneath her tan skirt swayed left, rebounded, threatening to come apart. She started, caught them, crossing her legs at the ankles. The gesture seemed oddly young, and it reminded him that she had been a pretty woman. She still was, he supposed, looking at her. They had been married forty years; he knew her movements and her

2

silences, but in that moment, with the sun full on her hair, he forgot those years and was struck by a sudden sense of oddity in time and place.

He flexed his hands on the steering wheel, as though to remind himself of who he was, and where. His hands were broad and capable, blunt-fingered, callused. He was proud of them. His arms, still tanned from summer work, were those, he thought, of a much younger man. He looked at himself in the rearview, surprised as always to find his face set in middle age, fleshier, softer than in memory, but he smiled at his own vanity, and was mildly comforted to find it still there, behind his eyes—a reckless, tender thing. Sleeping, he could tell by the slack way she held her mouth, Ida Grace shifted, her hip canted in an angle as familiar to him as his own hands.

After the Hill Country of central Texas, the land flattened out. He'd charted an inland route on purpose, so the surprise of the ocean would come upon them all at once. But the dun-colored landscape made him feel strangely heavy, low, as though he would have to drive uphill again to reach the Gulf. Ida Grace fidgeted with the air vents, worked the power windows: too hot, too cold. She sighed.

Outside Sarita, they stopped at a dusted-up convenience store. Jesse waited at a picnic table by a bumper-scarred palm tree while Ida Grace went inside. A rope of yellow plastic banners fenced a display of statuary. Donkey carts and bathtub virgins, she called them, but Jesse had stopped chuckling at her joke the third or fourth time she'd made it that day. He'd stopped pointing out signs that read "Welcome Winter Texans to the Magic Valley." He no longer tried to interest her in billboards about game fishing, in cantaloupes bigger than the watermelons they grew at home, in roadside citrus stands and fields of sugar cane. These things thrilled him, but he was irritated, now, waiting by the battered palm, that he was noticing not its exotic frill of fronds but the peeling brown debris beneath it.

"Pineapple pop," she said, crossing the parking lot toward him. She handed him a pink aluminum can. "I got you guava." She smiled. "I never dreamed they could make pop out of it."

"Sure," he said, heartened. He sipped his drink, thinking he remembered a taste something like it from his days at Schofield Barracks.

She sat beside him on the bench, then reached out to thump the trunk of the palm. "These aren't natural."

"Sure they are. They're all over the place."

"Native. Native's what I mean. They're transplants." She shook her drink can to give the soda more fizz, then sipped. "Pretty good. A little sweet, but good."

He wasn't ready to drop the subject of the palm trees. "Still," he said, standing to stretch, "the climate must be right. They grow everything down here."

"One hard freeze and poof . . ." She flicked her fingers off her thumb, then got up and walked to an oil drum to throw away the can.

"Think of it," she said, returning, making a shooing motion toward the drum, "bees and horseflies in the middle of November!"

It was dusk when they entered the marshy lowlands outside Port Isabel, the entry point to South Padre Island. Ida Grace dozed against the window. In the center of the road, across the median line, lay a huge snake. At first Jesse thought it was dead, but as the car drew closer he saw it, thick and black, appear to drag itself across the blacktop, sluglike, rather than move with the rapid undulations he was used to with the smaller snakes at home. The largest he had seen on the farm were the mean-tempered water snakes that nested in a stump along the Broken Moses. Those sometimes grew to six feet, big around as his arm. Sometimes, during spring flooding, he saw a ball of them dislodged and writhing in the stiller pools close to the bank, and once, with a rake handle, he'd hit one wrapped around a catalpa trunk, more to see what the snake felt like than to hurt it. He had been surprised by its bulk, at the thudding sound of wood against its girth, more muscular, less yielding even than the flanks of the Aberdeen Angus he sometimes nudged along with his basswood prod. This one looked twice the size of any he had seen before, and he didn't want the car to hit it. He tapped the horn, felt foolish when he remembered snakes couldn't hear. But the snake began to move faster, sliding onto the oncoming lane. In the sideview Jesse watched its blunt tail disappear into the marsh grass beside the road. He switched on the headlights. The road ahead was flat and clear, and he began to wonder if he had imagined the snake.

Ida Grace slept on, so he was alone when he entered Port Isabel and saw the mix of taco stands and neon signs, souvenir and bait shops, sand-rimed streets. He lowered the window and breathed the smells of hot tar and cooking oil, barbecue, fish— fresh and not-so, bay water, cumin, garlic, frying onions. The air was warm and moist, and when he exhaled, it was with a sense of perfect timing, the rightness of arrival. To the left of the entrance to the causeway bridge, on a rise overlooking Laguna Madre Bay, stood a thickset, bone-white lighthouse. Jesse saluted it, and as he steered the car and trailer onto the great bowed back of the bridge, he felt capable and strong, boundlessly resourceful. He had done it.

At the apex of the causeway over Laguna Madre Bay, Ida Grace woke up and screamed to find herself at the top of what she later said seemed like the rearing back of a huge brontosaurus. Below her flowed the night-dappled channel of the bay, but at the time she didn't know it was the bay, or where she was, only that she was high above a body of endless moonstruck water, supported by tall pylons that seemed to her like immense, lock-jointed legs. She would surely levitate or plummet; certainly she couldn't just remain in the seat beside her husband. She lost control of her bladder. Not much, just a little; a slight squeezing, then the voluntary catch.

Funny, but it hadn't surprised her. She remembered it from pregnancy. Her doctor told her it was normal. "The pressure," he'd said. "It's"—he laughed at his joke—"to be expected." Ida

Grace, laughing with him, had almost done it again, right there on his exam table. "Do your exercises," he told her. "We'll have to watch you for cystocele in later years, but don't worry."

She hadn't told Jesse about it, and she didn't think he would have wanted her to. Theirs was a marriage in which bodies were kept private, and she thought he seemed most comfortable that way. She'd taken care never to walk in on him when he was in the big family bathroom off the kitchen, and if he relieved himself outside, she turned away. She never mentioned that she'd seen his pale yellow name frozen in droplets into a snowdrift outside the granary. During her pregnancies, she hadn't bored him with details. Early nausea, swollen feet and ankles, the pangs and twinges; she weathered them herself. This was the way of her family, and she was proud she'd honored the tradition; it was no less than Jesse'd expected. Not a man to hover and worry, he had never, awed or curious, held a palm to her belly. The births of their children seemed to him no more out of the ordinary than foaling, calving, the flow of milk from her breasts no more miraculous than a mare come fresh. This was just the sensible, natural way of things, nothing to fuss over. Sometimes, though, lying awake while Jesse slept, she had felt the pulsings and stirrings inside, the glancing pressure of a baby's feet or elbows, and she had whispered softly, *Pregnant*. It was a lovely, swollen word, and it was her, the ripening inside her. She hoped it wasn't sacrilege that she felt vaguely holy, and heard over and over in her mind the words: *But Mary kept all these things and pondered them in her heart.*

Ida Grace's shriek as they hit the top of the causeway bridge startled Jesse. He almost lost control of the wheel. Though he rarely swore in front of her, he shouted. "What the goddamn hell?"

When she opened her mouth, it was with her breathy, familiar expression of surprise and relief. "Well," she said. "Nothing, I guess." She looked out the window. "Where are we?"

6

"The island's up ahead." He pointed toward the strip of lights in front of them, the dark Gulf beyond. "Ten minutes and we're there." Land's End, the trailer park where he'd made arrangements, was just off the causeway exit.

"We should stop and get a bite to eat."

In his excitement he'd forgotten they hadn't eaten since noon. "Sure."

"There's a McDonald's somewhere. I see the sign."

Inside the restaurant, Ida Grace commented on the jars of jalapeño peppers and bottles of hot sauce on the counter.

"They're not supposed to do that," she said. "I read once where they're only supposed to have the same things. World-wide."

She sipped her drink, and Jesse noticed the web of wrinkles around her lips. "I guess they have to adapt to wherever they are," he said. "A lot of people down here must like them."

She bit into her hamburger and made a face. "Spicy. It doesn't taste the same."

Jesse shrugged, bit into his, and didn't tell her he agreed.

The next morning he woke early and made coffee at the little stove. Wanting to see the water, he left the Airstream before Ida Grace was awake. No place became real to him until he walked around in it. As he crossed the dunes, a lizard scuttled across a rind of sand at the base of a lightpole. Jesse smiled. Heavy, heavy, he felt at sea level, as though his heart was closer to his chest wall, pounding there, swollen and excited. Gulls swooped and dipped around an open dumpster near the public beach, and a group of Mexican children clambered past him, squealing and laughing, wearing only underpants, then ran inside one of the vendor shacks that lined the beach.

He didn't want to stand at the water's edge, so he climbed to the crest of a dune where he could see how the land met the water, how the island was like a long, curved finger of sand that hugged the mainland. He took deep breaths, as though he would take in the place, himself in it, the change, along with the warm salt air. A map can only show so much, he thought.

7

"Why is it so gray?"

Ida Grace stood behind him. She stepped over a clump of grass to come up beside him, looking out at the water.

He shrugged. He'd expected it to be blue, too, blue as the map, blue sky, blue water, a long sight off until forever, like the Pacific off Saipan. Here on Padre Island, the sky was a low, hazed gray, the shallows murky, the deeper water on the flat horizon dull, metallic.

After the first days of settling in, both Jesse and Ida Grace fell into slumps. Jesse told himself it was normal, that having pushed so hard to get here, he would have to wait awhile before he adjusted. Still, he couldn't shake the feeling of heaviness, a feeling of time slowed down, a feeling that he'd forgotten something he used to know.

For her part, Ida Grace said little, only that the trip had been hard on her and she needed a rest. She started on a cycle of sleep and waking that was to last three weeks. She spent the hot part of the day tangled in the bedclothes of the trailer's bunk, drowsing in the slatted green light coming through the blinds. Messy and indulgent, she looked to Jesse, daysleeping in the dimness. He tried to stay out of the trailer during her naps. She rose after dark to heat a can of soup or peel an orange, then she would move outside to sit in a lawn chair on their little slab of patio. He didn't know what time she came to bed, and in the mornings when he woke, she had already left.

Freed of all her years in one place, Ida Grace was adrift on a strange sea of remembering. She wasn't alarmed, and she wasn't afraid of sinking. She had always known it was there, this sea, but she hadn't had time to wonder too much about it, busy as she was with one thing or another. She knew it would keep. Now she had the time, and what she did, lying in the bunk or wandering along the beach, was a sort of gathering of the far-flung parts of herself in order to pack them into a tight, firm ball, the way she did with wet sand at the water's edge, crouching nearly hypnotized over the impressions her fingers made, marveling at the trails and patterns.

The memories came upon her scattershot. She gave them equal weight. In one, she was nine years old, digging a hole to bury a borrowed book she had lost—later found—rather than tell the schoolmate she'd come to hate by then that the book hadn't, after all, been stolen. In another she was stanching blood from a pupil's cut chin, trying not to be angry with the girl for her loud crying. Some made her laugh: a brother's comic look, a prank involving a city cousin and an outhouse. Others didn't: she sat rocking a baby, looking out the window at Jesse walking toward the barn; rocking, *husband, husband, husband,* unable to remember what the word was supposed to mean. In all of them she tried to see herself, the Ida Grace who felt, not did, and all of them she summoned gently, as she would hens to roost, waiting until the fluttering and ruffling ceased before she counted and considered them. Then she closed the door, knowing what was behind it. She knew the mother she had been, the daughter, sister, friend and wife. She saw herself through many eyes, the way she'd moved through days and years, this to one, that to another, hollow, though, outside herself: see me rocking, hear this laughter, now I'm rolling pie crust; scattered, no one thing to all, nothing to herself. She had loved them all, she thought, these people, in her way. But what was that, her way? She wondered what things she'd done for love, what out of duty, and the answer horrified her. She spent one last, long night in the lawn chair under the trailer's awning, her head lolled back, stunned, immobile in the humid breeze. When the sun came up she rose, her face salt-drawn, exhausted, but forever done with regret.

Time, for Jesse, stretched like catnaps, like the coffee he con-sumed at the Jetty, a warehouselike diner at the tip of the is-land, his cup filled and then refilled before he realized he'd brought it to his mouth. His schedule was off, out of kilter, and so was his digestion. This he blamed on Ida Grace's defection from the kitchen. He began taking his meals at the Jetty. He'd memorized the names of the fish on the scalloped placemat: tarpon, sailfish, marlin, yellowjack, tuna. The other side was printed with a map of the Gulf. X's marked the places ships had sunk with cargoes of gold, so close to where he sat he imagined he could smell the coins. *Idiotenfreiheit.* The phrase snapped at him from a long way off, from his German grand-mother rebuking him when he and his brothers didn't get their chores done. *Idiot freedom.* He thought of this now, sitting at the Jetty with nothing but time on his hands, lunatic no-tions of pirate treasure filling his head. He looked out the windows at the wharf where shrimp trawlers churned through the water. He could buy a boat and live on it, shirtless as he saw the fishermen now, a scrap of cloth tied round his head, gulls wheeling above him. He saw himself agile and sea-legged, swinging belowdecks to his quarters. *His quarters.* He searched his imagination for Ida Grace, but he didn't find her. Along the skin of his arms where they were exposed to the breeze from the paddle-fan raced small shocks of fear, and a strange feeling of elation.

On the day Ida Grace returned, as she later said, "to the land of the living," this happened: Jesse met a woman, Sigrid Foss. When talking later about what had happened to them on the island, Ida Grace never mentioned this. Not because she didn't know—she did, Jesse told her, and she later came to see that this was one of the things that set them right with each other—but because she still believed certain things were best not dwelt upon.

He had stayed longer than usual at the Jetty counter that day. It was nearly five o'clock, and the dinner crowd was coming in; a few families, their small children gaping at the rows of shark jaws mounted on the far wall, but most of the patrons were Jesse's age or older, other snowbirds. Most of the women carried sweaters over their arms, which made them look suspicious of the climate or infirm; in either case, old. Jesse had just decided to leave, and he was reaching for his wallet when he heard her say, "Why don't you have a beer, *Schatz?*"

He glanced around, thinking she was talking to a man who sat two stools down, a man in seersucker Bermudas, whose underslung pelvis and soft-looking paunch made Jesse think he'd never done outside work, but the man didn't respond.

She repeated herself, setting a bottle of Chihuahua on his treasure-hunt placement. "See? I am even buying."

She settled herself on the stool next to him, so close they were almost touching elbows. He twisted slightly to give her more room, though she didn't seem to want it. She was short, late forties, he guessed, dark-skinned but not Mexican, at least not the mestizo blend he was used to seeing on the beach and in the stores. Her accent sounded European. *Schatz,* he knew, was German, but she didn't look German; more like a gypsy with her big silver earrings the size of the toy sheriff badges his sons had played with. Her eyes were large and striking, green. They reminded him suddenly of the cut-glass bowls of olives Ida Grace set out at family dinners. Her nose was high-bridged, almost hawklike. She wasn't pretty, and he wondered what quality she had that kept him looking, almost staring, at her. Beneath the gathers of a black peasant-style dress made of material so gauzy he could almost see through it, her figure looked compact but ample, and it occurred to him that beneath the dress she wore nothing.

He tipped the beer bottle toward her to show his thanks. "Do you work here?"

She laughed, a rich throaty sound. "You could say that. This place was my husband's." She gave the fishnet-draped rafters a baleful glance. "It will probably kill me too." Again she laughed, and Jesse didn't know whether he should say he was sorry about her husband, or laugh with her about staying away from the place.

She drank beer from a glass, tipping back her head, looking at him, her lips parted by the glass rim, the tip of her tongue a pink crescent. "Is this your first time here, to Padre?"

He looked at his red cap on the counter, its green and yellow seed company logo, and he thought, wincing, of Ida Grace's pun: DeKalb is on de korn. "I guess it shows."

She nudged him with her elbow. "Everything shows." Smiling, she extended her hand, "Sigrid Foss."

He was surprised by the roughness of her hand; it felt chalky, like his own when it was dusted with wheat chaff. He smiled at her. "I give up."

Her look was quizzical. "You don't know your name?" She released his hand.

"Oh," he said, realizing—he'd thought she'd said "secret pass," was playing some game with him. "Jess. Jess Folcher."

She touched the hair at his temple. "Good," she said. "Thick and coarse. Just the right bald on top." Her fingers moved to his forehead, then withdrew. She picked up her glass. "Men who lose no hair keep too much in them from their mothers."

It was a pronouncement, he decided, she had made before, but he was flattered by it all the same, and he wondered if all women thought this, if the business about not losing hair was something everyone else knew, or if it was just peculiar to this strange woman. He wanted to hear more. It came to him, as he drank the last of his beer, that he had always been interested in these things—what women thought of men—but he hadn't had anyone to talk to about them. Not even at Oklahoma State; he'd been studious and shy, had spent his time with other biology students, all male, none of whom, despite anatomy class, knew any more about women than he did. Ida Grace had been no help either; she kept things to herself. He wanted Sigrid Foss to go on.

"So," she said, "you want another?" She had walked around the counter to lean on it, facing him. She was flirting with him, he knew, her voice the taunt he remembered from the street girls in Honolulu. *Haole-boy,* they called, the corners of their lips turned up in a look of seduction and derision, a look that worked, making him want to prove, though he hadn't had the nerve, that he was neither too white nor too young for them. Funny, now, how with another dark woman, he wanted to prove he wasn't too old or too white.

He decided to have another beer, but before he could tell her so, she said, "I have a better idea. Come with me."

Compared to the dim interior of the Jetty, the glare outside was almost blinding. They walked through sand drifts along the side of the building. There was a narrow boardwalk, but Sigrid Foss said, "Take the sand. Always. Better for the legs."

When they reached the outside staircase that led to the second story of the restaurant, she started up. Jesse, following her, saw that she was barefoot, her heels flat and hard, her ankles silted with sand. He asked himself what he was doing. At the top of the stairs, she opened a louvered door and held it for him. "Welcome."

She closed the door, then pulled her dress over her head and off, hanging it on a peg next to other dresses of the same material but different colors. Too stunned to move, he stood by the door while she walked, naked, heavily, across the varnished floor toward a wall lined with shelves. She didn't apologize for her nakedness as Ida Grace did if he walked in on her when she was dressing, but Jesse looked away all the same, trying to keep his attention on the room.

Two walls were solid, broken only by small shoulder-high windows and a door, which he supposed led to a bathroom. The other walls were glass, floor to ceiling, overlooking the Gulf. In the center of the room stood a huge worktable. "Look at me or don't," she called. "It's all the same to me."

He heard her opening cabinets and he looked briefly, thinking she might be changing clothes. She wasn't. Uncertain about what he should do, he turned back to the worktable. A large sheet of smudged plastic covered the table, but through it he could see tools—adzes, awls, chisels, an array of knives, one big as a bolo, others small as Ida Grace's sewing machine screwdriver. In the center of the table were some light-colored objects, statues or pottery, he didn't know which. Irregular blocks of stone lined the wall beneath one window, and a large plastic-covered barrel stood in a corner. He had never felt so uneasy in his life, but it didn't occur to him to leave.

She came toward him, holding two glasses, offering one. "Sit down," she said.

He tried not to look anywhere but at her face and at the room. There were no chairs, only a folded mattress strewn with pillows. "There," she said, "On the futon."

As he lowered himself, trying not to spill the liquid in his glass, he realized the mattress was her bed; the smell of her, earthen, musky with a tang of sweat, rose from the pillows. She sat beside him, sipping her drink, smiling in a way he thought seemed oddly shy. "I hope you are not too shocked. This is how I live."

"Oh, no," he said. "It's fine." He raised his glass. He smelled pine resin, reminding him of the cleaning solution Ida Grace used on the kitchen floor. He sipped at the liquor. It tasted of turpentine and it burned his tongue. He coughed, then shook in an involuntary spasm.

"You don't like retsina?"

"What is it?"

"Greek wine," she said, her glance at him oblique. "Something else to get used to."

He tried another sip. "Are you Greek?"

She lay back against the pillows and closed her eyes. "A little of everything," she said. "Whatever you want."

Just when Jesse thought he'd gone beyond surprise, he surprised himself by lying back beside her, and it struck him that it was for this moment—though he hadn't known it was coming—he'd started on his trip, had chosen this place, driven halfway down the country.

She was not a gentle partner. She did things that surprised him, said things about what they were doing that he'd hardly ever thought to think, much less say, and when he left, nearly dizzy from the wine and what they'd done, walking up the beach road toward the trailer park, the memory of those things seemed to sear across his legs. He felt his belly tighten, only to go loose again with wonder. He walked along as though bewitched. He remembered the bull elk that had wandered onto his land one summer. He'd found it mired in a slough along the Broken Moses, spavined hocks collapsed against each other, a thousand miles from home, its mossy, battered rack weighting the head that still strained to lift its body, move it forward. The vet told him about the worm that sometimes infested the brains of these animals, causing them to roam in an unswerving course, across rivers, highways, even city parking lots, not eating or stopping to drink, going forward, always forward, until they died of exhaustion. The elk had to be destroyed. When Jesse arrived at the trailer park, he had to think about it to remember how he got there, until the Airstream door clunched shut behind him and he was back with Ida Grace.

"You lost your hat," she said, studying him. She turned to the stove and flipped a hamburger patty. "That's pretty dangerous around here. Sunstroke, they say." She handed him a jar of pickles to open. "You look a little bleary-eyed."

He loosened the lid and handed back the jar. "Just tired, I guess." He couldn't look at her.

She sniffed the air. "What's that funny smell?"

He sat down at the table. "I don't smell anything. Those pickles, maybe."

"No, it's pine-y. Or like fruit." She cocked her head to catch the smell. "Oh, well." She set a plate in front of him, then took her place across the table. "Jesse," she began, then lowered her eyes. "I guess I haven't been quite myself lately."

He knew this was all she would say by way of explanation for the last three weeks, and he nodded, picking up his knife and fork. But she continued to look at him, in a way that made him think she was waiting for something from him, an answer, a blessing for the food. He couldn't think of either. They began to eat, silent until she suggested a visit to the marine museum the next day.

15

At the museum, a pressed-concrete building the same color as the surrounding dunes, she went from case to case, aquarium to aquarium, looking here at a display of flotsam, there at a burnished tortoise shell. She zigzagged from one exhibit to another with no method Jesse could figure, and he had a sudden urge to take her hand, not in a companionable sense but for the same reason he'd held his sons' hands when they were small and would try to run wild in a store, more to corral her. Ida Grace seemed animated, energetic in a way that had nothing to do with work. He began to wonder if something was wrong with her, if she was ill.

"Jesse, look here," she called from across the room. "Can you believe this?"

"I haven't even seen it," he said irritably, weaving through displays to stand beside her in front of an odd-looking fish mounted on metal rods. He read the placard, "Coelacanth." He had once taught students about the fish.

"Think of it! From the Devonian period, it says. And this one was found live!"

He looked again; he'd thought it was just a model. The scales of the fish were large and mottled, blue, oily-looking, pendulous fins blunt and thick. The texture of the scales reminded him of the skin on Ida Grace's hand as she pointed to the placard, gnarled and spiny-looking.

"Listen, Jesse. It says their fins probably developed into the legs of land animals." She looked at him earnestly, telling him what he already knew. "They thought these were extinct. For millions of years. Then they caught one. Alive!"

"Then it's not that unusual after all, is it?" It was a peckish thing to say, but he didn't think she heard him. He moved to an array of shark teeth, anxious for the museum trip to be over. He wanted to go to the Jetty.

Though Ida Grace had returned and they established a more usual routine, he continued to see Sigrid Foss. He discovered she made her appearance in the Jetty around five o'clock, when she wandered through the kitchen, more to trade jokes with the cooks and waitresses, Jesse thought, than to keep an eye on the business. Then she would go to the cooler and take out a chilled glass and a bottle of beer. She would come around the end of the counter to sit beside him for a while, to talk. Then they would go upstairs. This was what he waited for, though he told himself each time would be the last.

In her studio, the ritual varied only with the color of dress she peeled off. They drank retsina. He had come to associate its paint-thinner taste and smell with what they would do later, after all the talking was done. He found himself telling her things he hadn't thought about for many years: stories of himself when he was young, stories of Saipan and Hawaii. He took the nods she gave as affirmation of himself, as proof of his existence before this time and place, and he felt vital, rich in lore, at the heart of everything. When he wondered why she had chosen him over other men, and what he meant to her, he didn't ask, knowing that such talk was not a part of the way she saw what they were doing, and when he was stricken by the frequent urge to tell her how lucky he counted himself, he held his peace for fear she would laugh at him, quote from one of the little books she had told him she'd written some high-sounding phrase that made him feel small and foolish in the face of all she knew. He was happy, that she wanted to be with him was enough.

He knew he was betraying Ida Grace, and he felt guilty but at the same time entitled. It was because of her self-containment all these years that they had come to this pass. Here, now, was what was real between two people, a man and a woman, and he wanted it. Whatever it was, and however it had come to him, he wanted it. At the same time, he had to silence his own voice when it asked him if he'd known enough, back then, to want it.

★　★　★

A strange thing was happening with his wife. She let her hair grow until it was long enough to gather into a nub at the back of her neck. She tied it with afghan yarn, and wisps of hair, lank at the crown but frizzled at the ends, blew around her face. The color grew out, the roots white along the centered part, the way snow sifts first into furrows, and he was surprised to discover she had been dyeing it for years. Her manner of dress changed. She gave up her polyester skirts in favor of a loose style of shorts that reminded him of army-issue boxers. At the T-shirt shack she bought five ninety-nine-cent bargains printed with flamingos, beer cans, palm trees. They embarrassed him. Her lace-up shoes were in a bin beneath the bunk; she wore rubber thongs.

Next her face changed. It looked smoother, the drawn, tight look around her lips relaxed, the contours of her cheeks plumped out. Her eyes looked larger, clearer. Her long legs, once wrinkled and slack-skinned at the knees, blue-veined as an udder bag, began to tan. She slathered them with a pale green cream until they glistened, and he noticed the swelling outline of muscle from her long beach walks.

Mornings, she scrambled eggs for both of them, then neatened the trailer and packed a raffia bag with bread and fruit, a notebook, pencils, and a plastic water bottle. She was gone hours at a time. Sometimes he saw her poking along the gray rocks at the inlet, squatting to examine something on the ground, holding her position so long it made his legs hurt just watching her. He saw her striding along the sand, swinging the bag, only to stop short, put down the bag and wade out into the water, peering into it as though tracking something that moved beneath the surface. She had gone back to the museum to gather pamphlets and field guides, and she kept a notebook of what she found.

One night, after she was asleep, he opened it. Neat drawings, captions in her even Palmer Method handwriting: *Jellyfish, a coelenterate, washed up 14 December; blennies and gobies, a mixed school, not afraid of me.* Shells and driftwood began to appear around the base of the trailer. When he asked her what she planned to do with them, she said, "Why, nothing. Look at them, I guess."

At night she cooked, sometimes fish from a market, mostly canned soup, sandwiches. He began to miss the pot roast and fried chicken of the country table she had set at home, and he was mystified by the changes in her.

"Sure is different here," he said one evening as they sat in the lawn chairs outside the Airstream. The day sounds of the trailer park had died down. He heard Benny Goodman on the radio from the Winnebago two slabs over, faint laughter, the jerk and squeal of a station being changed. Wind rustled the waxy leaves of the crotons that grew beside their slab.

Ida Grace leaned forward, rested her elbows on her knees. She looked up at the stars beginning to appear. "Yes. I don't ever want to leave."

Her reaction surprised him as much as the reminder of leaving; they weren't due back until March. "I didn't know if you liked it here or not."

She stood, walked to the edge of the slab, still looking up. "You can't tell?" She turned, smiling, and he saw the way her hair caught the light from the neighboring trailer. "I love it."

"Well," he said. "Well."

She ran her thumb and finger down the spine of a croton leaf. "This is silly, Jesse, but . . ." She let her hand fall and stood quietly, her face so naked, old and hopeful in the fading light that Jesse had to look away, afraid she would say something too full of feeling and embarrass him, embarrass herself, now, when he was least ready to hear it.

"Jess?"

He made a noise low in his throat to show he was listening.

"Did you ever feel real?"

He felt suddenly transparent. "How do you mean?"

"I can't explain it, really. Just, finally, for the first time, that you see everything that's happened and your place in it. You see the way you fit, and it just . . . is." She rubbed her forearms briskly, and the sound made Jesse want to get up and run. "That suddenly your own *skin* means something." She smiled. "Real?"

He went to the water hookup to check the hose. "Sure. Of course." He checked the faucet wheel, giving it a tightening it didn't need, then went inside to bed.

He hadn't talked to Sigrid about his marriage, but now he wanted to. They sat on her floor. She had brought a plate of chorizo from the kitchen and sat eating, listening. Grease from the sausage drizzled down her wrists like orange veins, and the spicy smell made his mouth water, but she didn't offer a taste.

"She was just what she was," he was saying. "Never one to say what was on her mind. She did everything, of course, but it was as if she was always inside herself, doing it. It's hard to explain."

"You think she is different now. That she has changed?"

"Something. She still isn't very talkative, but there's something different."

Sigrid wiped her fingers on a napkin, then dabbed a line of grease from her wrist. "This happens often here," she said in the tone that had begun, lately, to irritate Jesse for its air of knowing.

"If she just hadn't been so bound up." He shook his head.

She balled the napkin and dropped it to her empty plate. "You're saying that is why you're here with me? Because she was always so . . . what she was?"

"Maybe. I don't know." He didn't want what he did with Sigrid to have anything to do with Ida Grace, but here she was all mixed up in it. He realized it sounded like he was blaming her for what he was doing, and he knew it wasn't fair to think that way, but somehow, it was true.

"What *are* you doing here, Jess?"

He looked at her. "Talking. I don't know. The other."

She slammed her plate onto the floor. "The other?" Her eyes looked darker to him. "You call it 'the other?'"

He didn't know what to say. He had wanted to be delicate about it, and now she was angry with him. He had the feeling she would have found fault, though, with anything he'd said.

"What we do has many names. A thousand. You can choose. Call it what it is to you—a miracle, an accident, fun. Making love." She stood, walked away from him, making a gesture of disgust, as though pushing him away. "You call it 'the other.'" She stood beside her worktable. "Perhaps what is wrong is in you. You don't know what anything is to you. So quiet, always the grim face, as though it hurts you to make words."

He stared at her, dumbfounded, thought of everything he'd told her, more to her than to anyone else in his life.

"Oh, you talk. But never what is, never what it means, only what was. And now, what wasn't. And it is always you." She flipped up a corner of the plastic that covered her worktable, then flipped it down. "Do you ever think that maybe all the world does not have you at the center?"

He stood to tell her Yes, yes he knew that, but he didn't have the chance.

"Do you realize that you have asked me only one question—am I Greek?—why is that?"

She was waiting, he realized, for an answer, but he didn't have one. "I don't know."

She crossed to the door and opened it. "Come back when you do! When you can come into this place with something. With a question. With an answer. Passion. Come back when you *know* something."

For the first time in his life he began to have trouble sleeping, and he lay awake trying to make sense of what she'd said, to make it fit him. But he couldn't. He had been a good man, he thought, a man washed clean by work to go about his days with a clear conscience. To work, and to work hard; for everyone, for Ida Grace, his sons, the land, himself; so the sun and moon could rise and set and the part of the earth he held together with this work could go on turning and not fall apart.

21

But what was he, what Jesse? Not the man Ida Grace saw, the good provider, companion of her bed and table who had to be reminded to wear a hat: more. Not the man who went to Sigrid. What did she see: a faithless, silent fool who flinched at life? Was he the figure plowing through the seasons toward the end, or was there something more to him, something buried like the arrowheads he sometimes found along the Broken Moses where he'd walked a thousand times before, not noticing, until a facet caught the sun and he stooped to brush dirt from the ancient flint; something more? He tossed, and was to himself only the man now tossing, the skin and bone and muscle that lay alone, intact, itself and like no other, but told him nothing, only tossed and asked and got no answer.

As he signed his name to the Christmas cards Ida Grace provided, a scene of stars and palms over an adobe crèche, it occurred to him that he was only this: his name, his signature a wavering spiny scrawl haphazard on the vellum, committed in an instant to signify his presence in the memory of anyone. He felt lost and diminished, old, hanging onto a scrap of land at the bottom of a continent, connected to the mainland by only a bow-backed, frightening bridge. Sometimes in the night he imagined it crumbling, swooning into rubble, the island wrenched into the Gulf, and he thought he understood why Ida Grace had screamed.

He followed her one afternoon on her beach walk, keeping out of sight among the grass-grown dunes, watching her. She moved along the shingle, stopping now and then, squatting, arms between her knees, supporting herself on her fingertips in a way she never would have at home, monkeylike. *Wife,* he thought, but the word seemed foreign, sharp, meant nothing. He watched as she lay down at the water's edge, half in, half out, letting the tide lap around her legs and hips. He felt betrayed, somehow, by this act, as shocked as if he'd caught her in some solitary female ritual he hadn't known existed. He started to turn, but then he began to wonder how the water felt to her. Cold, first, then warming as it curled around her, a pull as it drew away; a pull, he thought, like birth must be, a pull as strong as the one he suddenly felt toward the Jetty. He turned to walk along the beach toward the restaurant.

She wasn't there, though it was almost five. He drank a beer, letting resolve swell inside him like the bubbles in his glass. He had a thousand questions now, and he would ask them, talk to her so hard she had to laugh, show himself to be so real it hurt to look at him. When five-thirty passed and she hadn't come, he paid his bill and went around the building to the stairway, laughing at himself for wasting half an hour. He plowed along through the heavy drifts of sand, then suddenly switched to the boardwalk. His legs were fine, just fine—her business about taking the sand was fine for her, but he was not obliged to mind all of her notions. The flex of muscle as he took the stairs thrilled him, and he couldn't wait to see her.

At the alcove in front of her door he stopped. He heard voices from inside, Sigrid's clear and strong, another muffled. He peered through the louvers and saw her, standing with her back to the door, her wild, dark hair, her wide, full bottom.

"A high and mighty miracle," he heard her say, "the fact that we are here at all," and he winced when he remembered the surge of power he'd felt when she had said the words to him.

She raised her arms toward the Gulf, and beyond her Jesse saw that sitting on the mattress, mother-naked though he held his glass over his lap, was a man—the man who'd been sitting down the counter from him on the day he'd met Sigrid. Jesse saw him gazing at her with a look of stupefaction, and in the man's expression he saw his own, the way he must have looked. He saw why Sigrid did the things she did, and he saw himself—outside the studio looking in, and also inside the man—and he knew that glimmers of the scene would haunt him for a long time to come.

"It is the accident of time that gives us life," he heard her say as he turned away. In his mind's eye he saw her arms fall as she made her pronouncement—not for the first time, he knew, and probably not for the last—and he saw in the old man's face a look of hope that made his own heart heavy with the memory of that longing.

He put a name to what he wanted when he turned to Ida Grace in the night, and it was comfort. She was in a dreamy, half-awakened state, her eyes closed, but she came to him with none of the sighing and shy twitching he was used to from her. Around her remained the aura of sea water, but warm, with a mineral hint of salt. She felt different to him, more liquid, the sound they made the soft *slup* of tide soaked into sand, dissolving. He wondered if this, then, was their only connection: the dissolution of the hard space (growing softer?) where their bodies met, the rhythmic impact of long habit? He didn't know, but he felt desolated and forlorn, and he wondered if this time would be their last.

He hadn't thought she was fully awake, but she moved her hand to touch herself where they were joined, something she had never done before. Her eyes were still closed, and he saw the pale green cream etched in beaded arcs along the creases of her eyelids. Behind the lids he saw the flickering movements of her eyes. He wished she would open them so he could see their blue irises, see them looking at him, but he had the feeling they would glance off, veer away to track the stars beyond the ceiling.

Her fingers, pressing, moved in slow, tight circles, and her breath came quickly. He felt her shudder, then contract and loosen. Something warm spilled out between them. Her eyes opened and he saw her look of astonishment, then she laughed.

"Well," she said. "It's cystocele, I guess."

She rolled to her side of the bed and covered herself. "Sorry," she said, then reached over to smooth her hand along his cheek and past his ear. She made a sound high in her throat that Jesse thought sounded like surprise and peace.

He lay still, listening to her breathing.

He wondered why she wasn't curious about the spot between them. It was big around as a dinner plate and cool, now, to his touch. He pressed his palm into the dampness then brought his hand to his nose. The scent was faint, slightly fishy, salt and bay, like shrimp boil. He had understood her to say she guessed it was just the sea, and he wondered if some water from the afternoon had been trapped, only to flow out later, now. He cupped his palm over his nose and mouth and breathed in again, deeper, but the scent still told him nothing.

When he was certain she had gone back to sleep, he got up and left the trailer to walk along the beach road. The Gulf was luminous and vast, in the darkness more sound than sight, a rushing vacuum-space. The air lay heavy from the day. He felt small and weighted, as though the air pressed him down into the earth until he was nothing more than the bubble of jelly-fish that washed up on the sand in front of him, its cystlike body flattening, fragile tentacles streaming useless trails behind it. Though the beach was strewn with jellyfish, their lustrous bodies thick and clustered as the stars, this one Jesse scooted gently, carefully, with the toe of his shoe, along the wet sand toward the water, until the tide caught it, sweeping it away, and he knew what it was he had to do.

He went back to the trailer and began to batten down. He disconnected the utility hookups, secured the hitch and brake-light wires. He thought of leaving a note, but how could a few scrawled words—gone, called away—explain what couldn't be explained. Later, when things settled down, he would worry about details, but for now, he felt he couldn't spare the time. Inside the trailer, he bolstered Ida Grace with bench cushions so she wouldn't wake up when they began to move.

As he turned onto the causeway bridge, the trailer wagged. He increased speed to correct for it, and the Airstream settled into a uniform drag as he pulled it up the incline. He felt queasy and sour-stomached heading up—the minute of forever it takes a roller coaster to climb toward the first drop—until he reached the topmost point where Ida Grace had screamed, until he saw what he was running from, in his mind's eye saw the pylons heave and buckle, the hitch uncouple, the trailer's lurch and yaw as it plummeted, splashed, a bullet-capsule in the green bay water, water sluicing through the trailer's airtight seams and over Ida Grace, still sleeping and serene, her hair fanned out and undulant, suddenly grown gilled; him here, still on the bridge, white-knuckled hands on the wheel all that kept him from that loss.

He drove on, shaken but relieved, through Port Isabel, then past the tended fields of cane and cotton, where he began to feel better. Then, above him, a crop duster flew so low he could see the pilot's eyes in the light from the plane's instrument panel, the pilot grinning, rakehell, buzzing him for fun, and suddenly he knew he wasn't safe at all, but so close to terror he could feel it pressing on his chest. As he pulled onto the shoulder to stop, he felt something break away inside him, deep, rising thickly to his throat. He couldn't swallow. Another bearing down, another something torn away, and this time he couldn't get himself to breathe beyond the ache. He wanted to yell out that this was wrong, an awful joke. Not fair. If he could have drawn his breath to laugh at himself for this— at feeling six years old again and nothing fair, and funny, how this mattered to him now the same way it had then, but even now there was nothing he could do, and at the bottom of it all was just his same old foolish, wanting self, and funny how he loved that self in the same sweet stupid way—he would have laughed, but he couldn't, and he gripped the wheel, looking at his hands as though they had the power—any power—to move him from the moment, knowing they didn't, and he felt ridiculous as he gave what he knew would be his final thought to asking the broken something deep inside him for another chance.

He sat, waiting to believe he was breathing, for his pulse to steady, until finally he let his hands slide from the wheel. He saw that his hands could move to open the window, to let in the familiar smells of earth and herbicide, tarry asphalt, oil, a slow night wind that held the scent of brush burning somewhere beyond his vision's reach. Here, with the land stretched out before him on its long way home, he began to feel calmer. He looked out the window, past the night and into space where other suns and planets moved, and he understood that there would come a time when he would cease to matter, but this wasn't yet the time. He looked at the moon, where men had gone, could walk, return forever changed to find the nothing they had known on earth grown greater in their absence.

There were too many questions and too much to know, and he understood that if to some was given understanding, he was not among their number.

He started the car, easing the trailer along the shoulder while he gathered speed. Bits of limestone chat, white gravel from the moon-washed road, popped against the wheel wells as he moved onto the pavement, and he marveled at the whole of everything, the mystery of his place in it, at all he couldn't know, but when Ida Grace, still sleeping, her strong legs scissor-kicking in a distant dream of lobe-finned fishes, swam up to sit beside him, he had known the very moment.

ALLIGATOR DANCE

I T wasn't the way he looked that made us hate Lonnie Olson. I'm not certain that we hated him at all, but his was the name that garnered all our fourth-grade disgust. He was pale, his face—Slavic, flat-cheeked, inscrutable—too wide for his head. At times his blanch-fringed eyes seemed nearly blank. At other times they looked old and wise, wizened like the winter apples we found stuck in the alley drainage grate behind Garden Homes School, pinched and desiccating. His hair was white-blond, flyaway and dry as the flaxweed in the ditch behind the Milwaukee Transit Authority bus barn where he caught me many afternoons as I walked home in my saddle shoes, white anklets, plaid tie-back dresses.

He wasn't the class bully. Two beefier boys—Richard Rogan and Jerry Schmidt—ruled the pike-fenced playground, aimed dodge balls at our flat chests, poked sticks along our dress hems to see London, France. Lonnie Olson played alone on the marshy ground behind a row of spruce, far from the dodge balls, marble circles, trading card exchanges. He was new to Garden Homes School that year, having moved from another Milwaukee neighborhood. My family had just moved from a country town in Oklahoma—Caddo—so I was new, too, and shy, but I escaped curiosity, probably because it centered on Lonnie Olson's dirtiness, and on the darkness of the things he did.

His neck was seamed with grime, and behind his ears were mottled patches; inside were specks the size of gnats. I wondered about his mother. My own lined up my younger brothers and me every morning, a soaped cloth in her hand, a bobby pin clenched between her lips. When she finished with our faces, they stung from air and friction. Then she dug in our ears with the loop end of the bobby pin. Lonnie Olson's mother, I imagined, wouldn't touch him.

In the schoolroom he spoke only rarely, and he had a way of ducking his chin, dropping his eyelids, sly, when Miss Doyle called on him. When he answered her questions, he picked at his palm, at clusters of fleabite-sized scabs, using a rusted safety pin that was attached to his belt loop by a length of raveled gray string.

"Lonnie." Miss Doyle's use of his given name startled me into remembering he was more than just the full, two-named entity—Lonnie Olson—who haunted the radiator side of the room. "Please tell the class the capital of South Dakota."

Sunlight from the tall west windows struck his head, spiked his hair with light. His chin dipped and he shrugged, scratching with his pin. "Pierre."

We snickered. The word, his rasping whisper of it in the breath-held room, sounded nasty, a bathroom word. We watched him, waiting to see if he would mouth his other word, his mysterious, Lonnie Olson tic-word. He picked again, clasped shut his pin, then his lips began to move the way we'd hoped, opened— "orty"—drew back, showing teeth, then closed—"teen"— holding between them for that moment our fascination and revulsion. He wouldn't ever tell us what it meant.

His clothes were dirty, too. In those days, the middle fifties, boys wore brown or navy trousers to school, plaid shirts and brogan shoes. Lonnie Olson's arms hung goose-pimpled and patchy from the too-large sleeves of his gray undershirts. The seat of his pants—roll-cuffed denim dungarees—was slick with dirt, and the knees were worn brown and thin from his crawling through the soil around the pylons of the MTA bridge. It was beneath this structure—at the place where the embankment met the girders in a row of cavelike hollows—that he lurked. Though I knew his house was nearby, I had to remind myself that he didn't, like the troll in the story, live beneath the bridge.

The ditch that ran under the bridge was flat and open, the nearest thing to meadow in the sidewalked, concrete landscape, wide enough for a dozen streetcars to pass one another in the days it had been used for that purpose. Now it was more like a low, dry riverbed grown up with goldenrod and burdock, a few small pines and poplars. High schoolers from Rufus King stopped there to smoke, to write on the stone abutments with chalk and lumps of coal. Neighborhood children sledded on the easy slope in winter, rode bikes along the weedy trails in summer. My brothers Jack and David, and the more daring primary school boys, often went beneath the bridge to pee, and once, the first summer we lived in the city, I had done it too. But even as I squatted there, the dirt-pack soaking up my stream, I felt a sudden shame—I was too old for this—and later, when I crossed the bridge on my way home from school each day, I remembered the mildewed dank, and I tried to forget what I had done. From the embankment beside this place, Lonnie Olson, one day in late October, called out to me.

"Hey, lookit." He stood below me, his head at the level of my feet.

I walked on, ignoring him, along the sidewalk where it buckled, shaling like a broken cookie.

Again he called, louder. "You want to see something?"

I thought of the time I'd peed; wondered wildly how long that smell, just beneath his feet there in the dirt, could last. "Me?"

He took a step up the bank. "It's a lady."

"Why would I want to see a lady?"

He shrugged. "Because it's keen."

He held his hand behind his back; a card, I imagined. Trading cards were big that year. Girls collected pictures of birds and flowers, Angora cats and Scottie dogs. Boys had baseball cards (the Braves were best, and everywhere—above the manila placards of the cursive alphabet in every Milwaukee schoolroom marched the pantheon of heroes: A, Hank Aaron; B, Bill Brutton; C, Del Crandall—the Yankees ran a distant second). They had Davy Crockett cards, and sometimes a dirty picture. From what I knew of Lonnie Olson, I imagined he had the one of Jayne Mansfield that was currently notorious. I wanted to see it.

"You have to come down here," he said.

I stepped off the sidewalk onto the incline, my shoes scrabbling on loose pebbles. The sun was warm on my bare legs.

He waited until I reached the first hummock along the slope. "Closer. Then sit down."

I moved closer, then sat on a heaved slab of concrete, careful to tuck my skirt under my legs. "You don't have anything," I said.

He sat beside me, close enough for me to catch his smell: damp and sodden, like the hamper behind our bathroom door. "Lookit," he said, his voice the whisper I knew from school. He held out his hand, palm up. "This is her."

At first I thought it was a tattoo, like the kind that came in Cracker Jack, but when I looked closer I saw that he had drawn in blue ink across his palm a female torso. Headless, armless, it showed the curves of waist, two small V's to depict creases where arms would begin, a large Y for the fold between her legs. He fished in his pocket for his pen, clicked the nib, then inked a spot for her navel.

"Her head is here." With the pen tip he indicated the fleshy place at the base of his middle finger. "But you kin't see it."

Like the rest of my classmates, Lonnie Olson said "kin't" instead of "can't." To my ear, developed in small, slow Caddo, the pronunciation sounded citified and northern; nasty. "I have to go," I said. But I shifted on the concrete slab, looked out into the ditch to make sure no one was watching us, and stayed.

He began to draw on the torso, and I saw smudges on his skin where he'd spit-erased earlier markings. He drew two semicircles, immense and pendulous, hanging nearly to the navel. In the center of each circle he made a dot. "Orty teen," he said, and I heard his breath at the end of the word, a soft, slow release.

He watched me as he fetched up his safety pin, unclasped it, and it seemed his pale eyes held me fast. "Watch."

He pricked at the right dot, then the left, meticulous, intent. Bright spots of blood appeared on his palm like small beads, growing. He held his hand out to show me, then ducked his chin. His eyes went narrow and oblique. "Then you suck on them."

I jumped up then, scrambling up the bank as Lonnie Olson brought the image to his mouth.

We called them "moles," my brothers and I, those dotted semi-circles Lonnie Olson had drawn on his hand. I don't know where we got the name; maybe the dark, imagined nipples of grown-up ladies' breasts reminded us of those skin marks we could more easily see; maybe it was the connotation of the word in its animal sense: soft-nosed, blind, burrowing, but we were fascinated by the hidden things the name stood for. Our Sunday School teacher, Mrs. Cookson, had "big moles," we said. "Did you see how big and fat they were?" my brother Jack whispered one Sunday after that ample woman had leaned over us as we sat filling in the cross-shaped crossword puzzles in our flyers, the cleft between her breasts squeezed into a wrinkled Y. Embarrassed and aroused, we giggled.

I had, that fourth-grade year, no moles of my own, or rather, what I had was the same as Jack and David, as baby Laura—two faintly brown circles, penny-flat areolae, nub-centered—but I knew that the fuller ones I was beginning to notice on high school girls, on women, held a secret I didn't understand. They were for feeding babies—my mother had told me—but I suspected there was something more.

That fall, in the middle time of childhood that I would later learn was known as "latent," there was plenty going on, though I understood none of it. One afternoon my father had taken my brothers and me to a movie, and as I sat in the dark theater and listened to him pointing out the marvels of animation on the screen, I felt a nameless, disturbing *something*. On the screen danced hippopotamus ballerinas, their scanty tutus ruffling in the cartoon wind. Then the music seemed to darken and from behind some columns rushed a group of alligator men, skinny, furtive, with narrow, wicked eyes. Each wore only a tiny hat with a long, streaming feather. Frightened, the hippo ladies danced away, but the alligators chased them. I squirmed in the scratchy theater seat. Finally, two—an alligator and a hippo—danced together, and it seemed their dance went on and on. I was glad when the movie ended and the lights went up.

Also that fall, I began to have the Dream: A room in our rental house had been cleared of furniture, then filled with dirt, a dark mound of it, like topsoil. I held a plastic spoon, and it was my job in the Dream to eat the dirt. But I never did. When I raised the first spoonful to my mouth, it was as though I'd already consumed it, the whole pile, without once swallowing, and I woke up sickened, phantom grit beneath my tongue, my stomach full, like the story wolf who ate the seven little kids.

In class I began to watch Lonnie Olson. He picked often at his palm, fingered his length of string. I caught him looking at me. Sometimes he smiled, sometimes he mouthed his word, and one day, toward the end of January, just as I was ready to cross the bridge, he stopped me again.

"Want to see my snow fort?"

He looked small, standing there below me on the bank in his lumpy gray parka, his brown-billed hat with earflaps, a button on the top center of his head. His smile seemed friendly. In the shadows beneath the bridge I saw the jut of a snow-packed wall, dirty-white, flecked with frozen leaves and twigs.

"Warm, yeah?" he said after I had picked my way down the ice and sat across from him in his shelter beneath the girders.

"It's nice," I agreed. I had pulled my muffler from my nose and mouth, the condensation from my breath cold against my chin.

He took off his oilcloth mittens and looked at me, his eyes hooded in the winter dimness. He smiled, as though something between us had been settled. "Orty teen," he said, then straightened one leg to take out his ballpoint pen.

I pressed the heels of my galoshes into the snowpack. "Why do you always say that word?"

"I just do."

"It's stupid."

"No it isn't."

"Then what does it mean?"

He began to draw on his palm. "Nothing. Just itself." He raised his eyes to mine, complicitous and secretive.

"But it has to mean something," I insisted.

He held up his palm. "Lookit."

I tried not to look. "It's a number, isn't it?" I had been thinking about his word, and I had decided that it had the feel of bulk, of multitude, like the dirt mound in the Dream. "Like forty? Then teen?"

He shrugged and began to unclasp his safety pin. I got up, clumsy in thick snowpants, and started, clambering and angry, up the slope toward the shoveled walk and home.

The house we rented was just off Olive Street on Twenty-second in a jumbled neighborhood of small German-style bungalows that seemed almost heaped upon each other, separated only by the narrow walks that led to the ash cans in the alley. The neighborhood was different from the grassy, open sprawl of Caddo, where houses were white and square and ample, where I knew every family, and their ways were comfortably the same, like ours. In Milwaukee, it seemed no one was the same. On our block lived Germans, Czechs, and Swedes, Italians, Greeks, Hungarians, all with different customs, wild, strange-sounding words that came out of open windows as I passed at suppertime during our first summer there, odd food smells mingling in the air that always seemed to hold a touch of chill; caraway, paprika, garlic, sausage, nutmeg, olive oil, and peppers. Our house smelled of plainer food: fried chicken, navy beans with bacon, biscuits; food I considered American and regular. I learned, however, on my first day in the new school, when Miss Doyle had us go around the room and tell where our families were from, that neither category constituted nationality.

"Just regular," I said, when my turn came. "American."

Miss Doyle pursed her lips while my new classmates shifted in their seats, craning their necks to look at me. "But where is your family from originally?"

The class—ethnic, wise—snickered when I said the town name that sounded suddenly stupid, then added, "But I have cousins over in Tishomingo."

Shortly after Halloween, Ruthie Wittenberg, round-faced, black bangs clasped at her temples by blue plastic My Merry barrettes I coveted, the only girl in the class shorter than I, befriended me. From Ruthie I learned many things: how to fold the Land O' Lakes butter box so the Indian girl's knees turned into boobies (Ruthie's word; I didn't admit to mine), the naughty version of the Bosco song. I learned why there were no Polish people in our school or in our neighborhood, though Milwaukee was full of them. They had to live, Ruthie told me, south of the Kinnickkinnick River, in basements. "Because they never wash," Ruthie explained. They used their bathtubs for storing coal. They farted all the time from the odd food they ate: dogs, Ruthie said, among other things. I nodded. Back in Oklahoma we had Indians, pretty much the same. When I asked how you could tell if somebody was Polish,

Ruthie said, "You'll know it when you smell one." The smelling part I knew about: my mother, worn out with four of us and expecting another baby in the summer, had hired a cleaning woman named Jennie Bronkala. A birdlike woman who wore brown socks that slushed around her thin, unshaven ankles, Jennie rode the bus to our house once a week. Though she told us wild, exciting stories in her thick, wet-sounding accent, though she brought us boxes of chocolate-covered cherries she swore her family wouldn't touch, my mother had to let her go: for hours after a cleaning, the house smelled strange.

Ruthie went to Hebrew lessons in an alley walk-up apartment off Teutonia a few blocks from Garden Homes School, and sometimes I walked her there before turning off toward home. I knew about Hebrews—they were all over the place in the Bible—but I was curious about what Ruthie did at a lesson about them. When she showed me her notebook with the squiggled writing, telling me they wrote their language, read it, backwards, I knew I had found the key to Lonnie Olson's word.

I didn't wait for him to stop me on the bridge, but sought him out on the soot-grimed snow of the playground the next day. "It's another language," I told him. "Swedish. Ha."

He reached out to pluck a clutch of needles from a spruce and brought them to his nose. "What?"

"That word. You said you were Swedish, before."

He shook his head, rolling the needles between his fingers to release the resin. He dropped them and held out his fingers. "Smell."

I turned my head away. "It's something backwards, then. Something backwards in another language."

He laughed. "It's only orty teen." A sly look came over his face. "You want I should make her? Here?"

"You don't know what it means," I accused. "You only say it."

"That's for me to know and you to find out."

I wanted to hit him on his pale, smug face, but I'd been taught that the first hitter was the loser because he wanted something most. I turned away. "You don't know," I yelled as I ran. "It doesn't mean a thing."

Though it was eight blocks farther, I started crossing the ditch on Roosevelt rather than on Olive, and in class I wouldn't look at him. But it seemed that ignoring him took up more time than wondering about him had, and the more I tried to ignore him, the more I wound up thinking about him. One afternoon in late March, when the thawing snow released the wet smell of spring into the air, I found myself, without knowing how I came to be there, on the block I knew to be his.

It was dark enough for the lights to be on in the rows of small bungalows along the block. All the houses looked alike, and I was just about to give up finding Lonnie Olson's house when a shabbier, dark-windowed one behind a fringe of arborvitae seemed to single itself out. The house looked squat and brooding, empty, but as I stood looking at it, I saw light coming from a basement window, falling dim and yellow across patches of melting snow. Suddenly a light came on behind a main floor window, and before I could turn to run I saw a shadow, immense and slow and human, moving behind the drawn shade. I felt caught, full of what I'd been caught at, curiosity and sneaking; known, though no one saw me, and at the back of my throat there arose the feeling of the Dream, that something was too much.

Spring came on. At school we played at hopscotch—ten steps up, ten back, again, again—skirted girls on one foot, skipping on the numbered squares, marking place with pebbles. Sometimes we jumped rope, nearly hypnotized by the cadence of our chant—"Call for the Doctor, Call for the Nurse, Call for the Lady with the Alligator Purse"—knowing without it being said that it was the Alligator Purse, and the unseen things inside it, that linked the Doctor and the Nurse in some suggestive way.

Ruthie Wittenberg and I had a private game we called Cheyenne. Lying across a plaster-dusted mattress in our bare-lathed attic, wearing only our underpants, we squirmed, summoning the image of Cheyenne Bodie, a buckskin-shirted TV cowboy. What he did with us after he crawled through the prop-set attic window, Ruthie didn't specify, though I knew it had something vaguely to do with our chests, which the game required us to stick out, our backs arched, shoulders back. I writhed wholeheartedly, though, along with Ruthie, calling his name in the breathless tones she said grown women used when they talked to men. I followed Ruthie's lead. If she drew her hands along her thighs and up to her waist and chest, I did it, too. When she raised her hips and threw her arms above her head, I copied her. When she asked me why I didn't make up my own things, I told her I just liked the way hers looked, that she did it better. All spring we played our game, and if the thought occurred to me that Cheyenne had anything to do with Lonnie Olson, I pushed it away.

His birthday fell in May. It was the custom at school to bring birthday treats. Cupcakes were the favorite; the fluted paper cups could be licked of frosting and crumbs, then chewed on in secret, yielding taste long after the cake was gone, until the wads became a bitter pulp and Miss Doyle made us spit them in the wastebasket. Next in popularity were Tootsie Rolls, with their deep segments, the grooves where we fit our teeth and bit, the nubs filling our mouths, chocolate sugar sluicing noisily behind our teeth.

The day before his birthday, Lonnie Olson came up to me on the playground as I stood in the jump rope line. He tapped me on the shoulder, then told me about his treats. They would be the biggest, he said, the best we'd ever had. He was smiling and excited, his face closer to mine than it had ever been. Suddenly I realized he thought his treats would make the class start liking him. Embarrassed for him, at knowing his wish, embarrassed at being seen talking to him, but torn, too, by a sudden feeling of pity, I moved off a bit from the line. "I bet it's cupcakes," I said.

"It's a secret. You have to wait."

"Candy, then." I felt the line of girls staring at us, and when I looked over my shoulder I saw Ruthie frowning at me.

"Nope. You're really going to be surprised." His eyes darted toward the jump rope line. "You want to see her?" He put his hand in his pocket and I heard the pen click.

"No." I turned back to the line, edging closer to it. Behind me, he said his word—"orty teen"—too loud. The jump rope stopped its rhythmic slap, and the girls stood still, watching.

Searching for the damning phrase, I turned to look at him. I saw his thatch of hair, his mottled neck, and I realized I was the only one he talked to, and that this somehow linked me with him. I had to say something that would make him go away, and I had to say it in front of everybody else. Though I said them because they were the only words I could think of, because they were the most devastating in the lingua franca of the playground, the words I said were to become an inadvertent prophecy: "You stink."

The next day after lunch when it came time for Lonnie Olson's treats, the classroom was too warm. The radiator, turned on that morning against the chill, now hissed and clanked, and the smells of mayonnaise and orange rind, brown paper bags and milk, washed across us as we sat at our desks, squares of rough brown toweling in front of us. When a knock sounded at the door, Miss Doyle motioned for Lonnie Olson to answer it. As he crossed the room, he tripped on his shoelace. He caught himself and his color rose. Ducking his chin, he looked across the rows of desks at me, his face half-smirk, half-smile, and I knew he wanted—needed—me to return his look. I looked down, pretending to smooth the creases of my paper towel. When he opened the door, I felt the cooler air from the hallway that carried with it the good smell of yeast and new-baked bread.

He stood aside as a woman carrying four large flat bakery boxes entered the room and made her way slowly toward Miss Doyle's desk. Shuffling across the room in wide brown brogans smashed at the heels, anklets so small and tight they looked like adhesive tape around ankles which flared into calves that reminded me of cartoon hams, she was the biggest woman I had ever seen. Her hips rolled widely, and her breasts—loose, immense—spread beneath a pale blue dress, flour-dusted, butter-splotched. The class was silent. As she passed my row, I caught another smell, like frying onions, only deep and human, like Jennie Bronkala when she swept our floor. I looked around the room to see if I was the only one who smelled it, who wondered who the bakery woman was. But I knew already: above the fleshy roll of neck, beneath the dark blonde coronet braid, was a larger version of Lonnie Olson's pale-eyed, Slavic face, and from the whispering that began after she had nodded to Miss Doyle and pinched her son's cheek in a loving gesture that made him cringe, after she had left the room, I knew that everyone had smelled it.

Miss Doyle tuned us with her pitch pipe and we sang while row by row Lonnie Olson passed between our desks, proudly placing a large round pastry on each paper square. They were prune kolaches, but at the time I didn't know what they were called. What I saw on my desk, butter already darkening the paper around it, was like a flattened nest, at its center a jellied pool, glossy as hot tar. The room was quiet except for the rustling of waxed paper as Lonnie Olson moved among us, and for the whispering of a word passed along behind cupped hands, a word that hissed like the radiator, like the sound for silence: Polish.

No one ate. We sat unmoving, the treats before us like black-eyed stones, as he returned to his desk. Beside me, Deborah Pagel reached out to push her treat away with a flick of her charm-braceleted wrist. Others followed her example until

Miss Doyle, for reasons either cowardly or wise, saved us from the moment.

"Lonnie, these are lovely," she began in a voice that seemed overly bright, "but I think that . . . since the time is getting away from us . . . we should . . . ," she faltered a moment, then her voice seemed to find its power again, ". . . we should wrap them up so we can enjoy them at home."

I couldn't, as some of the others did, throw my kolache in an alley ash can on the way home, yet neither could I bring myself to taste it. I hid it, wrapped in its buttery paper, in the bottom drawer of my dresser, and I forgot about it until I woke up one night from the Dream, an unnameable taste full and heavy in my mouth. When I opened the drawer in the morning, the kolache had been removed, in its place a stack of folded anklets my mother had put away.

Then it was summer, and the things that happened at school, if not forgotten, seemed to matter less. My brothers went often to the bridge to play, but I stayed away, spending my time riding my bike up and down the block and through the alley or playing with Ruthie in the attic. Though we started out by playing Candyland or Tickle-Bee or Cootie, our game eventually turned into Cheyenne.

One day in June, Ruthie suggested that since it was so hot we should take off our underpants. I agreed. Giggling, we removed the last of our clothes, telling each other not to look. Then we lay back on the mattress, parallel but farther apart than was usual, on our backs, our toes pointed toward the window through which Cheyenne would enter.

I liked it yet I didn't; it felt free and daring and the air was cooler on my skin, but it seemed too close to the secret thing I had begun that summer to experiment with before I went to sleep. I didn't know quite how I felt about Ruthie's variation, and maybe that was why I picked at her when, squirming, her eyes half-lidded, she whispered, "Oh, Chey . . ."

"His name's Cheyenne," I said.

She elbowed me. "I know. But I just like to call him Chey. Ann is like a girl's name, don't you think?" She closed her eyes again and moved her hands up her stomach. "Oh, Chey."

I sat up. "It isn't Ann, either. Cheyenne is his whole name."

Ruthie looked at me. "It doesn't matter. We know who we mean."

"But his name's not Chey. That makes him sound stupid. Like he's bashful. Like shy."

She drew up her knees. "Well, he is, isn't he?"

I laughed. "You mean you think his name's S-H-Y A-N-N?"

She looked away, and I knew I'd hurt her feelings. "You think you know everything." She sat up, her back toward me, and reached for her clothes.

"I don't," I said. "I only know his name isn't Shy Ann." I gave a little laugh to show her it was all right. "That's all."

"You ruined it," she shouted. I heard her sniffle as she pulled her shirt over her head. "And you're stupid. Anybody who comes from Oklahoma is stupid. A dumb Okie. Everybody knows that."

I grabbed my shorts and yanked them on, forgetting my underpants. "I'm not," I yelled, "and I never liked this game. You're the one who always makes us play it." I jerked on my shirt.

Ruthie, stomping toward the attic door, her My Merry barrettes dangling at the unmoored ends of her bangs like drooping insect antennae, like Cootie feelers, wheeled. "You! You started it! You're the one who made the whole thing up!"

"I did not!" I shouted, and I started toward her, thinking I would pound her the way I tried to pound my brothers when they teased me, but then the way her bangs reminded me of a silly, haywire Cootie we'd once made struck me funny, and I laughed. I wanted to stop fighting.

"It's all you ever think about!" Ruthie yelled. She slammed the door behind her.

"I don't," I shouted back, but Ruthie was already gone.

If I had to give an answer for what I did next, why I went downstairs and through the kitchen past my mother, her apron tight around her swelling middle as she stirred raspberry Jell-O powder into boiling water, the odor rising ripe and fruity, past baby Laura who sat playing with Cheerios in her high chair tray, why I went into the backyard where my brothers played at Black Bart, making their gunshot noise, the pharyngeal implosion only boys and grown men showing off know how to make, groaning as they fell into handy bushes, dead or dying, why I went into the garage and got my bike, meaning to head for the bridge and Lonnie Olson, I could not have said it was because of Ruthie or kolaches or the Dream, the jump rope chant, a butter box or Mrs. Cookson, Cheyenne or orty teen, pity, curiosity, atonement. If anyone had asked me why I did what I did next, I would have had to tell the only truth I knew, the truth that stands as fast now as it would have stood then: I didn't know.

The wind blew my shirt against my chest and I felt the blood-pulse ticking in my legs as I pedaled up Olive toward the bridge. I remembered that my underpants were still in the attic, but I didn't care, and when I came to the elm-root buckles in the sidewalk I didn't raise myself from the seat. At the bridge I got off the bike and wheeled it down the slope, then dropped it by the concrete slab where I had first sat with Lonnie Olson. I ducked down and went under the bridge.

He wasn't there. I sat in one of the smooth-packed hollows. The ground rose winter-cold through the fabric of my shorts. Cars went by above me, a heavy whir at first, then shadow flickers as they rolled across the expansion slats, a diminishing treadle as they passed onto the street. I looked out of my hiding place onto the bright expanse of ditch, the trails, the burdock, clover, purple thistle, and I thought about Lonnie Olson. I wondered what *he* thought about. I wondered if he hated me. I wondered what it would feel like to be him, and then, as though just thinking about him had summoned him, like the djinni in the story, he was there.

He approached from the opposite embankment, climbing the slope toward me. His dungarees had been cut off to make shorts, and his bare knees were dusky with limestone mud. He stepped into my hollow and sat across from me, then picked up a rusted can lid and began to scratch in the dirt with it, releasing the moist earth-smell of rain, night crawlers, mildew. I pressed my knees together, suddenly afraid he could guess about the underpants, afraid he could know about the activity that led to their absence. I picked up a flat stone and scraped it along the wall of the hollow until goose bumps rose along my arms.

"You din't eat it." He looked out onto the sunny weeds of the ditch, and I saw his pupils constrict as they moved beyond the shadow.

"I did," I said. "At home." I was prepared to defend my lie, if it came to that—in my mind, the wish that I had eaten it had become the truth—but he was silent. His face looked naked, close. When a car whooshed overhead, he flinched.

"I know about your word," I said.

His look was blank, unreadable.

"That one you always say. I know what it means."

"What?"

I looked at my hands, fumbling with the stone. "You know." I bent to scratch a row of X's in the dirt.

"You have to say it," he said. "Then I'll say if you're right."

I looked across the ditch, at the names and words chalked on the pylons. I made another X, then dropped the stone. "It means," I said, "what people do."

His shrug said maybe, maybe not, and it incensed me.

"Then what? You can't just say it!"

He smiled, smug, inscrutable, then said it.

I hit him—open-handed, an undershot girl-slap—my fingers glancing numbly off his jaw then flying, almost automatically, to my own. I sat still, shocked by what I had done.

His eyes tearing, he stared at me. Then he hit me back, in my same gesture, along the side of my throat. His blow was dull as mine had been, but my throat filled suddenly, and I swallowed. My nose began to run. I sniffed, swallowed again, and in that swallow tasted, felt, the confusing fullness of everything, the gorged feeling of the Dream, and though I didn't— though I felt for him something I couldn't name—I said, "I hate you."

He nodded. "So?" He had reached into his pocket and brought out his ballpoint. "You want to see the man?" He tried to grab my hand, but I drew it back.

"Orty teen," he said, and in the way he said it, the word took on the power of clear and simple reason.

I held out my hand, my left, palm up. He drew the torso of a man, its board-straight sides, the same small V's for arms, dots for nipples, navel. The pen's pressure tickled, but I held still. Where the torso's legs began he drew a long, full U, like Kilroy's nose, flanking it with C's, one of them reversed. He released my hand and began to draw on his own, inking the lady across the creases. Then he put away the pen.

I knew what we were going to do. I held up my palm. He fit his against mine.

We pressed—gently at first, then harder, like people pushing at opposite sides of a door, until it became a contest: he pushed, I pushed, our elbows locked, and neither arm would give or weaken. I felt his hand, foreign and intact, its other-ness against mine, the images pressing at each other, warming, too warm; hot, suddenly, as shame. I drew away my hand. He let his fall. For what seemed a long time, he looked at me, then he got up to leave. I watched until he disappeared along one of the trails, his narrow shoulders set, his pale hair fading into the color of the tall dry weeds he walked into until I could no longer tell where he left off and they began.

I stayed under the bridge and looked at the picture, at the way the lines folded on themselves and seemed to bend the figure as I cupped my hand. I rubbed at the ink. The dirt smeared slightly but the blue lines held. I licked my thumb and tried again to erase the man. Finally I brought the picture to my mouth, tasted ink and salt and dirt and skin that tasted suddenly like something I had just remembered, something I had already known. I rubbed at the damp spot on my hand until the blue began to smudge, to blend into the dirt, to fade until the spot became so faint that if anyone had noticed, I could have said it was a bruise.

THE WACO WEGO

B EFORE he lost heart for the practice of law and went
on to serve twelve terms as judge in our small town—a
post that called for warning harborers of goats within town
boundaries, fining hot rodders who careened through flocks of
hens on the county roads, and chiding those citizens of Pawnee
Wells (everyone in town) who coasted through our four-way
stop—my father was a reckless driver.

Not in town, of course. And never on the highway that
linked us to big meat-packing, airplane-building Wichita to
the north. But on the sand-bed roads that scored the fields of
milo, wheat, and soybeans between the little towns stationed
along U.S. 81 between us and the Oklahoma line, he turned
into an outlaw.

He called it "veering into the rough." The rough, to my
younger brothers and me, shrieking in the back seat, meant the
embankment of the levee, the wind-ribbed dunes of the Big
Slough—any place our family Ford would hazard. My mother
refused to ride with us. She maintained that these excursions
were a throwback to a boyhood wild and best forgotten, and
she dropped lead-heavy hints that the rearing of children
would proceed more smoothly without such rowdiness. She
pursed her lips at our breathless homecomings, speared more

47

violently the sizzling chops as we told about near-misses and close calls. "Think of what they're learning from you, Jim."

"Awful," she called us, our delight, his scofflaw attitude, "awful" being her strongest epithet. But only the harrowed Ford in the driveway—bug-bespattered, weed-festooned, engine ticking like a locust jamboree—managed to look chastened.

"Off scot-free!" my father would whoop to our success, and we were unrepentant. We loved the rough, and if it occurred to me to wonder if these rides courted the wrath of my mother's Texas Baptist God, I shrugged the thought away. I believed most headlong in my father's rakehell grin: he would outride, outsmart, and outmaneuver any obstacle fortune threw in his path, even if he had to go out of his way to find it. He never had a wreck.

In 1961, the summer I turned thirteen, something happened to my father, and the rough-riding stopped. After the biggest trial of his career, he gave up his practice and for several months he spent the days carving great blocks of Silverdale stone into Easter Island heads, which he set around our yard like rows of stern, stone judges. At night he read Dostoyevsky, and it seemed he hardly spoke to us. Though I understand now that much more than I could see went into this, at the time I held at center, as cause and reason for the changes in him, myself and what had happened on our last rough-ride.

That summer the papers had been full of my father's client, a lank-boned, one-eyed man named Daniel Long. He had been accused of a double murder: the bartender at the lounge where Long worked part-time as doorguard, and Ulla Ricke, the waitress, who was Long's common-law wife and the mother of his two boys. The newspaper photographer had caught Long in profile, grinning, the eye that showed askant, so the white stood out like an awful star in the shadow the picture had made of his face. The hank of black hair that fell across his forehead made me think of the mark of Cain, and every time I looked at the picture, which was often, the word "evil" fixed itself more firmly in my imagination. Ulla

Ricke's body had been dismembered, the paper said, bits of black cocktail dress still clinging to the parts that he'd wrapped in butcher paper, then stuffed into an oil drum and dumped into the Big Arkansas. The reason for the murder, the paper said, was a love triangle.

If my father was already a celebrity in Pawnee Wells—he was city attorney and one of the few white-collars in a town that piled into pickup trucks each morning for the factories of Boeing, Beechcraft, Lear, and Cessna, and our family rode on a float with other members of the town council each year in the Founders' Day parade (from which perch it did not occur to me to wonder if the waves returned me by the sons and daughters of burr-bench operators carried any measure of re-sentment)—his celebrity was clinched by his appointment as Daniel Long's attorney. The town couldn't talk enough about the trial, and people stopped to ask me what I thought.

When I went into the Rexall, Bonner Wilkie wouldn't hand over my lemon Pepsi until he delivered his opinion on the sorry state of law. "Your daddy's smart," he concluded, "but if he was really smart he wouldn't stand up in front of God and everybody's dog and tell lies for white trash. Long's guilty as sin and everybody knows it."

I told Bonner Wilkie how court appointments worked, but he shook his head and leaned across the counter, his face so close I could smell the sour lump of Red Man behind his cheek. "He knows Long did it, don't he, Paula?"

"He's not supposed to say," I said. I sipped my drink while he waited for me to go on, but I could not make myself admit to him that at home my father refused to talk about the case.

At the perfume counter, Mary Rose Reese and her girl-gang, smelling of Emeraude, My Sin, and Kool Filter Kings, stopped me. Mary Rose cracked her gum. "You scared?"

"He's in jail," I said.

Vonda Hardesty bent toward the counter mirror. She made a kissing mouth and began to apply another coating of white lip-stick. "Your dad's real cute."

Mary Rose asked me if I thought Daniel Long would go free. "I don't know."

She had narrowed her eyes. "Well, you think he killed 'em, don't you?"

I shrugged, and though I thought he was guilty, had come at big, blonde Ulla Ricke like the paper said, had stabbed her thirty-nine times, then hacked at her with his machete, I said, "That's for the jury to decide."

In those days when I held my father up to Ike or Solomon or Perry Mason, he came out ahead, and I loved best those times when I did something that would make him say, "Smart girl." When I heard myself saying to Mary Rose Reese the words I'd heard him say—the jury will decide—I knew I'd done the right thing, and I knew he would be proud of me. What surprised me was the sudden sense of separateness, of elevation, the words gave me, as though in saying them I'd grown wiser.

I hoped to show him how wise I had become when, on a Sunday morning in early August when my mother and brothers had gone to church, he asked me if I wanted to go with him to see Daniel Long's mother, who worked at a truckstop cafe called the Waco Wego, south on 81. "I think you're old enough to see how the real world works, Sis."

The day was still and hazed, the traffic light in that hour when Sunday school classes convened in cool church basements. As we braked at the four-way, the bank thermometer showed eighty-six degrees. Out on the highway, mirages shimmered in the tar-veined macadam. "It's done with smoke and mirrors," I said, hoping to get his attention, pointing to the bright reflection ahead of us, an old routine he'd started years before when I'd asked why we never splashed into the pools.

He laughed. "By Oz, the great and powerful."

Just past the town limits, we found a pasture access road that showed a promising tree line in the distance. My father slowed the car then turned off the highway. "You're not too grown-up for this, now, are you?" He was grinning his Wile E. Coyote grin.

I laughed, shook my head. "Oh, no." I braced my legs against the floorboards as we bumped across the pasture.

We drove through brome and buffalo grass and I heard the thresh of weeds beneath the chassis. Tall spiked heads of rattlesnake master struck the bumper. My father called out the names of grasses, weeds, and trees. "Poppy mallow. Bull thistle. Osage orange." It was a game: I was to call out the Latin when I knew it. "Goatsbeard!" he yelled at a tall weed with a silver head that looked like spun sugar. "*Tragopogon dubius,*" I shouted. "Ha!"

Down among the trees we found a dry creek bed, and we bounced along the hardpan until we hit a sand draw. "Trap!" he yelled. "Now we've done it!"

We lugged and fishtailed in the friable, false-bottomed stuff, and he mock-wrestled with the wheel. I laughed.

"Momentum!" he urged, and I leaned forward to make the noises my brothers and I had always made. But suddenly, without the boys, those noises seemed silly, ridiculous, and I was glad when we hit hardpan again, then left it to go back across the pasture toward the opening in the barbed wire fence. Back on the highway, we picked up speed.

He pushed the lighter into its socket, but forgot to pull it out when it clicked, his Winston resting on his lower lip. "This won't take long," he said. "It's a kindness more than anything. She's having a rough time of it."

I smoothed my cotton skirt and tried to match his tone for what I'd taken as irritation with the woman. "I can imagine." I wondered what the mother of a murderer would look like.

He had forgotten the cigarette. "Besides, you've never seen your old dad at work, have you?"

"Not talking to a client. Or at court. Only writing things."

"That's the smoke," he said. "The easy part." He laughed, then punched the lighter in, this time holding his fingers over the knob.

I wanted to keep the conversation on the trial, to show how much I knew about it. "It was pretty awful, wasn't it?"

"It?"

"What he did. How he cut her up."

He lit his cigarette, then expelled smoke in a tight, down-sped flume. "Who?"

I realized my error. My father had taught us not to make assumptions, to be specific in our references. I supposed this made him a good lawyer, but it often turned a talk with him into a trial, and left me feeling on the shaded side of dim.

"Daniel Long," I said. "Him. Assuming he did it. It was pretty awful."

"We can't know for certain. He says he didn't kill them, and we have to operate on the presumption . . ."

I finished his phrase. Along with stories about his daredevil boyhood, I had heard the lecture on the presumption of inno-cence many times, along with lectures about the burden of proof, the spirit and the letter, habeas and all the corpora, prima facie and circumstantial, malice aforethought, as well as post hoc ergo propter hoc and what seemed like a thousand other logical fallacies. These were the precepts he carted out to settle arguments when my brothers and I couldn't settle them ourselves, and he drove my mother wild with fury when he brought them into husband-wife disputes. I listened while he went on, but I was ready to show him that I was wise enough to go beyond the abstract. "I know all that," I said. "But what do you really think? He did it, didn't he? All that blood on that axe."

"Machete," he corrected.

"There's motive," I said. "And opportunity. That man who saw him coming out of the lounge." I persisted. "Daniel Long is guilty, right?"

He drove awhile, smoking, then put out his cigarette. "The jury will decide, Sis. It isn't up to us."

Stung, I turned to look out the window as we moved along the highway past the fields, the stands of cottonwood and wil-low fringing the shallow Ninnescah that now and then curved toward the straight-line highway as though it was the river rather than the road that had to yield. We passed plywood sheds whose painted sides offered squash, tomatoes, roasting ears. In black lightning-letters one sign promised "Cantiloap," and I pointed at it. "Stupid," I said, trying to catch his attention; "stupid" was his most damning curse, even worse than "harebrained" or "irrational," and if I happened to be anywhere near an act or an idea that he deemed stupid, I smarted more than if he'd struck me. "If they grow it, why can't they spell it?"

My father was quiet, busy making the turn from the highway into the rutted parking lot of the Waco Wego. Farm trucks were parked haphazardly in front of the Alamo-shaped facade of the cafe. We pulled in under the branches of a Chinese elm and parked beside a wooden sign where tin plates had been nailed, their letters spelling out the cafe's name. He took the keys from the ignition.

"He says he didn't do it, Paula, and I have to believe him. You understand that, don't you?"

I nodded. Two shirtless little boys darted from behind a Bunny Bread sign and ran around the side of the building into the trees at the edge of a ravine. "Are those his and Ulla Ricke's boys?"

He nodded. He took his briefcase from the seat between us. "Mrs. Long isn't . . ." he began, then stopped to zip his case. "She isn't the kind of person you're used to, but try to see past that and understand how she's feeling."

I opened my car door. "Oh, I will."

Outside, he looked at me across the hood of the car, as though considering me for the first time, and I wondered if he suddenly regretted bringing me. But he smiled. "I wouldn't have brought you if I didn't have faith in you, Sis."

I gestured toward the tin plate sign. "What does the name mean?"

He shook his head. "Something Indian. It's an old place name, I imagine." He tucked his briefcase under his arm. "To tell the truth, I don't really know."

"Eat at Joe's, maybe," I offered, and he laughed. We walked toward the screen door of the Waco Wego.

The cafe smelled of cigarettes and coffee, field dirt and sweat and cooking grease, the sharp, hot animal smell of bacon cut from a boar let go too long before gelding. Men in seed caps swiveled on their counter stools to look at us as we came through the door. I heard a coin chink into the jukebox behind the door, the selector whirring, then the whine of a slow, high fiddle.

From behind the counter came a large, thick-torsoed woman, her huge shoulders tapering buffalo-like to legs that looked impossibly thin. She wore gray twill men's trousers and a chambray work shirt, the sleeves cut raggedly off, showing upper arms that looked huge and mottled. She drew an order pad from the pocket of her tiny apron as though on reflex, then jammed it back. "Well, now," she said. "Here's Jim Franklin." She fumbled at the pencil tucked behind her ear, and for all her bulk, she appeared uneasy and apologetic.

My father smiled at her. "Hello, LaFaye."

She giggled, covering her mouth with her large, red-knuckled hand. "Shoot, you're the only one that calls me that, Jim. Makes me feel like a girl." She pulled at her earlobe, coy, then gestured toward the line of farmers at the counter. "I sure get tired of them all calling me Laffy." Her expression turned mournful, and I almost laughed before I realized she didn't mean her look to be comic. "When there don't seem all that much to laugh about."

My father put his arm around her big shoulders. "This won't take long," he said. "I just want you to know what's going on when the trial comes." He squeezed her shoulder. "Don't be nervous, honey."

I started: this was the first time I'd heard him call a woman by a pet name. He called my mother Jo or Josephine, and me he called Paula, Sis, or Sister. In the way he called LaFaye Long "honey," I heard a kind of tenderness that made me wonder if he genuinely liked her, that made me feel left out of something. I tried to remember if he'd ever used the name on me.

54

When he introduced us, she grabbed my hand. "How do," she said. She smiled; two lower teeth were gone. "How do."

"It's nice to meet you, Mrs. Long," I said. I tried to pull my hand away.

She pumped my arm; her hand was moist, her grip tight. "Your daddy says you do real good in school." On the word "school," her voice seemed to crackle. She cleared her throat. "You make him proud, now, hear?"

"I'll try." I made my hand go loose so she would let go, but she held on.

"Your daddy's one fine man," she said. "One damn fine man. He's got the common touch and he don't forget we all come from the same damn monkey." She laughed, and I heard a loose, phlegmy sound. I pulled a bit at my hand. "And Jimbo, I'll say that to any son-a-bitch that asks!" With her free hand she gestured extravagantly toward the line of men hunched at the counter. "'Course, I don't see no sons-a-bitches askin'!" She beamed, then released my hand.

My father directed us to a booth by the back window. I slid in and sat at the center of the bench, expecting him to take the seat opposite me. But he slid in beside me. "Scooch over, Sis." I realized this meant that Mrs. Long would sit with us.

But she remained standing, shuffle-footed at the edge of the table. "Get you coffee, Jim?"

"Sounds good," he said. "And maybe Paula would like a doughnut." He shifted in the booth to look at me. "Or wait. You've never had a real truckstop breakfast, have you? How about it—bacon, eggs, a side of spuds?" He nudged my elbow and grinned.

I didn't know how to take his sudden, folksy change. Was he teasing me, pointing out the difference between us and the other people in the Waco Wego; was he serious?

"Aw, Jim, don't tempt her." Mrs. Long winked at me. "She don't want all that. I bet she's trying to keep her little figure. See how she's all buddin' out?" She directed a sly look toward my chest. "Why, I bet there's boys around like buzzards!" She giggled, smiling at my father. "And don't I know how trouble-some that can get!" She rapped a knuckle on the scarred Formica as though she'd suddenly had a revelation. "Old Laffy knows what she wants," she said.

I felt my face grow warm, and I looked down at my hands in my lap. I wished she would disappear, that the floor would swallow her up, but then I understood that, like someone who refuses to tell a joke's punchline until everyone is listening, she was waiting for me to look at her before she made her pro-nouncement. I made myself look up.

"She wants a soda pop. The diet kind!"

I turned to look out the window, pretending interest in the trees by the ravine. "Coffee," I said. "Black."

Her voice sounded hurt. "You sure, now?"

I nodded, still looking out the window, and she went away, her step heavy.

My father reached over to pull the ashtray toward his place. He brought out his Zippo, and I heard the metallic click, smelled the familiar lighter fluid. "This won't take long," he said.

I looked around the cafe. "I see what you mean." I rolled my eyes to show what I thought about the twang of the juke-box, the work-worn, dirty men at the counter, the scuffed-up, beaten feel of the Waco Wego, Mrs. Long's embarrassing dis-play, but he didn't catch my look.

He exhaled smoke, stretched his free arm across the seat back. "This place is like those little cafes your grandpa used to take me to when we went on harvest," he said. He was leaning back, his legs extended into the aisle. "This kind of place makes you feel more like yourself."

I stared at him. Then, suddenly, I understood the message he was trying to send me: that we were supposed to be big enough to see past what these people were and give them the impres-sion that there was no difference between our kind and theirs. I felt better knowing this, and I relaxed a little in the booth. "Sure does," I said. "It sure does."

When Mrs. Long returned, she set the coffee cups before us and sat on the opposite bench. The plastic wheezed as she put her weight on it, and I caught a whiff of stale foam rubber and sour clothing. While she settled herself, I stirred my coffee.

When I reached for the bowl of sugar packets and took one, shaking it by the corner, my pinkie finger raised the way I'd seen my mother raise hers, my father nudged me, grinning. "Thought you took your coffee black, Sis."

I stopped shaking the packet. The cup was my first, and he knew it.

"Don't pester her, Jim." Mrs. Long smiled at me with her gap-toothed grin. "Me, I can't take it black, neither." She shook her head, and I saw that her hair had been dye-burned, the ends frizzled, sparse growth on the crown. "It's them damn calories, though. Why, I just so much as look cross-eyed at that rabbit on the molasses bottle and I blow up a hundred pounds." When she patted her belly, I looked away from the strained buttons of her shirt. "But I just think, oh, what the hell—what's a little fat?" She winked at my father. "More to love on, right, Jim?" She reached across the table to pat my hand. "You have your sugar, hon."

Sitting back, she grinned at us as though she was proud of her speech, then again reached out to pat my hand. "Us girls have to stick together."

My father said, "I guess you're right, LaFaye."

"Oh, hell," she said. "You call me Laffy, too." She giggled. "I guess I'm just the kind of gal that can't stay down too long."

She was trying to charm us, I realized, and I smiled at her so my father would see I understood. I was relieved when he brought out his pad of foolscap and his fountain pen and began writing across the top of the page.

"The docket's set for September nine," he said. "The first thing is jury selection."

I sat, spooning up little drinks of coffee, sipping at them, stealing looks at Mrs. Long, the mother of the murderer. She didn't seem to be listening, but picked with her thumbnail at a burn-blister in the Formica. From time to time her mouth worked around words that seemed to want to come out. I imagined her tongue poking into the empty spaces inside her mouth. I put down my spoon and sat up straighter, hoping she would take my posture as an example. My father talked on about juries, newspaper accounts, sequestering. I nodded at the points he made.

The next time I looked at her, I saw that she was crying. Her face puckered, her mouth straining to cover her teeth. She lowered her head and moved it slowly back and forth, cowlike.

"My heart is broke," she moaned. She wiped her nose with the back of her hand. "Daniel didn't do it."

I stopped stealing looks and stared openly at her.

My father handed her a napkin. "Don't let this scare you, honey. That's what we'll try to prove in court."

She blew her nose. "Just broke." Again her mouth stretched wide. "I raised him right." Her head jerked up and suddenly she looked angry. "I raised him right!" I saw the color rise into her scalp.

My father reached across the table to pat her hand. "Of course you did. Now, all we're doing here is going over a few things so you'll know what's happening in September."

"You don't know," she said. "You don't know what it's like. You got it easy. Never all these problems." She pronounced it "prollems."

"It's been hard for you," my father agreed.

She sniffed, seemingly mollified. "You just don't know him like I do. I'm his mother. A mother knows her own." Her face had gone mottled, her nose reddened at the tip, a sick-looking green along the sides. She tried to smile at me but I looked away, pretending to rub at a speck on the window glass.

"Why, when he was a little kid, you never saw a cuter squirt. This was before he lost his eye." She wiped her own eyes, rubbing them so hard I heard moist, clicking sounds. "He had this calf one time. A little black bull calf. Bought him

over to the auction yard." She gestured toward the trees outside the window, as though the location of the auction yard
proved the calf's existence. Outside, the two little boys played
in the mud flats at the bottom of the ravine. They chipped at
the slabs of cracked, curling mud, making piles that looked
like wattled huts.

"He loved that calf. Made a little pen for him out back.
Called him Feller. Lord-a-mighty, it was Feller-this and Feller-
that. All I ever heard. Loved him like a baby. That calf'd bawl
out in the night and up Daniel'd be, out there loving him and
petting him."

She wiped at a ring on the table, then blew her nose into the
napkin. I waited for my father to change the subject, to talk
again about the trial.

"Some mean boys came around once and tried to ride on
Feller. Daniel wasn't having none of it. Them boys came back
at night and we heard Feller out there bawling. Little old
Daniel got him a board with some nails drove in the end of it
and he was after 'em." She smiled. "You never saw such. Why,
I believe if anybody'd hurt that calf, old Daniel would of killed
'em."

Her laugh was hopeful, then it trailed away. "I didn't
mean . . ."

I heard my father's Zippo click open, smelled lighter fluid.
"A figure of speech." He lit his cigarette, waved away the
smoke that was blowing my way.

Mrs. Long shifted in her seat, glancing wildly around the
cafe. It seemed her gaze was seeking some safe place to fix itself. "I only meant . . ."

He flipped through his legal pad. "An expression." When I
felt his knee press into mine beneath the table, I realized I'd
been clanking my spoon around my cup rim.

"Now, the prosecuting attorney will have a few things to
say, and you need to be prepared for them."

I let out the breath I'd been holding. He resumed talking but
I scarcely heard. I hoped he would soon finish.

Suddenly, Mrs. Long turned toward me and rapped her knuckles on the table. "You damn kids! You kids don't listen! You think you're so damn smart. You think you're just above the rest of us!"

I stared at her, or rather, I couldn't look away. Her eyes, narrow and accusing, seemed to pin me to my place, and for an awful moment it was as though the truth had switched from our side to hers and that as long as she held my look that truth held, too. Then her face crumpled into grief. "I taught him! I raised him right!"

"Of course you did, LaFaye." My father gave a rueful laugh, and I knew that he would hold up the example of my brothers and me as proof and that this would feel like a betrayal. But I saw now that with the kind of wild, irrational person who was LaFaye Long, you said whatever you had to. Still, I wanted him to defend us, to defend himself, to say that maybe if she'd been a different kind of person—a normal, smart person—her son wouldn't have grown up to kill people and then lie about it. "I know how it is, honey," he said. "I've got kids, too. You can't blame yourself, LaFaye, you did the best you could."

She chortled then, and seemed satisfied. Again my father began to go over the details of the trial. I tried some more of my coffee, but it had gone cool and bitter.

Mrs. Long fidgeted with her order pad and from time to time she sighed. Then, suddenly, she spanked the table top. "I just remembered!" She licked her lips. "He was with me that night! Daniel was right here with me!"

My father laid down his pen. "It's a little late for this."

"I had this trash that needed burned, see. And he said to me, Daniel said to me, 'Well, Mama, why don't I just come on down and burn it for you?'"

She fingered the top button of her blouse. "That's the kind of person he is. He said, 'Now, Mama, there's no earthly need for you to wear yourself out like that. I'll just do it for you.' I had this mess of egg flats, I remember, and they needed burned." She pointed out the window. "Right out there."

She wiped her hand across her forehead and looked at my father. "Boy-howdy, Jim, I'm damn glad I remembered that!" I felt the blood rush to my head, and my ears seemed to ring with every word my father had ever spoken about what was right and what was wrong. Mrs. Long had committed every offense against logic, had done everything he had taught us not to do—lying foremost—and still he sat there, listening to her, seeming not to judge her.

There had to be an end to this; if you let the little breaches pass, you might as well give up the law, the right, altogether. There had to be a point when you stopped feeling sorry for people, stopped doing all the understanding for them, and made them pay for what they'd done. There had to be a point beyond which there was no excuse.

I banged my spoon on the table. "That's a lie!"

Mrs. Long's mouth fell open. My father stood. "Paula, wait outside."

Refusing to look at them, I slid out of the booth. The men at the counter watched as I walked across the room, but I didn't care. I knew the sun outside the Waco Wego would be hot and blinding, but I didn't care: I knew it would welcome me into a better world. I knew my father would apologize for my behavior: let him. I was right about LaFaye Long, right about her evil son, right to say that she was lying.

I crossed the parking lot and walked north along the highway shoulder. Grasshoppers ticked in the dockweed and jimson grass of the ditch, and when cars went by, I felt the windblown dust pepper my ankles. A grain truck rumbled toward me on the opposite lane, and the farm boys standing in the truckbed waved and yelled at me, "Hey, baby!" as they passed. I felt suddenly—unbearably—exposed, that there was nothing but my feet to hold me to the earth, nothing between the girl who walked along the highway in her silly white flats, her cotton skirt and blouse, nothing between me and the high, wide sky. I turned around and went back to sit on the bumper of the Ford.

Daniel Long's little boys came up from the ravine, hauling a wagonload of chipped mud slabs across the lot toward the highway. They hid the wagon behind the "Cantiloap" sign. When cars went by, they pelted them with the chips, which broke across the windshields into shards and dust. The boys laughed wildly each time, then ran back behind the sign. This was the kind of prank my brothers pulled, but when Daniel Long's boys did it, the act took on a different, darker color. Anyone, I reasoned, would have to acknowledge this. My father, I decided, would think it simple mischief. He would call them "honey."

From the highway I heard rumbling from a line of heavy custom-cutter trucks moving south along 81, returning from harvest in the Dakotas. The lead truck turned slowly into the parking lot and the others—carrying huge green and yellow John Deere combines—followed, roiling dust into the leaves of the overhanging elms. Texas, from the tags. Daniel Long's boys watched, but held their fire.

The cab doors opened and the cutters jumped down. A girl who looked only a little older than I was stood in the doorway of the first truck. She wore ragged cutoffs, tight around plump thighs, a red bandanna halter top. Her hair hung in greasy lanks down her neck. She called to one of the men. "Hey, Rucker, catch me!"

A man held out his arms and the girl jumped. He set her down, then reached around to pinch her. She squealed, slapping away his hand. "Cut that out, you nasty old hog!" I heard her giggle as they slap-boxed each other.

The man said, "How 'bout a little sugar?" He grabbed at her.

The girl said, "Get bent, Rucker."

Rucker's expression went dull, but then he smiled, in his eyes a wicked, teasing glint, and he snapped the shoulder strap of her bandanna. "Hey, how's come you call that thing a halter top? It sure ain't got much to halt. Haw!" He doubled over, holding his belly.

She tossed her hair in a sassy way. "You just keep your old paws where they'll do the most good, Rucker Massey. In your own damn pants!"

He guffawed and they walked toward the cafe. Just as Rucker and the girl reached the door, the boys behind the sign let fly. Mud chips shattered against the side of the cafe, against the backs of Rucker and the girl. Rucker wheeled, doubling his fists, looking around. The girl caught sight of the boys running for the ravine. "Goddamn brats!" she yelled. "Forget it, Ruck." She tugged at his hand and they went inside.

I let myself into the car and sat, the windows rolled up, the doors locked. The air was hot and still, heat-radiant, close. I thought about the girl. How would my father like it if I were such a girl?

I sat in the hot car and smelled the bitter coffee-breath that seemed to fill the car when I breathed out, a sour, heavy tang when I breathed in, highway dust, the creosote smell of tar that had smeared my shoe, sweat, the cloying chemical sweetness of the hairspray I'd put on at home when I'd felt so grown-up about being invited along, now liquefying in the heat. I said words to myself. "Awful," I said. "Stupid." And it was a long time before I realized that in the company of those I meant to curse—LaFaye Long, her son and grandsons, the farmers at the counter, Rucker Massey and the girl, the murdered Ulla Ricke for ever hooking up with such people—I had to include myself.

At last my father came out. I watched his face as he walked toward the car, the way the elm-leaf dapple shadowed his eyes and seemed to hood them. He would be angry. I tried to think of what I could say against the rebuke I knew was coming.

He opened the car door and I felt the outside air break the seal, the wash of moving air. He rolled down the window, put the keys in the ignition, started the car. He backed out, then began to circle through the lot past the trucks.

I waited. His silence seemed worse than any punishment. I slouched in the seat, felt mean and hot and put-upon, and before I knew I meant to say anything, my stomach seemed to rise into my chest with the wrong Mrs. Long had committed. "She lied!"

My father steered the car around a chuckhole. The car lurched as a back tire slipped into the rut.

"That's perjury," I said. "And it makes it even worse! She *knows* he did it. How can she say he didn't?"

I expected him to call into doubt how I could know she was lying, but he didn't. He braked slightly to ease the car along another rutted spot just before the pavement began.

"I don't know," he said. His words had come slowly, as though he was puzzling something out. "A thousand reasons. She loves him. She wants to believe it." He eased his grip on the steering wheel, flexed his fingers, then tightened them around the wheel once more. "Maybe she feels that somehow she might be to blame. That in some way it's herself on trial."

If I had had my senses with me, if I hadn't been so angry, I would have heard in his words and in his tone his admission of what he believed about Daniel Long's guilt. I would have heard myself admitted to the inner circle of the law. But I was twelve and hot and angry. "That's just plain stupid." I cranked the window down. "*She's* stupid."

He brought the car to a full stop at the edge of the highway and looked over at me. "Paula," he said. "Honey, do you understand that what you did can be seen as an even greater wrong than hers?"

Stunned, I could only stare at him as he pulled onto the highway. He was wrong, and I wanted to pound at the dashboard with my fists to prove it. At the same time, something sad and different in the way he'd spoken to me made me want to cry. When the mud chips began to break against the windshield, cobbling the hood and roof like brownish hail, I felt as though they were aimed at me. "No."

The mud rained faster, and one clod hit the dash and ricocheted. The window glass grew clouded, brown with swirling grit. He hit the brake. "What the hell?"

When I realized he couldn't know where the mud was coming from, I felt strangely pleased, that this was somehow just. A proof.

I waved my hand at the sign where the boys hid. "Go on," I shouted. "It's just those brats."

He accelerated, and when we were beyond their range, I said, "Those goddamn brats!"

I felt his shock. He had never heard me swear. I'd never sworn. But there was nothing he could say about it. Nothing that I didn't have an answer for. And if that answer wasn't rational, so what? I was done with reason. All it ever did was make you see how you were wrong and everybody else got off scot-free. LaFaye Long could swear.

We rode in silence. He smoked. I looked out the window.

Finally he spoke, and his voice sounded tired, as though he knew that nothing he could say would make a difference. "Paula, I'm . . . we . . . none of us is perfect. You can't expect . . ." He fell silent, then began again. "The law itself is far from perfect, but it's the best way we have to get at things we can't ever know for certain. To make things fair for everybody."

He was looking at me, and his expression, clouded by what must have been confusion about how everything had gone so haywire, seemed to clear, as though he saw the reasoning behind the way I'd acted. Then, as quickly as his face had cleared, it again grew clouded with what looked like a sudden, heartsunk understanding of the place he'd held in all that reasoning, and in a tender voice it hurt to hear, he asked me, "Sister, have I led you to believe I'm without fault?"

The answer that he must have wanted was, "Of course not." But I knew a loaded question when I heard one. The truth was Yes, I had believed that he was perfect. And Yes, I had been led to this belief—by everything he'd ever told me about right and wrong, by all he knew, by his insistence on the truth, the sacredness of oaths and words and honor, by his knowing which laws were insignificant enough to break. I saw then that another truth was No, he hadn't intended for me to make of all this a belief that he was faultless, that it hurt him to consider what he'd done to cause me to believe this, and so the greater truth lay somewhere in the middle, closer to a No, but this left only me—alone—to hold the blame. I looked down at my hands and answered, "Yes, you have."

He slowed the car. The change made time seem heavy, damped the sound of rushing wind around my ears. I looked at him and saw that his gaze went beyond the trees that lined the road, the ribbon of macadam, and seemed to move into the distance. "You need to learn . . ." he began.

I looked away. I knew enough. I watched the trees roll past and gave them names I'd learned from him: Chinese elm and cottonwood (*Populus deltoides*); bitter-green black walnuts with their oily thick-skinned fruit (Put them in a gunny sack and run over them with a pickup truck: Oklahoma Nutcracker); mulberry (of the family *Moraceae*); dusky Russian olives (Shelterbelt Project came through here in the thirties, Sis, planted twenty thousand); catalpas with their blooms like hothouse orchids (from the Creek *kutuhlpa,* a head with wings). I knew all this.

He couldn't seem to find the words for what I didn't know. "To learn . . ."

I knew the names of fields: hard winter wheat, the Turkey Red kind brought by Russian Mennonites; kaffir corn and milo, sorghum, still threshed, when he was young, by mules hitched to the mill to make Great Plains molasses; melons ranging broadleafed, low; grass, the thousand nameless kinds that cover our part of the world in a way that looks like nothing less than grace. If I didn't know the words he wanted, I knew their meaning, but I held my silence.

For a long time I imagined that it was at some time during our speechless ride back home that there had come the moment out of which my father would give up his practice, take up the once-a-week town bench where he became the teller of stories at the heart of which he placed his own among the human fooleries he couldn't judge for knowing his own failings, or presume to pardon for believing justice rested somewhere far beyond the realm of law; where he became the tenderhearted grouch, the lover of lost souls, the easy touch that small towns shake their heads at, love and—finally—take up as their saints. But this, as I wish he were here to say, is speculation, and more likely it is true that nothing I said or failed to say on that ride had any bearing whatsoever on the changes he went on to make. Daniel Long spent twenty-seven years in Leavenworth before he died from drinking home brew made with cleaning fluid, and I know no more about him now than I did then.

What I knew, in August 1961, as the trees and fields rolled out of one another lost as any other moment, was that if our ride seemed to take forever, eventually there would come an end, that we would soon be home to order, to the Sunday table over which he would return our thanks for countless blessings. I knew that in three weeks I would be thirteen, that school— where I still knew the rules, where I would still be smart— would start again. I knew the world was bigger—better—than the Waco Wego, where I would never go again, where I believed I had left nothing.

When we passed the pasture road we'd taken earlier on what had been our last rough-ride, I saw along the fence the sign we'd disobeyed: No Trespassing. I looked at my father to see if he would notice how it seemed to hang between us like reproof, but I couldn't tell, and then we were beyond it.

Mountains, Road,
the Tops of Trees

T HE man I called my husband had a God who made him
do some things I couldn't cotton. For forty years I told
him that his hard head was the one true bone of our contention, but he just laughed, and looked at me like I was joking,
which I was, but only half. He was a tall, too-quiet man, easy
to get mad at, hard to stay that way with. Many said he was a
long way off from wonderful, but that was fine with me, because I stopped some short of wonderful myself.

The way I met him was when Daddy got the idea my sister
Ella could be a movie star. She was the image of Betty Grable,
only with red hair, and she had movie magazines strung all
over the house, piled up in the corners of our room like dirty
clothes. She knew all the beauty habits of the stars. "Little
Lou," she'd say, "if you'd part your hair to the side and dab on
this Crimson Passion, you could look almost like a real short
Rita Hayworth." It was all she ever talked about, and it was
enough to make me scruff my hair and bug my eyes like Peter
Lorre's at her.

Daddy thought she had something, though, and he figured
to cash in on it, so he packed us in the car and hauled us out
west, Mama in the front seat pregnant with number seven and

us all in the back, hot as popcorn and fighting like cats, everything we owned bumping along behind us in a two-wheeled
trailer Daddy bought for a dollar. It was World War II, and lots
of people were on the road.

We had the whole summer to get across the country. It was
Daddy's plan to drive awhile then stop and work and that way
keep us in road money and not have to dip into Ella's movie-
star nest egg. He had it all mapped out, and we wound up in
Trinidad, Colorado because somebody told him it was a railroad town and he'd find a restaurant where he could hire on.
Back home he was fry cook for the Ozark Queen, known in
those days for fine food, and Daddy could cook like an angel,
anything you wanted, steak or catfish, chicken-fry to break
your heart. Mama used to tell me, "Little Lou, when your time
comes, find yourself a cooking husband. That kind will love
you sweetest."

I was next oldest after Ella. She could never be depended on
to do much in the way of help—her nail polish was too wet or
too dry or else she had her elbows stuck in half a lemon—and
it seemed like Mama always had one on her lap and another on
the way, so it got to be my job to look after the middle ones,
Arliss and Bobby. They were nine years old and twins, wild as
jackrabbits. We'd pulled into town and Daddy found a job
right off, so the rest of us sat around the car waiting for him to
get off so we could find a place to stay. Arliss and Bobby
couldn't tolerate sitting. They started walking up the hood and
over the top of the car and down the trunk. They messed with
the trailer, scattered things to kingdom come. Mama poked
her head out the car window and called out, "Sister, take those
boys and see if you can find them some ice cream."

She wasn't talking to Ella, who was in the driver's seat doing
something to her face with tweezers and the rearview mirror
pulled out of whack, so I looked around and the only place I
saw was across the street and down. The sign on it said "The
Ute." It looked pretty seedy to me. I said, "I don't see why
they should get a reward for acting awful."

Mama fished in her pocketbook for change.

"That looks to me like a tavern," I said. "Why can't they just go in Daddy's?"

She looked at Arliss and Bobby, then rolled her eyes at me so I would remember El Reno, Oklahoma and the horn-toad in the pie case and the price of two meringues and one banana cream, squashed.

"Here," she said, dropping some dimes tied up in a hankie into my hand. "You get one for yourself, too."

"I'm not hungry," I said, "and besides, isn't this the last?" Mama was the kind to spend her last red cent on a sack of jaw-breakers and laugh doing it.

"Well, now, Miss High and Mighty Finance," she said, "since when did you get to be the expert on money?"

I said I supposed I knew enough about it to know it didn't grow on trees. I figured I'd catch it then, for sassing, but I didn't.

"Might as well, honey," she said, and she laughed. "Some tall, tall trees." Mama had a laugh to make you think everything would turn out fine, no matter what it was. "Now you go on and do what Mama says."

So I did. I hitched up my skirt and tucked my blouse in and I took Arliss and Bobby over to the Ute. It was dark inside, and by the time my eyes got adjusted and I got the boys to stop jumping up to touch the deer heads on the wall and get settled in a booth, it was clear to me that the whole deal was unsavory.

Nobody was at a booth or any of the tables, just a handful leaning on a long dark bar and way in the back around a pool table some drunks in checkered shirts and faded dungarees who I now know thought they ran the town. They were whooping it up and poking each other in the hind end with pool sticks, but they stopped when they saw us and started nudging each other. Before I knew it, they were all around our booth and blocking our way out.

My hair was curly red in those days, and I was used to people making remarks about it and sometimes even touching it, but I didn't take it as a compliment when the rangy, popeyed one with long sideburns reached out and pulled up a hank of it right above my ear and said, "Hey, Pretty. You're just as red as a little mama fox."

I turned my chin up and away the way I'd seen Ella do when she didn't like something.

A squatty one who wore what looked like thirty dollars worth of Stetson on a ten-cent head, and who I later found out was named Royce Lashley and owned the biggest sheep ranch in the state, leaned on his pool cue. "Why, she ain't talking. She's too good for us." He waggled his behind and drew his voice out slow. "She must be in the moo-vies. She's a movie star, boys. Haw."

"You're a corker, Royce, I swear," said the popeyed one.

"You must be thinking of my sister Ella," I said, snappy, but they were laughing so hard I didn't think they heard me.

One I hadn't noticed came around from behind Royce Lashley. He had a little scarf tied round his neck and a shirt with pearl snap buttons, and from the way he stuck his belly out and made his legs go funny, I could tell he thought he was just dandy with the ladies. "We'll take your sister, too, honey. If she's pretty as you."

He had an evil-looking smile and I remembered the last time anybody smiled that way and it was Spencer Wilkes because he wanted to stick his hand down my dress front, which I didn't allow, and he got mad and tripped me down the ramp of the Ferris wheel and I almost broke my leg, so I figured I was in deep because this bunch looked a good deal meaner than Spencer Wilkes ever hoped to be.

If I'd been able to see around corners to what was on its way to get me out of one fine pass into another, I could have just sat tight, but naturally, I couldn't. And right then I was as mad at Ella as I'd ever been—her being the true author of the whole sorry mess—and if I'd had her in front of me, I would have pinned her down and tweezed every one of her eyebrow hairs with a red-hot pair of pliers.

"Oh, she's a lot prettier," I said. "A whole darn lot. I'll just run and get her and you all can introduce yourselves." Meaning to head for the door, I started to slide out of the booth, but Royce Lashley stopped me by putting his boot on the seat.

"One in the hand worth two in the bush." His laugh sounded like a goose's honk.

The popeyed one picked at my hair again. "I never knew no moo-vie gal before." He looked over at Royce Lashley like he'd gotten off a corker himself.

The dandy with the pearl buttons elbowed him. "Aw, hell, Wink. You know you never known *no* gal before."

Then they really hooted, and I could smell sour whiskey and dirty jeans and a chemical smell I now know is sheep dip, and I realized that unless I got some help or got out, things were going to take a turn for the far worse.

All this time Arliss and Bobby were jumping around and riding the back of the booth like a horse and not paying any mind to what was going on. I grabbed Bobby by the shirt and pulled him close and grit my teeth in his face. "Tell Mama," I said. "Go tell Mama."

Bobby misheard me to say that I was going to tell Mama on him and Arliss, so he grabbed Arliss and they scat under the table and set up a ruckus for ice cream and root beer, so there I was with the nasty bunch fiddling with my hair, the twins acting like wild animals under the table, and me rooted to the spot. The dandy one petted his little scarf in place and asked me what my name was.

Even though I was scared, I was still acting Sassy Jane, so I made a pruney mouth and said, "Puddentane."

"Well, now, Puddentane," he said, "what say we dance?" He grabbed my hand and pulled me out of the booth and Royce Lashley took my other hand and they started twirling me back and forth between them like we were all three dancing while the popeyed one named Wink stomped and clapped until I got so mad and dizzy I could hardly see. Then, of a sudden, they stopped. Just ceased. And there I was with my eyeballs skittering around, and when I came to, they were gone, and standing off to the side of the back door was the biggest man I ever saw.

This was him the first time I saw him, not smiling or saying anything, just looking at me with his deep, deep eyes. He wore blue jeans, too, like the others, but where they had on old faded shirts with the sleeves rolled up, his was smooth and tan as saddle leather, creased along the sleeves, so starched it looked like it would crackle if he moved. He wore a silver bracelet with flat green stones, and of all things, suspenders and a red bow tie. I never saw anyone like him in my life. He later told me he had felt the same, that he didn't know if he was looking at a woman or a wildcat. He had black hair, a brown face that looked to be all sheared-off angles, handsome in the way you can't stop looking at. He held a heavy book—his crumbled-up black Bible he never would give up for new—like it was no more than an envelope in his big hand.

I never heard him say a word, but just the sight of him must have been enough to scare Royce Lashley and his sheep-honchos off. They were long gone, and Arliss and Bobby and I just stood there staring at him. When he turned to leave, I noticed another thing that nearly floored me: he had a ponytail so long it was halfway down his back. Then it hit me, and I said to myself: That man is an Indian. The only other Indian I'd ever seen was Shawnee O'Connor back home, and she was only eighth or quarter and didn't look it except for the long black hair that hung down past her bottom. He looked full, or near as you could get. The next thing I knew, it seemed like I just blinked to get a better look and when I opened my eyes, he was gone.

I didn't stay around the Ute another minute. I swatted Arliss and Bobby. "Get now!" I said, and we got. We spent the rest of the afternoon waiting for Daddy to get off and I just sat on the runboard and drew little beards and tails and devil horns on all the pictures in Ella's magazines, I was so mad. When Mama tried to make me tell what happened, I wasn't sure how the part about the man would come out, so I just shook my head and said, "You don't want to know." I practiced looking dark and put-upon at Ella so Mama would see who the real guilty party was. When Ella pitched a fit at what I'd done to her pictures, Mama took my part and told her to leave me alone and that made me feel even madder and sorrier for myself. And a little bit good.

We stayed three weeks in a little motor court off the highway, and it was nice enough until the Dorcas Circle of the Rocky Mountain Methodists got wind of us and decided we were needy. All tricked out in flowered hats and dresses, they knocked on our door one morning and handed Mama two big sacks of clothes. Mama smiled back at them and set the sacks down just inside the door, but when Daddy came home, she was mad enough to spit.

"We had some visitors today," she said. "A bunch of Gussies." She showed him the sacks and told him all about it.

Daddy just shook his head and said, "A woman in a hat can be an awful thing." Those sacks sat there the whole three weeks.

There was a market down the road where you could buy bread and milk and lunch meat and that was where I saw him for the second time. You couldn't miss him, ponytail and bow tie, this time drunk as a skunk from the look of things. I was just paying for some groceries when I heard a commotion outside, so I took my change from the clerk and left the sack there on the counter and went out to see what was going on. He was out there, holding a little skinny man in a too-big shirt under a water pump, the water splatting on a cement slab and the little skinny man squalling like a cat with its tail in a socket. A crowd had gathered, so I sneaked up and looked around a lady's shoulder and that was when I heard his name.

"It's just Samson Cloud," somebody said, "baptizing a Chinaman."

The lady in front of me said, "Must be time for one of his spells."

It didn't look to me like the Chinaman much wanted baptizing, and it came to me why that bunch at the Ute lit out. I watched until it was over and the Chinaman had run off like a dog in wet pajamas and the crowd trailed away. Then it was just me and him and I saw him looking at me kind of soft around the eyes, and I figured he was getting the idea for me to be next.

"Oh, no, you don't," I said. "Oh, no, you don't."

I ducked around the market and took off running for the motor court. I forgot about the sack of groceries I left on the counter. When I remembered it, I stopped running and dodged behind a stand of piñon to catch my breath. I scouted around to see if he was behind me. He wasn't. I figured Mama would skin me if I came back without the groceries, so I headed back to the market. The sack was gone. I walked back home, wondering what I was going to tell Mama and how a person would look with no skin, but when I passed the piñons for the second time, I saw a paper sack sitting there on a rock. I looked inside and sure enough. Somebody left it for me and it was no mystery who it was. I knew it like I knew my own breath.

All the next day I couldn't get him out of my mind—the thought of him was like a thing you can't quite see, but know is there—so I put on my best blouse with the horses printed on it and pinned a hankie to my pocket with my horse pin with the rhinestone eyes. I sneaked some of Ella's Crimson Passion, but I couldn't get my mouth to hold still long enough, so I wiped it on a sock from one of the Gussy sacks. Then I told Mama I'd found a nice place for the twins to play, and why didn't I just take them there right now? I was thinking about the rocks in that piñon stand. What I meant to do was take a side trip to the market and see if any baptizing was going on.

When we got to the place, I noticed something red and white on the rock. It turned out to be a whole Baby Ruth candy bar, only a little melted from the sun. I divided it up between us and the boys gobbled theirs right down, but my part I rolled around inside my mouth for the longest time because it was the first time anybody ever meant a thing to be for only me.

The next day I went to the rock alone.

People have a way of wanting to know why, and even if they didn't, it's a thing you have to ask yourself. "Why'd you do a thing like that?" "What made you decide to do it?" Like everything you do in life is something you decide. I'm not sure why I went there by myself, but I do know this: the *why* of a thing doesn't matter once it's done, and all the reasons in the world won't make it right or wrong, they just make it done, and once it's done, it *is*. It's just a thing you did, whyever. Sometimes you have to put the cart before the horse on purpose, do the thing and figure out the reasons later. Or make some up. Either way, it doesn't matter. The closest I can come to why is that I figured I was half in love with him. So I went to the place and sat on a rock and one minute I didn't see anything and the next he was standing right in front of me.

He looked me full in the face and said, "Do you know Jesus?"

Well. I wanted to say, "Jesus who?" but something stopped me and I'm glad it did, but I always hated that, when people asked you if you *knew* Jesus. Like they're the ones with the personal road map to heaven. If you said you didn't, they'd look at you like you were Adam's off ox and tear into you until they got you confused and ready to say anything just so they'd let you alone. If you said you did, they started up a holy-contest and wouldn't stop until they satisfied themselves that they knew Him better than you all the way down to His shoe size. I always figured I or anybody else had as much claim to Jesus as the next person, and no slick-headed Pastor McRaney back home or his daughter Iris Ann with her precious name stamped on her white Bible in gold letters, and certainly no pump-happy Indian wearing a bow tie was going to shake me from that notion. He was either everybody's or nobody's, and way down deep, nobody's business what anybody else believed. All that question ever did was get me riled. I narrowed up my eyes, and I said, "You fixing to dunk me if I do or dunk me if I don't?"

That got him off the track. "Hmmph," he said.

"Hmmph, yourself," I said. He didn't say anything back, just looked at me quiet, like I'd hurt his feelings. Then I remembered my manners and I said, "Oh, and thank you for that candy bar. It was real good."

The corners of his mouth turned up a little. I sat there and gave him a good looking-over. I couldn't really tell, but I thought he might be even older than Daddy. "I know your name," I said.

He was looking at me funny, and I began to wonder if there was something worse wrong with him than what I'd already noticed. "Mine's Lou-Rita Simms," I said, "but everybody calls me Little Lou. That's because my daddy's name is Lou, too. Louis." I had started talking, I guess, to put him at his ease, but then I wasn't ready to stop. I told him how Daddy first wanted to name Ella after himself, but Mama insisted on Ella because of her sister who died. I went on about how pretty Ella was, how everybody said so and how he'd think so too if he could see her, and how Ella was the reason we were on the road, but that I didn't care much about the movie business and if you asked me, the best actor out there was Gene Autry's fine horse Champion.

"Little Lou." He said it out of nowhere, all surprised and sweet, like he just woke up and found a piece of taffy in his mouth.

"That's right," I said. "Lou-Rita Simms and we're from Arkansas on our way to California."

He shook his head like he was saying no, no we shouldn't. "You could come up to the ranch with me."

I looked at him out of the corner of my eyes. The way he was acting made me feel funny, and I didn't know what to say.

Back home, you sassed the boys and they liked it. They were used to it and it saved a lot of trouble. This one was no boy, and it didn't look to me like he'd ever been sassed in his life. I didn't say anything, but sat there fiddling with my hankie and pretending I was all of a sudden concerned about the eyes falling out of my horse pin.

"Do you like horses, Little Lou?"

I stared at him. What on earth kind of question was that, do I like horses? I was sixteen, and my middle name might as well have been Horse. Daddy thought I would outgrow it, but I never did. That question brought my sassy-bone to life again and I said, "No. I don't like horses. I flat *love* horses."

He said something, quiet and low, and I barely heard it but it sounded like he was saying, "I love *you.*" To me. I dropped my mouth open and shook my head like I didn't believe what I was hearing, but the truth is I did believe it, right off, and I knew that things for him were like they were for me, that once something was, it just plain *was,* and no sense backing up to take another look.

"What?" I said, and I could feel this smile sneaking onto my face, just sneaking and sneaking until I thought I must be lit up like a pumpkin I was smiling so hard. "What?"

He wouldn't say it again.

"Well," I said, "that's a fine how-do-you-do." I picked up a little skipper-stone, plunked it at his feet. I didn't know what to say. "Hogwash," I finally said. "Most likely hogwash. I bet you say that to all the girls. Before you dunk the living day-lights out of them."

He looked at the ground with that hurt look, and I could see he didn't know how to take me. I plunked another pebble at him to get his attention, and when he looked up, I smiled and gave a little laugh to show him. He smiled then, and I could see his teeth, white and even. His whole face changed from that serious look and I thought what a handsome man he was, even with his ponytail and bracelet. Again he asked me to come to his ranch.

"I'll think about it," I said. "If you promise not to dunk me."

"My word on it," he said. "No baptizing." He smiled. "Unless you want."

I wouldn't want, I said. I double-dog guaranteed it. Then I spit a little on my hand to show my word was good and held it out for him to shake. But he just stood there, smiling. I got up and started for the motor court. I didn't look back, but I knew he was watching me all the way and I also knew that nothing was going to keep me from going to that ranch.

The next day, when he turned up in a gray Ford truck, Mama wanted to know what was going on. I told her about the Ute and how I'd seen him again at the market. I left out the part about him being drunk and baptizing the Chinaman. I also left out the part about him loving me. She still looked skeptical, so I told her he wanted to take us all to his ranch for a nice visit, and that worked. Mama said it would be good to have a rest from being cooped up. We piled into the truck, Mama and I and the babies up front with him. Ella had to ride in the truckbed with Arliss and Bobby and some hay bales, which messed up her hair and made her mad as a mud dauber, but Mama told her he was my friend and this was only right.

It worked out fine. The little ones got to sit up on a horse and climb on the corral fences, and later we ate fried lamb and pinto beans at a long table on the front porch of the main house. He wasn't much of a cook, but only Ella turned her nose up. The rest of us said how being in the mountains certainly made a person hungry and it was the best food we'd ever tasted. He told us that the ranch was a mission started by the Catholics. He was born there and the brothers named him. Then it got taken over by some Baptists for a boys school. "Rio Grande Indian School" it said on a signboard over the schoolhouse, spelled out in deer antlers. The river running through it was really the Purgatoire, but the Catholics didn't like the sound of that so they told people it was the Rio Grande and for a long time everybody believed them.

"That figures," I said. Mama poked me. I could tell she wanted me to mind my manners in front of such a man.

Twelve boys were living there and he ran it all by himself now. The Baptists had bailed out years before.

"Good riddance," I said, and this time he laughed to show Mama it was all right. He was thirty-five years old, I found out, and when Ella's mouth dropped open at the news and she nudged me under the table like wasn't that hilarious, I looked at him and learned I was in love for certain.

Two weeks later Daddy and Mama and the rest packed up, and I announced I was staying, hiring on at the school as cook, and I would be paid for it. If I didn't like it and wanted to go on to California, he would put me on a bus. He wanted to get married but I said no, I was too young and it more than likely meant a dunking first, to ask again when I turned eighteen. He promised not to baptize me or even look at me cross-eyed like he wanted to, but I didn't tell Mama and Daddy any of that. I'd worry about it myself. Daddy said he thought there might be laws against this sort of thing, but he'd never been one to stand in the way of progress.

"I hope to think I never raised a senseless child," he said. "You do what you think's best, Little Lou."

"Thank you," I said. "I will."

When Mama cried, I pointed out that she was married and had Ella by the time she was sixteen and it hadn't seemed to hurt her any. She laughed, then, that old sweet laugh, and said, "Sister, I just wish I could be around to see you get your comeuppance."

I did too, I said, and we hugged each other. She felt soft and womanly, and I felt to myself all hard and angles, bones and elbows, grown, but not yet full.

Ella said she'd always known I'd find a harebrained way to wreck my life, but that she had no idea I'd be in such a hurry to do it. I figured she was jealous because he was someone who never had an eye to flirt with her, so I hugged her for that. Arliss and Bobby set up a howl to stay and I told them they could visit any time, a whole summer if they wanted. I hugged the babies tighter than I thought I would, then everybody got in the car and I got in the truck and we went our separate ways, them to California and me up into the mountains.

When we got up high enough, I could see the way the world spread out around us, sometimes rolling, then heaved with rocks, falling into valleys, how one part gave onto another in a way you couldn't figure, and I tried to make the world be a picture of the way things were with men and women. But every time I got close to thinking I could understand how things fit together, I'd see the sky, how it was bigger and held itself above things in a way that showed them up as only what they were—mountains, road, the tops of trees—and I saw that if I never understood the picture, it didn't matter, that we were here and in it just the same as these, with understanding always just beyond us.

We bumped along the road and he looked over at me. He could see me crying a little and he started to say something, but I shushed him. "I know what I'm doing," I said, and I hoped I did. I looked straight ahead at the mountains we were driving into and I thought about a thousand things. I thought about Mama and Daddy and how it was with them. I thought about Spencer Wilkes and Ella and Catholics and everybody gathered on this world and I thought: who am I, one lone speck on this green, green earth and how big things are and how small I am and who am I to think a thing I do makes any difference whatsoever? Still, it somehow does.

I looked over at him, at his hands on the steering wheel, and I thought what would have happened if we hadn't stopped here, if I hadn't taken Arliss and Bobby in the Ute and if all the things that happened after that hadn't happened and I almost cried for that, to think I never would have seen his hands at just that moment. I remembered a song from Sunday School called "I Have Decided to Follow Jesus" and I began to sing it to myself except in the places where it said Jesus, I stuck his name in. I laughed at myself for what I was doing, but I began to think that maybe what makes people want religion is the same thing that makes a woman want a man, to hook her life up with his, and it's a powerful, powerful thing and I guess it's supposed to be. It can make you grit your teeth, you fear it so, and yet you want it past all reason. You know it has the power to swallow you whole and there you are all wanting to be swallowed. I reached out and ran my fingers along his arm. He had big wrists, flat as axe-heads. It was the first time I ever touched him.

II

I never got on any bus to California. Mama wrote to tell me Daddy had a job at a studio commissary and Ella was working at a luncheonette while she waited to be discovered, which almost happened three or four times but somehow never took. It turned out to be Arliss and Bobby who went on to be big in Hollywood, where reckless habits qualified as stunts, and people paid good money if you could make it look like you were just about to break your neck. On the day I turned eighteen, he went into town and came back with a bunch of daisies stuck in an empty Nehi bottle and a little moonstone ring.

"Oh, no, you don't," I said.

"I want you to be my wife."

"You're just having one of your spells," I said. "I can smell it from here. And besides, I've been more or less your wife since the first week I got here." It's not that I was all that proud of the way things happened between us, so quick it had to be either that we knew our minds or lost them, but that was the way it happened and I'm not ashamed of it either. We both wanted to, and it was the one thing we always had, almost up until the last, and it was sweet and tender as the day is long.

"I'll hire another cook," he said. "That way you won't have to work so hard."

"I like work," I said. "It pays, and wifing doesn't."

He looked at me like he was going to cry. "Little Lou," he said, "the way we live is sinful."

I almost laughed, but I got mad instead. "Sin? It seems to me that's the way the world got started, the part with people, anyway, and more than likely that's the way it'll end." I was getting wound up, like my mouth was running away with my head, but I couldn't stop and I knew I was saying what I'd always thought.

"Don't talk to me about sin," I said. "I decided a long time ago not to mess with it. All I know is what I think is bad and what I think is good. And this," I said, "is good. I think." I waited a little to see if he would laugh at the way I said it, but he didn't. He wouldn't look at me.

"We're not hurting anybody, are we?"

He wouldn't answer, and I got so mad I wanted to shake him. "Besides," I said, "it didn't seem to bother you all that much last night, sin."

He gave a low moaning sound and turned away. Then he turned back around and quoted the Bible at me. "'And a man shall leave his mother and father and cleave unto his wife,'" he said. "It says *wife*."

"Cleave all you want," I said. "Cleave to your heart's content, but that's not something you have to get married to do." I wanted to make a joke and say if marry turns to marriage, do you call cleaving cleavage, but I held back. It wasn't the right time.

"It's been two years," he said. "It would be such a simple thing."

He was working on me about the years, how good they'd been, about getting married being such a simple thing. But to me it wasn't, it only seemed that way to anybody else, to him, and that was what pulled at me.

"You don't understand," I said. "You're not me. You're you and you believe in things I don't have figured out yet. Every time you get a snootful you baptize anything that will hold still. Every last one of those boys ten times over whether they wanted it or not, and I'm not going to be next. I've thought about it a thousand times. You won't marry me unbaptized, so that would come first, and I don't hold with it. It wouldn't mean the right thing to me and it would be wrong. I flat won't do it, not even for you." I was about to stomp off, but something stopped me. "Besides," I said. "I'm happy."

And I was.

Every so often he'd pester me to marry him, but I always got around it. He'd pout and lick his wounds awhile and then we'd just go on. Several times he tried to trick me, come up behind me while I bathed and I'd hear him breathing and I'd turn around to catch him before he could dunk me, splash him until he was soaked to the skin, both of us laughing and joking-mad. He could have forced me if he'd wanted, but even he didn't want it that way, and it got to be a little game with us, on the edge of fun if we hadn't been so stubborn.

Like anybody else, we had our troubles, too—those times when you think somebody else would appreciate you better—but they never lasted long. And there were all the normal things that come with having all those boys around in the almost forty years we were together, but we always got through them. Our biggest trouble was his spells.

He made the wine himself. The Catholics had started it, of course, but when the Baptists came, they let the vineyard go to waste and spent their time having revivals and putting a baptismal font in the chapel and painting the Cedars of Lebanon on the backdrop. Because he'd lived with the Catholics, he knew how to go about it, so when the Baptists packed up he took it up again and used the tank to smash the grapes. That tank bottom was purple as a berry bucket by the time I saw it, but he kept it clean and filled with pretty violet-looking water in the off-time. It was good wine, too, but every six months or so he'd get into it. Then a fever seemed to take him and he couldn't be stopped. I never even tried. Mama used to say that there were two things that drove a woman's life, wanting to have babies and trying to change some man's ways, and only one was worth the trouble. All I ever said was, "Why don't you just let people come to it of their own free will?" but he never listened. I don't think he could, he believed in it so hard.

There were those who liked it and came to him every so often, his regulars, and once a crowd of migrant pickers walked the whole way up the mountain and camped here just to have him dunk them. Those were the times he loved best. The worst was when he went to town and tried to catch people.

From time to time there were complaints, and we had a whole stack of newspaper editorials Royce Lashley tried to write, which we figured was a mighty effort since he only knew a couple dozen words and half of them were "dang." He called the spells "a dang abomination," and always wound his letters up by calling "men of stature" to rise up to rid the land of this dang blight. These men of stature always came around at night in pickup trucks and neckerchiefs up over their faces and only wanted to race around the yard a couple times and raise the dust and yell, and they were easy enough to scatter off with rock salt. But one morning some ladies drove out in a caravan of fancy cars, all bird-print dresses and bird-y hats. It was the Gussies, ten years holier and broader in the beam. I invited them in.

They turned up their noses at the syrup cake I offered and sat around with knees clamped and their bottoms stiff as starch. About half of them were pregnant. One in navy blue with covered buttons the size of biscuits looked me over close, as if she hadn't ever seen me in town or driving around in the truck.

"A child, dear," she said, "why, you're really just a child, aren't you?"

I knew what she was getting at, so I straightened up in my chair and even though I must have been twenty-five or six by that time, I said, "Why I'm fully sixteen years old, Ma'am."

That got them going. Their hands flew up to their little bows and collars and all the hat-birds started bobbing.

"We came to help you, dear," she said. Her voice was smooth as buttermilk. "Why don't you tell us why it is you stay here with him?"

The rest leaned forward and opened their eyes wide like they expected me to stand up and announce he tied me in the cellar with a dog chain.

"With who?" I said.

"Why, *him*. That man. What has he done to you?"

"What man?" I said.

She'd gone spluttering by then. "That Indian! That drunken Indian!"

"Oh," I said, like I was just beginning to understand, "him." I stood up. "Madam," I said, "I'll thank you not to refer like that to my husband."

That sent them through the roof. They clucked and shook their heads and I decided I'd had enough.

"That man," I said, "that drunken Indian, is my lawful-wedded husband, and a better man never walked the face of the earth." I was stretching it some, a whole lot, maybe, but I didn't care. I never had much use for busybodies, or for people who just can't seem to understand how a person can be more than one thing at a time and how the little boxes they'd fit everybody into have a way of leaving out the most important parts.

"That man, ladies, loves me. Drunk, sober, and in-between, he loves me. And that's enough for anybody." This was something I'd never said before, never even thought, but the minute I said it, I knew it was the truth. Even though I knew I was going to give him the holy dickens the first chance I got, for putting me through the whole thing, even though I knew I was going to make his life a misery for the next few days and have a fine time doing it, I knew what I'd said just then was the truth.

"That's enough for anybody," I said again. I stomped over to the door all full of myself. "And maybe it's a damn sight more than you can say about your own husbands," I said. I looked hard at their maternity smocks. "Presuming you got husbands, that is."

The lie—the part about lawful-wedded—was worth it. Those ladies scratched like squirrels to get out the door, and they never came back. What was true was that he loved me, mad as he sometimes got. I was sassy, stubborn, muleheaded, and a tease, but he loved me. And mad as I sometimes got at him for all the things he was, I loved him.

I teased him something awful. He'd be in the schoolroom with the boys and I'd poke my head in and grin and say, "Say, tell me that Bible story one more time. I just can't get it through my head how one man smoked all those Filipinos with the jawbone of an ass." He'd steam over like a pot. Or if I happened to be sewing something or trimming a turkey for the oven and he came around, I'd snip the scissors at him and sing the shave-and-a-haircut song.

He could have teased me back, about any number of things, but he never did. It wasn't in him. He called me Little Lou all his life, and it got to be almost funny after a while because I'd stopped being little a long time back, but that was the way he saw me.

I called him nothing, because he was everything. I somehow never got in the habit of saying his name, and then it got to be too late to change. It would have sounded funny in my mouth. Until the day I came upon him in the empty schoolroom and saw what he was writing—over, over—on the board, and that his old, strong letters had gone rickety and thin, I was fool enough to think he hadn't noticed.

III

It never seemed our life together passed in years or seasons, more in batches of boys that rolled along and overlapped each other until the last ones left and it seemed we woke up one morning and discovered it was just us and all the time had gone too fast. We never had any of our own. Maybe if we had, it would have made deciding easier, but even then, I wasn't sure. I only knew I'd fussed with it so long, I didn't know how not to.

The baptizing had long since stopped, and when it stopped, something seemed to go out of him. Or maybe it was the other way around. At first he tried to keep up with the ranch work, but then it got to be too much and it seemed like every little bug that came along he caught. Finally he just stayed in bed most of the time and I read to him and bathed him and toward the end I had to feed him and clean up after him, which shamed him so that he could hardly look at me. He got so small and shrunk up there in the bed, and every time I went into his room the air felt colder, thin and still, like that time in late afternoon when the sun is bright and red on the high rock face but down below the air is shadowed and blue and chill. You almost don't believe what you feel because the top face looks so warm, but you feel the cold and you know you have to believe it.

Now all this time I'd been thinking and thinking about what to do and I felt like a fool for taking so long, but still I wasn't done. Daddy had died and Mama was wheeling herself around Ella's house in San Diego, even Ella had grandchildren, and here I was still thinking. Sometimes I thought I was selfish and wrongheaded and other times I thought I was right, and the only thing I knew for sure was that my stubbornness had kept him from a thing he wanted, and that I had in me the power to make it right, even though it was late. But if I said I *knew* Jesus and He was everything to me and that I wanted to dedicate my life to Him it would be a damn lie. Jesus was in there somewhere in all the things I knew I believed, but He wasn't *all*. And I'd be doing it for the wrong reason. It was too deep a thing to lie about. I lay awake at night thinking and thinking until I was almost sick.

And then there comes a point when things are past deciding. When there's nothing left to weigh, when all that's left is want, and what you do, you do to fill the want. I went into his room and woke him and wrapped a blanket around him and helped him from the bed. I held him up and we walked out of the house, across the yard, slow, so he could keep up. The skin on his arms was slack-feeling, dusky, that olive-color of new bark under white on a paper birch. He leaned on me, and beneath the blanket I could feel his old, old bones moving against each other, pushing him on, and for a minute I thought he wasn't really with me, it wasn't really him, just some spirit, some little live thing left in those long bones that kept him with me, walking, and I began to think some words that came rolling toward me out of somewhere, not a prayer, more like a poem that doesn't rhyme, and I said them to myself, and they were beautiful and true, the words we'd say if we could see into each other's hearts and tell what's in our own, past all the things we do, the words we'd use to fill the space between two people, the space where one leaves off and the other begins, the words we want at night when it seems we can't hold each other close enough to make the space go away and us be one, and they moved me forward, saying them and holding him, until we got inside the chapel and down beside the tank.

I undressed myself and slipped off his blanket and kissed him in all his places and led him down into the water. It was warm and pale, a purple almost lavender. I put my hands on his shoulders and I wanted to say the words to him the way I'd said them to myself, but I couldn't. They had flown out of my mind and the only thing left of what they meant was that I loved him.

"I'm doing this because I want to," I told him. "It doesn't have an earthly thing to do with Jesus, and everything to do with you." I told him I was sorry, and I said his name.

I stood there waiting, wondering if he'd gone past caring, but then his hands were on my shoulders, strong again, and warm. He dipped us down together, under to the quiet where my throat filled wide with everything, the words again, his name, that thing in me that wouldn't budge, and I choked them back and swallowed, and then we drew each other up, gasping, me all crying, and there we were, two naked, holy people with the water running off us, and it made us look so serious, so old and new and sorry, so wet and stubborn-foolish we just had to laugh, for everything we ever did, for gladness and the maybe-hope of heaven.

NOSOTROS

I T was always hot in the little house, her mother's house, even in December. Licha, lying on the floor, arms above her head and braced against the mirrored bedroom door, thought how cool it was here in Madama's house where the big air conditioners hummed, pumping cold air through all the louvered vents in the spacious rooms. Madama's son Raleigh strained above her, drops of his sweat pooling like warm coins on her breasts and belly, his movements grinding her hips into the wool carpet until they stung, but it was cooler. Licha drew up her knees and curled her toes; even the carpet was cool, and she wondered how far down the coolness went.

All the houses in the Valley were slab houses, built on concrete. There were no basements; hurricanes came this far inland. Few peaked roofs; there was no snow here. Ever. Under the slab, Licha knew, and in the space between the walls, lived thousands of lizards: stripebacks, chalotes, green anoles. They came out to bask on the hot packed dirt around the foundation, to crawl up the screens. Madama hated them. If she saw too many she called the exterminators down from McAllen. Then Licha's mother Catalina was set to draping the furniture in sheeting, removing dishes, food, and clothing from the house so the pesticide wouldn't contaminate Madama and Raleigh.

When the exterminator's immense plastic tent was pulled from the house and all the lizard carcasses were shoveled into bushel baskets, Licha's mother would come back in to give the house a thorough cleaning: Pine-Sol the terrazzo, scrub the pecky cypress walls, shampoo the carpets. Then she would move everything back in, washing each dish and glass and fork in hot detergent water while Madama supervised, giving orders in her tight rough voice.

At the little house behind Madama's, where Licha and her mother lived, lizards entered and departed through the gap between the screen door and the flagstone sill, unremarked. Geckos made their way around the walls, eating insects, spatulate toe pads mocking gravity. But it was so hot there. Licha thought about the house she and Raleigh could have when she finished high school and moved from the Valley, a little college house with a peaked roof and an air conditioner in the window, a Boston fern hanging above the table, her biology texts and notes spread out beneath it.

"Squeeze your titties together," Raleigh said. "I want to see them that way."

She braced her feet against the floor and took her hands from the door. She tried to place them on the sides of her breasts, but his movements inched her too far up. "I can't. I'll hit my head."

Raleigh balanced on one arm, pushing his glasses further up on his nose. Licha didn't understand how he could sweat so, when it was as cool in the room as it was in the big Anglo stores downtown. His glasses were fogged. She wondered why he wore them, what he saw as he watched in the mirror, if he saw the two of them as a watery image, the edges of their bodies blurred and running together. She looked up at him, under the rims, at his eyes, and their blue startled her. It was an uncommon color, she thought, a surprise of a color, a color she marveled that the human body, with its browns and tans and pinks, could produce. She couldn't look at it long without imagining it was from another place; foreign, vaguely holy, like the blue of the Blessed Virgin's mantle at the church of San

Benito; cool and infinite, like the blue of the sky when the heat
lifted and the haze that sealed the Valley blew away in the wind
of a norther. It was a blue like ice and snow.

It snowed sometimes in Austin, even in San Antonio. Where
her brother Tavo had gone, to Fort Dix, New Jersey, it was
probably snowing now, great fat flakes floating and floating,
covering the barracks until they looked like rows of sugared
cakes, and Tavo, inside with other soldiers, maybe some from
other warm places, would be laughing from the surprise of it.
As much as she hoped Tavo wouldn't have to go to Vietnam,
she envied him his chance to be away, to open a window and
draw the coolness in. She closed her eyes and imagined she
could smell the snow. It must be sweet and powdery, she
thought, like coconut. She looked again at Raleigh, his neck
cords straining, watching in the mirror. "Have you ever seen
snow?"

"Don't talk," he said. "I'm almost there." He clenched his
jaw, and Licha knew her question had irritated him.

Raleigh went to school in Tennessee, to Vanderbilt. He was
home for winter break. Madama had picked him up at the
Brownsville airport, taking the yard man Perfilio along to drive
the big car. She refused to drive the road alone. Raleigh's father,
called Papa by everyone in the little towns along the highway,
had been killed on this road, on an inspection tour of his groves.
As he'd pulled onto Farm-to-Market Twelve, he'd been struck
by one of his own trucks, the driver drunk and running with no
lights, a load of stolen television sets concealed by cotton bales in
the truckbed. On the day of Raleigh's return, Licha had seen
Perfilio pull the car into the driveway, Raleigh and Madama in
the back seat. When Perfilio piled Raleigh's red plaid luggage on
the *porche* beside the tall white poinsettias, Licha thought they
looked like Christmas packages from another country, from
England or Scotland, not like they should belong to Raleigh,
whom Licha and Tavo had grown up with, the three of them
playing in the shell-flecked dirt around the roots of the live oaks
in the back yard, none of them wearing a shirt, Raleigh's hair

bleached almost white with the sun, tanned until he was nearly as brown as Licha and Tavo.

Licha was nine when she'd overheard Madama's order. The children were not to play together any longer. Madama stood by the laundry shed, her mother at the clothesline. "Catalina," she said, "that girl of yours isn't mine to boss, but she's about to bust out of herself."

Her mother pretended she didn't understand Madama's English, and it irritated Licha; her mother smiling, nodding, an impassive, half-comprehending look in her eyes, wiping her hands on a dish towel or patting little balls of dough into flat round tortillas: pat-pat-pat, smile, nod, shuffle around the big *cocina* in her starched blue work dress and apron, her backless sandals. She had lived in the little house eleven years, since Licha was five, but still she pretended she didn't understand, or understood only dimly, forcing Madama into a fractured mixture of languages: "Catalina, *deja* all that laundry *sucio en el* whatchamacallit."

Licha and Tavo had laughed about it, about their mother getting the best of bossy Madama in such a sly, funny way, but it made Licha angry that her mother could let Madama think she was stupid; her mother understood everything Madama said. After Madama's bridge club meeting she entertained Tavo and Licha with stories and imitations until they collapsed on their beds in the little house, wrung out from laughing at the dressed-up stupidity of Madama and her henna-rinsed friends. On the day of Madama's order, she had pretended not to understand, but she complied, keeping Tavo and Licha from Raleigh. Licha remembered how unfair it seemed, and that Madama saw it as her fault: *that girl.*

"Hurry, Raleigh," she said. "They'll be back."

"Maybe if you did something more than lie there," he said. "Move a little."

She tried moving her hips in a small circle. She wasn't sure if it was the right way, the way he expected or was used to, or if there was a right way. Their first time, two days earlier, when they had stood behind the door in Raleigh's bedroom, she hadn't had to move at all, and it had been over sooner. That time, Madama and her mother had gone to the grocery store, and Raleigh had come around the side of the big house to the clothesline where Licha was hanging towels. He held a radio to her ear, as though the years they spent avoiding each other had been no more than a few weeks. She heard a rasping female voice.

"Janis Joplin," he said. "Great, isn't she?"

He lowered the radio when Licha nodded. "Bobby McGee," she said. "I heard it at school."

Raleigh looked the same as he had in high school, when Licha would see him in the halls or at a football game, surrounded by other boys in the same kind of clothing, madras shirts, wheat jeans, loafers they wore without socks. They dressed as if they were already in college, and everyone knew it was where they would end up. The other Anglo boys, those who would stay in the Valley to work and marry, to hunt whitewing dove in the fall, javelinas and coyotes the rest of the year, wore blue jeans and white T-shirts. Raleigh's hair was still cut in Beatle bangs, but he had grown sideburns, the ear-pieces of his new wire-rim glasses cutting into them. "Are you at Harlan Bloch?" he asked.

She looked at him, trying to decide if he was joking. She reached for a clothespin to clip the corner of a towel over the line. He should know she wouldn't be at Blessed Sacrament; she was the daughter of a maid, and the public high school was her only choice. When she nodded, he asked her what courses she was taking.

She wanted to tell him about the frog dissection they had done the week before in biology, how she had cut into the pale, pearlescent belly to expose the first layer of organs, the ventral abdominal vein like a tiny, delicately branching river, the tor-sion of the small intestine giving way to the bulk of the large intestine and how both of them, when held aside, revealed the deeper viscera, the long posterior vena cava, the testes, kidneys, and adrenal bodies; how the heart and lungs lay over the perfect fork of the aortic arch; how surprisingly large the liver was, its curves, its fluted edges, and how she could hardly catch her breath, not because of the formaldehyde or out of revulsion, like some of the other students, but from awe, for joy at the synchrony and mystery of the working of the body laid out before her, its legs splayed on the cutting table, the fragile mandible upturned and yielding to her touch. She wanted to tell him how she felt as her probe and scapel moved through the frog's body, about the sacred, almost heartbreaking invitation of it, but she couldn't. "I'm taking biology," she said.

"Does Mohesky still teach it?"

She nodded. "I really like him." She became aware of Raleigh looking at her breasts, and when she stooped to pick up another towel from the basket she checked the buttons of her blouse. She hoped he hadn't noticed the downward glance that meant she knew he was looking at her.

"Come in the house a minute," he said. "I want to show you something."

When they were just inside his bedroom he closed the door, telling her how beautiful she was, how sweet. She was all he thought about during his first semester away at school. Her breasts were beautiful; titties, he called them, and he'd bet they'd grown—would she show him? She was surprised to feel her nipple tighten when he took it into his mouth, the whole breast seem to swell around it. He lifted her skirt and eased his fingers past her panties until the middle one was inside her. "You know all about it," he said. He unzipped his pants.

"It hurts," she said, and he stopped moving his fingers. "A little."

"You don't act like it," he said. He slid his fingers out and guided himself into her, knees bent, his hand pressing against her hip.

"That doesn't mean it doesn't."

"You like it, though." It wasn't a question, and Licha didn't bother to answer. She did like it. She liked it that he wanted her. She liked the push of it, the tip of him pushing past the part of her that felt like a small, rugate tunnel into a bigger part that had less feeling, more like a liquid cave that seemed to swallow him. She worried that she was too big. Anglo boys said Mexican girls were built for breeding. She wondered if this was what they meant, so much room inside. She wondered if Raleigh was small. She had seen other men; several times she had surprised Tavo, and she had seen braceros relieving themselves in the groves after siesta. She hadn't looked closely, but it seemed that most of these were more substantial, their color fuller, more nearly like the rest of their skin. Raleigh's was the color of sunburn, almost purple at the tip.

When it was over he had gone into the bathroom. She'd heard the tap running, a flush. She'd cleaned herself with her panties, not wanting to use the lacquered box of tissues beside Raleigh's bed. She noticed only a slight pink tinge, no more blood than from a paper cut. She'd tucked the panties into the waistband of her skirt and pulled down her blouse to conceal them.

This time, two days later, he had come up behind her as she emptied trash from the little house onto the burn pile at the back of the property. "*Nalgas,*" he said, patting her bottom. She laughed at the pachuco word for buttocks, at the growling, mock-salacious way he said it, the furtive waggle of his eyebrows behind his glasses, and she had gone with him again to the big house, this time to Madama's bedroom where he locked the door and showed her the full-length mirror behind it. Facing it, with Raleigh behind her, Licha watched his hands, nervous and more intent this time, move up her body, the tips of his fingers tapered, almost delicate, nails bitten to the quick. She could see ragged cuticles and dark flecks of dried blood as his fingers worked at buttons, at the elastic of her shorts. He pressed himself closer, sweating already, his breathing shallow and uneven, and when they were on the floor, Licha on her hands and knees, Raleigh upright, kneeling behind her, she looked at their image in the mirror, at Raleigh watching, his head thrown back and arms extended so his hands grasped her hips, his movements regular and insistent. She thought of the mice they had mated in biology lab, of the male, a solid black, his motions powerful and concentrated in mount, of the female, a pink-eyed white, hunched and holding her ground to help him, her neck at an angle of submission, and she knew they were more alike than different, the mating mice, herself and Raleigh; that this impulse shot through all of life, through male and female, and made them do the things they did, made men and women lie down together. We are mating, she marveled.

He seemed to go deeper this time, deeper than when they stood against his bedroom wall. She felt her belly swell from him, a soft cramping like her menstrual cycle, pleasant at first, then almost painful. She'd asked him to stop, and he had waited while she turned over to face him, her arms braced against the door, then he had continued. Again she tried to hold her breasts for him and to move her hips at the same time. "You have to take it out," she said. "Before." She had forgotten to tell him this the first time.

He said nothing, concentrating on their image in the mirror. Finally he moaned, withdrawing, and Licha felt slow, warm spurts against her thigh. She squirmed beneath his weight, and when he rolled over she got up. "We'll leave a spot."

She went into the bathroom, looking for a cloth for the carpet. She didn't want to use the pale yellow towels folded in a complicated way across the bar, so she tore a length of paper, setting the roller spinning, and hurried to dab at the wetness where they had lain. The paper pilled and shed, leaving lint on the close shear of the wool. She tried to pick it off with her fingers, but it stuck here too. Raleigh laughed and got up to go to the bathroom. "Don't worry so much," he said, closing the door. "Catalina will get it."

His mention of her mother startled Licha; she and Madama would be back soon from McAllen. She dressed quickly, tucking the wad of paper into her pocket. She was halfway down the *galería* to the stairs when she heard the bathroom door click

98

open and Raleigh calling out, but she didn't want to risk the time to answer.

The little house felt hot and close after the expanse of the big rooms. Even before she opened the door she smelled the heat inside, the dust, warm *cominos* simmering into the beans in the big cast-iron *olla* on the hot plate. As she crossed the room to her bed she compared what she had seen upstairs in the big house with her mother's attempts to brighten things, a scattering of second-hand bathroom rugs across the dull linoleum, knickknacks cast off from Madama, paper flowers at the single window. Licha's bed was the lower bunk of a government issue set, curtained with a sheet tucked under the mattress of Tavo's top bunk where boxes of clothing and household things were stored now that Tavo had gone. The beds were white, but the paint had chipped, exposing leopard-spots of army green. At the head and foot the letters "US" were carved into the wood. When Licha was learning to read, she thought the letters meant herself and Tavo; us, *nosotros,* and she felt special, good, tracing the letters with her fingers, with a purple crayon, lucky: no one else had a bed that told of herself and her brother, of their place in the world. She hadn't wanted to believe Tavo when he'd laughed and told her what the letters stood for. Her mother slept on a daybed in the opposite corner, behind a partition made of crates and a blue shower curtain with a picture of an egret wading among green rushes. Licha lifted her sheet curtain and lay down, letting the heat and dimness envelop her.

She heard the car pull into the driveway, the sound of car doors closing and Madama's voice telling Perfilio to wash the car. She heard the slap of her mother's sandals on the flagstone path, coming toward the little house. She wished she had washed; the girls at school said other people could tell by your smell if you had been with a boy. In the stuffiness of the room her mother would notice it. She lay still and hoped her mother would think she was asleep.

Through the sheet Licha saw her come in, silhouetted in the light streaming through the doorway. She could see well enough to tell that her mother still wore her apron. Madama insisted on it, especially when they went to town. Licha watched as her mother took off the apron and folded it over a wooden chair, then began taking dishes and pots and pans from the crates that were stacked to form shelves, wisps of hair springing from the bun at the back of her neck.

She tried to remember how her mother looked when her skin wasn't glistening with sweat, when her hair wasn't escaping from the bun. Saturday before church, sometimes for whole days in winter if a norther came in and work at the house was light. Even through the sheet Licha could see the patches of darker blue under her mother's arms, around her waist, between her shoulder blades. They were as much a part of her mother as the starched work dress, as the apron, as the low song she sang while she worked, a song that irritated Licha for its persistence, its quality of being a song yet not a song, more a droning, melodic murmur made low in the throat that had the power to remove her mother, lift her beyond Licha's reach and back into the time before Licha, a song from her mother's earlier life in the barrancas of the East Sierra Madre, a place she never talked about, the place she had left to come here, first to work for Papa in the fields, then for Madama in the house.

When Tavo and Licha asked about it she said little. All they knew was that Papa had found her walking along the road, fifteen, pregnant with Tavo, on one of his trips below the border to find workers. He didn't like the migrant teams, the braceros, but preferred to find whole families who wanted to come across the river, to live in the block houses at the bend in the levee until they found something better, or even asked about something better, and then Papa would help them, with papers, by getting their children into school, with medicine and food. Her mother had been alone on the road, in the last month of pregnancy, but Papa had idled the truck alongside her, asking questions in Spanish, inviting her to join the families in the truckbed. Tavo had been born in the block house by the levee. Licha was born

three years later. Her father was a Latino from Las Cruces working a few months with the Army Corps of Engineers on an irrigation project before he moved on. This was all she knew. She
and Tavo had stopped asking; their mother didn't welcome
questions about the other life.

A stack of Melmac plates clattered to the floor, causing
Licha to jump. Her mother stooped to pick them up, her eyes
on Licha's curtain. "*¿Estás aquí?*"

Licha swung her legs over the edge of the bed. "I'm here,
Mama."

She made it a practice to answer her mother's Spanish with
English, as though she were talking to a toddler just learning
the words for things. "What are you doing?"

Her mother ignored her and continued picking up the scattered plates. Licha sighed and repeated the question in Spanish.
Her mother was stubborn enough to ignore the question all
day if it was a matter of will.

Her mother smiled at her, setting the stack of plates on the
wooden table. She told Licha that she and Madama had gone to
an appliance store in McAllen. She described the shining rows
of silver and white, and a new color for stoves and refrigerators
called avocado green. They had picked out a new stove for the
cocina in the big house. It was to be delivered tomorrow. And
guess who, as a gift for Christmas, was to have the old one?
Licha smiled in spite of herself. "We are!"

Her mother crossed the room and stood behind the big chair
next to the window. "*Ayúdame, chica.*"

Licha helped to move the chair. They placed it at an angle by
Licha's bed, then lifted the table from the corner where the
new stove would go and put it by the window. While her
mother dusted the tabletop, Licha went outside to get one of
the potted aloes that lined the step. She arranged it in the center of the table.

"*Mira,* Mama," she said, gesturing grandly toward the plant.
"*Better Homes and Gardens.*" They laughed, and Licha felt
good, good and happy, like Licha-nine-years-old, Licha of no

secrets, her mother's *chula niña* in a ruffled skirt and braids stretched tight for church. She watched her mother poke the broom into the cleared corner and shoo a lizard along the baseboard toward the door, her throaty song rising in the heat, happy with so little, and suddenly Licha was angry.

"A stove," she said. "An old stove. How much did the new one cost?"

Her mother continued sweeping, the hem of her work dress swaying stiffly with the motions of the broom. "*No importa.*"

"It *does* matter!" She felt like grabbing the broom away and forcing her mother to listen. "We don't need a stove. Let her sell the old one and give us the money. Let her buy us an air conditioner. She has enough. She has everything." Licha thought of nights in the little house, of trying to sleep with only the old black fan to cool her, its woven cord stretched from chair to chair, tripping her if she got up to get a drink of water, the frayed fabric encasing it reticulated like the backs of the water snakes she sometimes saw in the canal. "It will only make it hotter in this place!" She pushed against the screen door hard enough to wedge the flimsy frame against the bump on the edge of the step and walked out.

She cut through the live oaks, through the rows of oleander set out like railroad tracks to shield the little house from view, around to the back of the property to the overgrown area that she and Tavo and Raleigh had called the jungle when they were growing up. It was mostly scrub pecan choked with ololiuqui vines, avocado trees, crotons and yucca, but a few banana and papaya trees survived, making the place seem exotic and lush. The spears of saw palmetto slashed her legs as she ran past the boundaries. She looked down to see the thin lines like razor cuts across her thighs. She darted through the algarroba thicket and came out on the other side, to Grand Texas Boulevard. A fine name, she thought, for the rutted road that led to the highway toward Reynosa.

She slowed down, thinking about what had just happened, thinking that she now knew what made people run away. It wasn't a simple matter of not liking home, it was far more complicated than that, and at the point when things became too complicated to think about any longer, people ran away. For whatever reasons they had that were too entwined to sort out. She imagined her mother, a pregnant girl from the barrancas, walking along the road, and she imagined a man in a truck, a man in khaki work pants and a Panama hat, a smiling, red-mustached man. She would have climbed inside the truckbed, too. She saw herself riding away from the Valley to a different place, any place, maybe a place with snow. To Fort Dix where Tavo was, Tavo a soldier in uniform, able to be what he was without people thinking they *knew* what he was just by looking at him, by knowing where he came from, a place with more to get excited about than avocado appliances, where he made his own money and didn't have to depend on a bossy old woman like Madama, where he didn't have to care what such a woman thought of anything he did. Tavo would understand how she felt. He had been glad to leave the Valley.

She picked up a stone and threw it at an irrigation pump. She knew what Tavo would think of what she and Raleigh were doing. He would spit, and make the jerking upward jab with his wrist, like stabbing. He would stab Raleigh if he knew. He wouldn't see that Raleigh wasn't like the others, but more like Papa. Tavo would see only his side of it, the pachuco side that hated all Anglos. He wouldn't see that it was different with Raleigh, that the two of them were what they were, male and female, Raleigh and Licha, as simple as that. Raleigh wanted her, he found her beautiful. The feeling made her stomach tighten as she walked along, slower now. She held her shoulders straighter and began to sway her hips the way she had seen other girls do, feeling the heads of her femurs articulating deep in her pelvis. She knew now why those girls walked this way: a man wanted them.

She stopped to watch the sun go down behind a grove of Valencias. The fruit hung ripe and brilliant, orange as the sun, as the bright new tennis balls Madama kept in canisters on the laundry shed shelf. She heard the big trucks start up, loading braceros for the trip back to the colonia by the canal. Traffic on the highway quickened and Licha turned to go home, the trucks rumbling by. When she heard the clicking noises the men made, their high-pitched yips of appreciation, she toned down her walk, but she thought: let them look, let them want.

Raleigh didn't come for her the next day, or the next, though she made many trips between the house and the laundry shed, the laundry shed and the burn pile, watching the back door of the big house. She began to think she had been a fool, that Tavo's version of the way things were with Anglo boys and Mexican girls might be right. She could hardly bear her mother's excitement about the stove, and she snapped at her to stop polishing it so often, she'd polished it every day for eleven years, to speak English, to pick up her feet when she walked and stop shuffling around like a cow. Her mother stared at her when she said this, and Licha had seen her face close down.

On Saturday Perfilio brought two chickens and her mother baked them, filling the house with a rich yellow smell that made Licha queasy. She couldn't touch the chicken and she didn't go with her mother to church. She knew it was far too early, improbable, given the dates of her cycle, but she began to worry beyond reason that she was pregnant.

At sundown Saturday a norther blew in, rattling the rickety door and filling the house with random pockets of cold air. Licha pulled a sweater from the box under her bed and put it on. She slid the shutter panel across the window and shut the heavy hurricane door. She sat at the table in the dark, not bothering to pull the string on the light overhead. When the first knock came she thought it was the wind, but it kept up and finally she opened the door.

Raleigh wore a zippered red windbreaker and his hair blew up behind his head like a rooster's tail. He was smiling. "Did you miss me?"

She wanted to slap his glasses away so they would skitter across the flagstone into the potted plants and he would never find them. She wanted to tear off her blouse and sweater and show him her breasts, press them into his chest so hard that they burned him. "No," she said.

"You're mad at me." He tried to look around her to see inside the house. "Can I come in?"

She looked behind her into the dark room, at the silly rugs and the shower curtain and the stove in its corner like a squat white ghost. "I'll come out."

They walked around the house to the jungle, Licha with her arms folded across her chest, her hand tucked into the sweater sleeves, Raleigh with his hands jammed into the pockets of his windbreaker, neither of them speaking. Licha sat on the rim of a discarded tractor tire where Tavo had once found a coral snake. She shivered, glad it was too cold for snakes. Raleigh sat beside her. He bent to flick an oleander leaf from the toe of his loafer.

Alarm surged through her. He had found someone else, she wasn't good enough. Madama had found out. She wanted Licha gone—that girl, her mother gone.

"I'm busted at Vanderbilt," he said. He looked at her. "Kicked out."

Licha hoped she kept a straight face, kept from smiling: this is *all*?

"Mother's been hauling me all over south Texas for the last two days, throwing her weight around." He laughed, but Licha could tell he didn't think it was funny. "She thinks she can get me into A and I or Pan American. They're piss-poor schools, but I guess it's better than getting drafted."

Licha waited to see if he had anything else to say, but he was quiet, drumming his knuckles on the thick black tread of the tire. "Maybe it's not so bad," she said. She wanted to tell him what Mr. Mohesky had said, that if she continued to work hard he would help her apply for a scholarship to Pan American, but she couldn't think of how to say this.

He shrugged, then pulled a jeweler's box from his pocket. "Anyway, I got you these." He handed her the box. "For Christmas."

"Not yet," she said.

"You don't want it?"

"I mean, it's not Christmas yet." She held the box, stroking the nap of the black velveteen.

"Soon enough," he said. "Open it."

Inside was a pair of earrings, tiny gold chains with filigree hummingbirds at the ends, red stones for each eye. In the moonlight she could make out the store name on the inner lid: Didde's of San Marcos. She imagined him on the streets of the college town, going into the jewelry store while Madama waited in the car, poring over hundreds of boxes until he chose these, for her. "Thank you," she said, and when he stood and held his hand for her she went with him through the jungle to the laundry shed. He waited while she removed the silver hoops she wore, then he inserted the posts of the new earrings into her lobes. She tilted her head to each side to help him, and she was reminded of the female mouse. The thought came to her that staying still was just as powerful an act as moving, just as necessary, and she again felt linked to the everlasting, perfect cycle of things.

They made love on the floor of the laundry shed, her hips lifted, supported by a pile of towels. They felt damp against her skin and smelled of Lifebuoy soap and Clorox. Her carotid artery throbbed from the rush of blood to her head, but she didn't complain, and she didn't tell him to withdraw. She wanted to give him this, a sign of trust, of utter welcome. It would be all right, no matter what. What they were doing, this act, was a promise of that, a pact. She felt the earrings slide back and forth against her neck.

She made it back to the little house and into bed before her mother returned from church, and when she woke up Sunday morning, the first things she felt were the hummingbird earrings. She thought of Raleigh. Was he waking up just now in his room in the big house, remembering what they had done? She moved her hands down her body to the warm pocket between her legs and wondered how she felt to him. How could they ever know, male and female, what each felt like to the other? She heard her mother stirring and she sat up to part the curtain. Her mother was tying her apron over her work dress.

"¿Café?"

"Coffee," Licha repeated automatically. Sunday mornings they usually sat at the table drinking coffee. It was her mother's day off. "Why are you wearing that?"

There was no answer. Licha sighed, repeating the question in Spanish. Her mother explained that Madama needed her to help with a party. She had to clean, prepare food, set things up. She would come home in the middle of the afternoon to rest, then she would go back in the evening to serve.

"On Sunday?" Licha pulled out a chair and sat at the table, pouring coffee into one of the Melmac cups, adding sugar.

Her mother shrugged, and the helpless gesture irritated Licha.

"Why didn't you tell her no? You always do everything she says. '*Sí*, Madama, *no*, Madama, *¿algo más*, Madama?'" Licha rose from her chair and went to the small refrigerator for milk.

Her mother stood at the sink, calmly tucking wisps of hair into her bun with bobby pins, her back to Licha. Licha thought she may as well have been talking to the stove, for all the effect her words had. Even her mother's back looked obstinate, her hips wide and stolid, square and stupid, the apron bow at her back as ridiculous as the daisy garland around the ear of the cow on the milk carton she took from its shelf. She stirred the milk into her coffee and looked at the older woman. She knew her mother's life would always be the same, shuffling back and forth between houses, going to church, easing her knees and elbows with salve she made from Vaseline and aloe, waiting on others, obsequious, stubborn in her obsequiousness, taking her small revenge in pretending she didn't understand English, forcing Madama into pidgin silliness, and all of it because of stubbornness, because she wanted nothing more, because she thought no further than the day after tomorrow. Licha banged her cup onto the table, sloshing coffee over the edge and onto her cotton shift. "Why didn't you get papers when Papa offered? You could get a better job."

Her mother turned, and Licha saw her face, hurt, defiant. "You could *learn* to read, Mama." She felt suddenly defeated; there was nothing she could do. "It's your only day off," she said weakly.

She watched her mother rinse her own cup and dry it; she took it with her to work because Madama didn't believe in sharing dishes with the help. Her mother left the house, closing the screen door gently, leaving Licha alone at the table sipping coffee she could barely swallow for her welling sense of injustice. She got up from her chair, then ran after her mother, catching up with her along the flagstone path. "Don't do it, Mama. Say no. Say it for once in your life. Show her what you think of her."

Her mother shook her head. "I think nothing. I only work." She resumed her walk.

"You work for nothing. For a house too little and too hot. For a stove!" She grabbed her mother's arm and shook it. Her mother looked away, across the yard toward the laundry shed.

"*Dejame en paz.*"

"English, Mama. Your English is good. Use it. Make her *see* you!"

Her mother looked at her hard, and Licha felt suddenly exposed in her cotton shift, as though she was standing naked on the path. Her mother shook off Licha's hand. "No."

Perfilio came around the corner of the house with a wheelbarrow full of sand and a box of candles. He began placing the luminarias around the patio. Licha stood still, watching her mother walk toward the service entrance. Her mother had almost reached the door when she whirled, throwing her cup to the ground. She started back down the path toward Licha, her face dark and angry. She reached out and with a violent flick at Licha's ear set one earring spinning wildly. "*¡Éstos son de Madama!*"

Licha's hand flew to her ear, to the sting. She was dumbfounded by her mother's anger until she realized she thought
Licha had stolen the earrings from the big house. "They are
mine," she said, proud that they were, glad her mother was
wrong. "Raleigh gave them to me."

Her mother's eyes widened. Licha watched as her mother
took in the information, as she looked at her daughter for clues.
She felt her mother's eyes on her body, looking through the
thin shift at her breasts which seemed in that moment huge and
bobbing, giving away her secret. Then her mother slapped her.

"Fool!" She slapped again and Licha reeled. "It is worse!"

Licha ran to the little house, to her bed, where she cried until her eyes were red and swollen and her throat was raw. She
got up to dress. Her hands felt limp as she pulled her skirt up
over her hips. She didn't want to be home when her mother
came back for her nap, but she didn't know where to go. She
didn't want to go for a walk, and the few girls at school she
could call her friends were just that, school friends; they rarely
saw each other outside, and if they did they only teased Licha
about studying so hard and taking everything so seriously.
When she opened the refrigerator to look for something to eat
she realized it was Raleigh she wanted to talk to. She sat at the
table most of the afternoon, pushing cold rice around her plate
with the tines of a fork, watching the activity at the big house,
Perfilio arranging the luminarias, raking palm trash from the
drive, pulling the car around for Madama. When she saw her
mother come out the service entrance, she left the little house
and hurried to the laundry shed.

The pile of towels was still on the floor, flattened slightly
from when she and Raleigh had lain on them. She fluffed them
up with her foot to make them look more natural. She looked
out the window to see her mother going into their house, then
she took a tennis ball from one of the canisters. She planned to
stand behind the poinsettia bush outside Raleigh's window and
throw the ball against the screen.

Her first throw fell short of the window, and her second, thumping against the wire mesh, was louder than she imagined it would be. The ball bounced into a plot of white azaleas. Its presence there looked miraculous and unreal, like one fully-ripened orange in a grove of still-in-blossom trees. Licha thought of leaving it there and giving up, but she wanted to see Raleigh. As she crossed the front yard to retrieve the ball, she heard the heavy carved door swing open on its wrought-iron hinges.

Raleigh stood on the *porche,* the fingers of his right hand kneading his left biceps, the blue stone in his class ring glinting in the sun. He stepped from the *porche* and walked toward her. His face looked fuller, younger; he had shaved his sideburns. She remembered her mother's slap. She couldn't make herself meet his eyes.

"What's the matter?"

She still couldn't look at him. "My mother knows," she said. She felt bad and stupid, as though she alone was responsible for what they had done. It was her fault her mother knew. "I'm sorry."

She hoped he would tell her it was all right, that he didn't care, that he was glad: now they could be together, without hiding.

He laughed. "Is that all?"

She looked at him, relieved beyond words.

"It's not like she hasn't done the same thing," he said. "She's been around the block."

She was puzzled. "What?"

He winked at her. "You know. When we were kids."

Licha never thought of her mother in that way; her mother was just what she was: aproned, blue-dressed, patting tortillas, sweeping; working. She started to ask Raleigh what he meant, but all of a sudden she knew. She remembered when they had first come to live in the little house, her mother, younger, thinner, sitting on the floor with them, showing them how to cut circles of colored paper and twist them into the shapes of bougainvillea, oleander, the blue trumpets of

jacaranda, her hair loose and fragrant from the castile shampoo she kept on the shelf above the sink. Laughing, her
mother had tucked one of Licha's flowers behind her ear, and
in the hollow of her throat a small blue vein seemed to pulse.
Licha had reached up to place her fingers on it, moved to joy,
to longing at the happy mystery of how beautiful her mother
was. Her mother had scooped her up and hugged her with a
strength that surprised her. In the hot still nights after she and
Tavo were in bed, her mother would leave the house. Just for
a walk, she said, just to cool off. Licha would try to stay awake
until she came back in, but the hum of the fan would always
put her to sleep. In the morning her mother would be at the
sink, running water for coffee, draining the soak water from
the beans, and Licha would forget. But it was Papa who
brought the fan, Papa with the red mustache that fascinated
her, taking off his Panama before he entered the little house,
patting the top of her head, "*Qué chula, niña.*" Papa who
brought the beds.

"Come inside," Raleigh said. "You can see the preparations
for Mother's big shebang." From his tone Licha could tell what
he thought of Madama's party, but she hesitated.

"She's not here," he said. "She's at the club getting a bag on."

She followed him into the house. As they passed through
the big hall she caught a glimpse of the *sala* with its grand
Moorish windows she had seen only from the outside. At the
far end of the room stood an enormous fir, its branches
flocked with white, shimmering with gold and silver birds.
She thought of the plastic Santas she and her mother would
hang on the potted Norfolk pine they would bring in from its
place among the other plants that rimmed the little house, the
red suits nearly pink from sun and age, the white of the beards
and fur trim gone yellow.

"She's got it all decked out," he said, starting up the stairs to
the *galería*. Licha followed him. She nodded though she knew
he couldn't see her. When they were inside his bedroom he
locked the door and took a mirror from the wall, propping it

on the floor against the bed. He fingered one of her earrings. "Beautiful," he said.

She pushed his hand away, but then stood still, her arms lifted as he pulled her blouse over her head. He kissed her, unhooking her bra. She felt her nipples draw and tighten. "My mother isn't what you think," she said. The words surprised her.

He eased himself down and took her nipple in his mouth, but she drew away. "She speaks English. She only pretends she doesn't so your mother will look like a fool." She felt the beating of her heart, shuddering and rapid, almost hot, astonishing as sudden anger.

He laughed, nuzzling her, pulling at the elastic of her skirt. "I know," he said. "It's been a joke for years. I used to spy on Mother's bridge club just to hear her do the Catalina imitation. She's really got the routine down."

Licha stared at him as he unbuckled his belt and stepped out of his jeans. "Lie down, *chula.*" His hands on her shoulders, he pressed her down with him until they were kneeling beside the mirror. She looked at him, at the dark triangle of hair against his pale skin, at his penis rising, then to the mirror where she saw the flexion at the side of his buttock where the gluteus inserted. She saw herself, smaller, a fool looking up at him, a fool somehow more beautifully made, browner, smoother, more round. She tried to meet his eyes, fixed on his own, but couldn't, and she had the feeling each of them was seeing something different in the framed rectangle, like two people looking at the same slide under a microscope, trying to adjust the focus to accommodate both their vision, failing. She removed his hands from her shoulders and stood up, gathering her clothes, starting to dress. "I have to go," she said.

She walked out into the early dark of December. Light shone from the little house, and as she got closer she saw her mother's form moving back and forth against it. Licha knew she would be eating her supper, standing over the *olla* eating beans rolled into a flour tortilla, alternating beans with bites of pepper, waiting to go back to work. She looked up when Licha entered, but didn't meet her eyes.

"*Café,*" her mother said, gesturing toward the pot on the stove. Licha saw that the light came from behind the pot, from a small bulb under the hood of the stove that cast the shadows of the *olla* and the coffeepot onto the floor. She sat down at the table. Her mother took cups from their hooks, poured them full and placed them on the table. Then she sat down across from Licha. Licha looked at her, at the crease from her nap across the smooth brown of her cheek, her hair freshly brushed and fastened back, in her eyes the sleepy distance of the saints, the prophets. Her mother lifted the lid of the sugar bowl. "*¿Azúcar?*"

Licha nodded. Her mother spooned the sugar into their cups. They were small things, not objecting to her mother's Spanish, sitting still to let her mother serve her, but Licha could tell she was pleased. She heard the low song begin in her mother's throat, masking for a while the faint metallic buzz of the stove light rattling under its enameled hood. Then the song trailed away. They sat for a long time at the table, speechless, beyond apology, and even the presence of a small green anole skittering across the top of the stove to bask briefly in the harsh white glare, the ruby throat it expanded when threatened now a flaccid sac, was not enough to disturb their silence. After her mother got up and left the little house to go to work, Licha sat for a longer time, drained and quiet, stunned before the complex living heart of grace.

WHITEWING

ALTHOUGH she liked to say she was a law unto herself in our small south Texas town, my mother listened every morning to Waldron Ming's phone calls reporting the fires and prowlers, deaths and mischiefs within the city limits of Martha. He called each weekday at exactly seven-thirty, just as my sister and I were getting ready to go to school, Evelyn-Patsy to her sheltered elementary outside McAllen, me to Harlan Bloch High in Martha, where I served a lackluster term as vice-president of the sophomore boys' swim club and slogged through every course but English, which I liked. When we heard our mother say, "Yes, Waldron, and you have a fine day, too," we went in to breakfast.

My mother cracked an egg against the side of the griddle. "Mr. Ming tells me the plate glass window at the Luz Palmetto looks like a bloodbath. They think it's V-8 juice." She slid the egg into melted bacon fat, then turned to me. "You wouldn't know anything about that, would you, Will?"

"No, ma'am," I said. When she turned back to the stove, I looked across the table at Evelyn-Patsy to see if she would give me away, but she was staring out the window at a humming-bird hovering over a firecracker bush. My mother often said she was a "simple spirit," but my sister seemed sometimes preternaturally wise, and knew the very things I wished she didn't.

"I didn't think so," my mother said. "I told him you wouldn't." She cracked another egg onto the griddle, sprinkled water on the hot fat, then clamped a pan lid over the eggs. "I hope," she said, fixing me with a look, "that I'm not defending you injudiciously."

I flicked my knee so my napkin would fall and I could duck to retrieve it. "No, ma'am." My voice was thick with the rush of blood to my head.

"That man," she said, warming to her subject, "can be such a pest."

"He sure can," I said. I hoped she would go on awhile about him, so I shook my head and said, "Boy-howdy, he sure can, Mama." I drank some orange juice, waiting, half listening.

Waldron Ming was a turkey-necked old cotton grower who wrote a weekly column for the *Valley Evening Sun*. Years before, when he was young and the lower Rio Grande Valley was at the height of citrus-planting fever, he had written the words to "The Magic Valley," a booster-anthem that had since been bastardized by several generations. Most of the versions supplanted the word "citrus," used in the song as profusely as the orange groves that lined our roads, with the word "Meskins," who were also profuse, but a good deal more indigenous. By the time my contemporaries got around to their own version, which was in the early sixties, no one except perhaps Waldron Ming himself remembered the original lyrics, and by now they are probably as lost as the way of life in the Valley when I best knew it, when Mingo, as we called him, made his daily round of calls to express the wattled outrage he divided between the Anglo teenagers who raced between the palms along our flat caliche roads, and the people who lived in the dusted-over tangle of *taquerías,* domino parlors and wooden shacks set among bright rows of cannas on the northern edge of town.

But my mother tolerated him, and in those days it seemed to me she suffered fools too gladly. Widow of Martha's once and only lawyer, my father, she was a lightning rod for the culturally deprived of Hidalgo County. She numbered among her friends several devotional poetesses, a mad-eyed sculptor of custom coats of arms, half a string quartet which scoured the Valley for a bassist (my mother was their cellist), and the unforgettable Mr. Boelker, a tortured wrack whose handwritten manuscript *My War With Mammon* spilled from three bushel baskets he carried on the back seat of his oyster-colored '49 Chevrolet, occasional sheets of foolscap flapping out the windows like yellow birds set free, him after them in hot pursuit.

My mother was from an odd, artistic Louisiana family, and used to eccentricity. Born Evangeline Garb, she had been, as my father loved to tell our guests—always in her hearing—the only Cajun-Jewish cello player at Sophie Newcomb, and he had married her—here he liked to pause, straight-faced, stage-reflecting, the pause holding her smile, his laugh, their love, and us, as surely as his broad hand held his glass of Beam—because somebody-by-God-had-to. It had been their plan, my mother had once told me, to rear their children with progressive artistic, spiritual, and social attitudes, even in a place like Martha. Especially, said my mother, in a place like Martha.

Much of this was lost on me. I preferred the company of Brush Dudley and Snakey Hurdman, white-socked, wheat-jeaned Texas boys who knew beans about art and music, who, if asked, might have said that Mahler's First was one god-awful round of tag-team wrestling, rooting for the Mauler. Our taste ran to the gunfighter ballads of Marty Robbins, "El Paso" at the fore, though the steel guitar of Santo and Johnny's "Sleep-walk" could twang in us a rapturous chord as we drove around the Valley in Brush's rusted Dodge, the Green Latrine, so called for its odor and condition. How could I tell my mother, when she wondered aloud what I saw in my friends, that it was for these inexpressible reasons I loved and defended them? She was a dark-eyed, pretty woman, with the gentle affect of her southern upbringing, but with opinions about honor and conduct set as hard as I liked the yolks of my eggs.

She brought our plates to the table and set them in front of us. "Don't stare so, Pats," she said. She tucked a strand of hair behind my sister's ear, then followed Evelyn-Patsy's gaze toward the hummingbird. "Such a pretty creature," she said. "Just think how fast its heart must beat." She sat down, poured cream into her coffee, then turned to me.

"I wish you didn't see so much of that Dudley boy."

I picked up my knife and fork, planning to chop my eggs and bacon into a red-and-yellow, pepper-flecked mash I would then fork onto a piece of toast. "Brush?"

At the sound of my friend's name, Evelyn-Patsy turned her attention to the table. Brush Dudley said sweet teasing things to my sister, flustering her into prettiness.

"Where do you suppose he picked up that awful sobriquet?"

I jammed a mash-spread toast corner into my mouth. Brush was Brush because he was the first among us to sport a full and wiry pubic escutcheon, which he liked to show off in gym class. His real name was Marion. None of us could remember the origin of Snakey's name, and only his mother called him David. "Mmnnh," I said, my mouth full, "good chow."

My mother gave me a look of disgust, then turned to talk to Evelyn-Patsy about school, allowing me to finish my egg project and to go over our steps of the night before. I was trying to decide if we'd left anything that would tie us to the juice-smeared window of the Luz Palmetto, a *taquería* on East Seventh.

It was Brush who led us on our raids. Vigilantes, we thought ourselves, and we had a name, the Valley Lords, and a special handshake that featured a lot of brace and shove. The Luz Palmetto had been our target because little Lupe Palacio had called Snakey a *maricón* when we went in to try to buy some beer. Brush decided things were getting out of hand if a seventh-grader could call one of the Valley Lords a faggot. Juicing was the perfect retaliation, as just that day Brush's father, manager of the canning plant, had caught two wetback workers pissing into a vat of tomato juice. It had to be thrown away, so we had all the material. We'd been sure to park the Green Latrine a block away, and we threw the five gallon cans in the arroyo. I didn't think we'd left any traces. I got up from the table, picked up my books, kissed my mother and sister, and went outside to wait for Brush.

From our front porch I could see the stretch of Mile Six Road down which the Green Latrine would come before it turned into our long flat drive. Just as I saw the flash of chrome in the distance, a movement near the mesquite thicket at the edge of our property caught my eye, and a dark-skinned stranger—the man who would become my mother's husband—came out from behind the trees and walked across the yard toward our tool-house. His walk was quiet, but determined, a guarded walk, but not particularly sneaky. I wondered what he was trying to do, walking toward the shed in full daylight, Brush's car approaching, its radio blaring. I watched until he popped the complicated door latch, so easily I thought he must have done it before. When Brush pulled the car up beside me, I set my books on the hood and stuck my head in the passenger window. "Some guy's in the toolhouse."

"A wet?"

"Looks like."

"Don't just stand there, man. Run him off." He reached under the seat for his Indian club. "You want the masher?"

"Nah," I said. "Guy's a runt." I gave the roof of the car a smart pat and started across the yard.

The door stood open and I could see him by the workbench, rummaging in a bin. When I was close enough, I called out, "Hey, buddy."

He looked up, then grinned. He held a few tools, a wrench, an auger. He extended them and grinned again. "Sí," he said. "Okay."

"Put 'em down," I said.

He continued to hold the tools, nodding.

"Com-prend-ay," I said. "Down." I didn't speak Spanish, just what was necessary to get along with our maid Remedios and what I picked up in the halls at school. I pointed to the tools, then to the workbench. "Put the damn things down."

"Okay." But he continued to clutch the tools, nodding.

I took a step toward him, blocking his exit. He wasn't acting like the thieving wets Brush always talked about running off, and I wondered what I should do, tried to imagine what Brush would do. I stepped inside and grabbed the tools. "Get out," I said.

He stopped smiling and dropped his hands to his sides. I stood there, breathing hard: who did he think he was? I clenched my jaw. I felt mean and ugly and stupid. "Move!"

Something about it—the close, hot smell of him; the way his shoulders set, somewhere between challenge and surrender; maybe just because it came to me that I could—made me wheel as he passed me, slam the heel of my hand into the flat place between his shoulder blades. The sound he made as the breath heaved out of him was thick and dull, hollow-sounding. He kept walking, not looking back, not acknowledging the blow, across the yard toward the mesquite. I shook my arm. My hand felt heavy and swollen, the way it felt if I slept with it hanging over the edge of the bed.

"You get him?" Brush asked when I got into the car.

"He's gone, isn't he?"

Brush shifted into first, narrowed his eyes at me. "You chickened out, man. Didn't you? Level with ol' Daddy Brush."

"I got him."

"Whoo-boy!" Brush beamed. "You're getting there, boy." He popped the clutch and we lurched onto the drive. "Damn wets," he said. "Kill you as look at you." He went on about a grower in Mission who'd had his shotguns stolen. I listened, rubbing the heel of my hand along my jeans leg. "The Valley's getting worse," he said. "Tell your mama to lock up better."

"Mingo's wise," I said, remembering the Luz Palmetto.

"Mingo doesn't know diddly. They already got that crazy old Fidencio on it. The Palacios fired him for being drunk again. They figured he did it to get even. He already confessed, I heard. Cried like a baby."

We pulled into the Hurdman's driveway where Snakey waited, black horn-rimmed, skinny. He got into the back seat. "Men," he greeted us. "A perfect day for tomatofish."

Snakey was a reader. His hero that year, and several before it, was J. D. Salinger, for the chapel-fart scene, which Snakey could recite. If Brush was the muscle for our excursions, Snakey was the brains.

"Snake the Great," Brush said. "We pulled it off."

"Vengeance is mine." Snakey leaned forward, resting his arms on the seat back as we drove along Mile Six toward school.

Brush looked in the rearview. "What's that gunkus all over your face?"

I turned to look. Snakey's forehead, cheeks, and chin were covered with puckered spots, like dried egg white. Flecks sprinkled his shirt like chips of mica.

"My secret formula." He flicked a speck from his glasses. "Equal parts alum and Elmer's Glue-All. Cheaper than Clearasil."

"Man," Brush said, shaking his head, and we all hooted, just to hoot. Brush turned up the radio to Richie Valens singing "Donna," and we pulled into the Harlan Bloch parking lot, howling and moaning with the song. In the swell of students entering the doors, I forgot about the intruder for a while, and if I thought of him, or of the way I'd treated him in the tool-house, in the days that passed before I saw him again—this time in our living room—it was with the uneasy notion that I had somehow wronged him, and that the wrong would come home to sit on my shoulder when my mother found out about it. I decided not to tell her.

Friday night Brush and Snakey and I went to McAllen to cruise the main street. Radio at full volume, we drove through the business district beside carloads of teenagers from other little towns along the river. We rested our arms on the rolled-down windows, trying to look uninterested. All the songs we heard seemed to be about girls, Donna, Carole, Peggy Sue. The Valley Lords had none, unless we counted Brush's fruitless bouts with Paula Rainwater. Cruising along on warm Valley nights, though, singing the girl-songs, we felt the promise that we were getting closer to some great something that was just around the corner, and I imagine each of us thought he was alone in pretending that promise meant nothing. The pretense was easy during the tough, macho songs, the driving songs, but when a tender lyric came along, I turned into wishful, hopeful, moonstruck mush, mush I would have hooted if Brush or Snakey had confessed to it, mush so fraught with yearning it was almost holy.

"I bet old Phoebe Caulfield turned into the greatest girl," Snakey said, his sneakered feet resting on the seat back.

Brush slowed the car beside a group of Mexican girls on the sidewalk outside the Rialto theater. His voice low, he said, "Look at that."

"Cowabonga, Buffalo Bob," Snakey said.

I slid down in the seat a ways, holding the girls in the corner of my vision until we passed. I didn't dare look at them full on. White, black, brown: if they'd been parrot blue they couldn't have looked more beautiful to me, innocent, mysterious, all of them, all of girlkind, and none of them, except the knowing ones you didn't want, could know how much you wanted them.

Something about the night laid us low. Maybe it was the lack of women, or rather, girls; it could have been the changes brought about by September and the start of school; even the weather, which had a lonely touch of coolness in it. Whatever it was, it seemed to swirl through the open windows of the Green Latrine as we drove back to Martha, subdued and disheartened, and when I walked onto our porch to let myself in, I felt for the first time empty, wanting, that even home was not enough.

Music came from the living room, from the old Deutsche Grammophon recording of the Ninth Symphony, the final movement with Schiller's *Alle Menschen werden Brüder* refrain, my father's favorite. I opened the front door and walked down the hall toward the sound.

A single lamp was on behind my mother's chair, its yellow light gathering all the sadness of our manlorn house the day-light made me forget. When I saw her reach out to touch my father's chair, and I saw the jut of a knee, I realized she wasn't alone. I moved sideways into the room to stand just inside the doorway.

I didn't try to make sense of what I saw. My mother's guest was the man from the toolhouse. He had cleaned up. He wore black trousers and a short-sleeve white dress shirt. Even in the dim light I could see the comb tracks in his hair. Flat-handed, he was wiping tears from his face. My mother touched his arm. I remembered how my hand felt on his back, and it came to me that I wanted to shove him again.

When the music ended my mother rose to lift the needle arm. Seeing me, she said, "Come in, Will."

He stood, wiping his palms on his pants.

"This is my friend Andrés." She took my arm and pulled me closer. "Will," she said to him, "my son, *mi hijo.*" He extended his hand.

Jackass, I called myself as I took it. My mother talked, but I didn't hear what she was saying, and when I took my hand from his, it was moist.

She went on talking, out of breath, overbright. Finally, she said, "He plays the violin," and sank into her chair.

Andrés and I faced each other. He said something to me in Spanish, but I didn't catch it. He spoke to my mother then, and she looked at the two of us and said, "Yes, that's probably best." She rose and they walked toward the front hall. I followed them. She turned on the porch light and opened the door for him. Moths began to flutter around her and she made girlish shooing motions.

He caught one of her hands, kissed it. "Evangelina," he said. Something in Spanish. Then, "Thank you." He looked at me, and for an instant I wondered if he had told her about the toolhouse.

"Bye-bye, Will," he said. My mother closed the door.

I followed her down the hall to the kitchen. "Bye-bye?" She wouldn't look at me. "He was a guest in our house." She ran water into two wineglasses that sat on the drainboard.

"I caught that guy out in the toolhouse, stealing."

She dabbed at a lipstick smudge on the rim of the glass. "I told him he could borrow things. I must have forgotten to mention that to you." She lifted the drainboard, then picked up a sponge and began wiping the counter. She wrung out the sponge, then looked at me as though from a distance. "I forget how big you're getting."

"He's a wetback, Mama. What do you think you're doing?"

"Keep your voice down, you'll wake your sister." Her eyes seemed tired, and her face had the bruised look that made me feel responsible for it, for my father's worn-out heart. "I just wanted him to have a nice evening. He's a nice man. And he isn't Mexican, Will, if that's what your trouble is. Really, you *must* stop using that ugly phrase." She opened the cabinet and began straightening glasses. "And I'll entertain Eskimos and Hottentots in this house if it pleases me."

A glass tipped over, rolling along the shelf in a bottom-heavy arc. She righted it, then giggled, oddly.

"What's the matter with him?"

"Nothing's the matter with him. He was an engineer. Is. He played with the symphony in San Salvador."

"Looks like he slept in a bale truck."

She brightened. "He's living out at the Seabury place, in the fruit shed. Miz Seabury told me about him and I went to visit." She shook her head. "No running water, no electricity. He sleeps on an old *lona,* Will. He's helping her with some . . . "

"What the hell's he used to, the Taj Mahal?"

"Keep your swearing outside. I won't have it in this house."

I got a glass, ran water into it, and started to drink, but the warm, mineral-tasting Valley water reminded me suddenly of the way he had smelled in the toolhouse. I swallowed. "Looks to me like you'll have everything else in here."

She closed the cabinet door. "You are treading on thin ice, Mister."

"If he's so great, what's he doing up here? He kill somebody?"

"It's political. He supported the wrong man. Or wrong for him."

"Stupid."

"That's not for us to say."

"How do you think this makes me look? Don't you think people are going to start talking?"

She laughed. "This place," she said, "this *place*. And what do you suppose they'll say that they haven't said a thousand times?"

I set my glass down. "That you're breaking the law."

She was silent, considering, and for one moment I imagined that this would be the end of it. I decided to press my advantage. "He show you his papers?"

Again she laughed. "Oh, Will, I don't need papers. And you needn't stand there glowering at me like a county judge." She pulled out a chair and sat at the table. "I suppose this has something to do with your friends."

"They don't know about it."

"I mean your attitude." She sighed. "I can't imagine what your father would think of the way you're behaving."

Her words struck me like a punch, and I felt sick. "Daddy wouldn't have let any wetback kiss his hand." I turned to leave. "Or his butt."

The next day I avoided my mother, spending the afternoon with Brush and Snakey. We cleaned our guns for the opening day of whitewing season, which would be the following Saturday. I had a Remington 20-gauge, Brush a Winchester, and Snakey used an old .410 we hooted routinely, but which Snakey maintained had mystical, lucky properties. My father had left me his beautiful Parker Brothers double-barrel 16 I could have used, but I was happy just to know I had it if I wanted it. Brush and Snakey and I had gone on opening day since we were eleven, and we waited for it all summer, resisting the urge to bag a few before time. None of us saw the irony in our strict observance of the season rules while at the same time using those shotguns to turn road signs into sieves.

That night my mother seemed careful with the things she said to me. She talked mostly with my sister, and I took a measure of mean satisfaction in my silence, in picturing the state of things if I were gone. Later, as I lay on my bed listening to KRGV, she came to stand in the doorway. The Coasters were singing "Poison Ivy."

"Try to understand, Will."

"What's to understand?"

She looked at me for what seemed a long time. "I'm helping him with his English."

"Right."

"Was that smart-lip, young man?"

"No, ma'am." I rolled over and turned up the radio, then closed my eyes and felt a wave of longing for my former self, for the times I'd lain in bed content to *think* about being a man—bigger shoulders, deeper laugh, a hat maybe, a pipe, wide hands that unscrewed jar lids—before this mystic urge to *be* one. I don't know how long she stood in the doorway, but when I turned over she was gone.

My mother set a table as hybrid as her pedigree. Coca-Cola baked ham, boiled greens and butter beans, gumbo, dirty rice, borscht, latkes. She left the Mexican cooking to Remedios, who made tortillas, cornshuck-wrapped tamales, pots of *olla podrida* with chorizo and garbanzos. My mother said she couldn't get the hang of it. When I came home from school the next Friday and found her in the kitchen chopping onions, Evelyn-Patsy beside her, the counters and table strewn with peppers and cornmeal, an oddly spiced meat mixture simmering on the stove, I knew something was up. I set my books on the table. "What's that smell?"

"Finer, Pats," my mother said to my sister, "they need to be the size of little grains of rice." To me, she said, "We're making *papusas*. They're Salvadoran."

"For him?"

"If you mean Andrés, yes. And for you, of course."

"He can't find his own food?"

She banged her knife on the cutting board. "I won't have this attitude!" She hacked at the onion. "He is an educated man."

"If he's so educated, why's he living in a fruit shed?"

She shook her head. "Someday," she said, "someday perhaps you will learn compassion."

I would like to say that her remark stung me, made me see how stupidly I was behaving. But I was fifteen, and I have since discovered that any lesson learned by me is of the head-bang, hard-knock, bashed-forward-from-bullheaded stripe. Her remark stung, of course, but it served only to give me a tighter grip as I clung to my Valley-logic, to make me dig my thick-wit ditch a little deeper, so that when I peered out of it I saw what I wanted to see, what everyone else in the Valley (except my mother) knew: that Mexico was a hopeless, dried-up dirtball of a country and that El Salvador, at the bottom of it, could only be worse. There was no beauty there. They all wanted to leave, cross the border any way they could. What they touched turned lurid and pathetic as their painted saints, as the bright red cannas that concealed tumbledown shacks, turned into the trashy leavings of a carnival. No music but the yipping seesaw of mariachi bands. No honor; they stole everything you didn't nail down. They wanted what we had. I yanked open the refrigerator and took a bottle of Coca-Cola. "I won't be home for supper."

"He's going to play for us," Evelyn-Patsy said. Her vague gaze seemed to go beyond our kitchen walls.

"Great," I said. "Just great."

I found Brush and Snakey on Hurdman's screened porch, playing with Snakey's parakeets, Holden and Phoebe. Snakey let them fly around the porch. "Don't let them out," he warned. I closed the screen door and sat in a seat-sprung lawn chair. Blue Phoebe flew to perch on my shoulder, pecking at my collar. "Tell her not to crap on me."

"She has her pride," Snakey said.

Holden, a small green missile, buzzed my ear as he flew to the screen behind me. I heard his claws picking their way along the mesh. "You know that wet?" I told them what was going on at my house.

Brush took out his pocketknife and began to clean his nails. "It's no secret, man. I heard the guy's just about camped out on you-all's doorstep."

Snakey nodded. "Mingo. The Voice of the Valley." He made a clicking noise to call the birds. "There's a lot of that on TV. Look at Louis Prima and Keely Smith. Xavier Cugat and Abbe Lane. Lucy and Ricky Ricardo. Shoot. Maybe it's not so bad." He shrugged.

"It's not like that," I told them. "She just feels sorry for him."

Brush slouched in his chair, giving me a heavy-lidded look. "What you going to do about it?"

That night the Valley Lords went riding. We drove out toward the Seabury place, swinging by Paula Rainwater's so Brush could see if Mason Vestring's car—a blue Plymouth sedan we called the Dipmobile—was there. It was. We drank from bottles of home brew Snakey filched from his father. The more we drove around, the clearer it became that we should teach Andrés a lesson of place.

Brush suggested tomatoes.

"Too close to Operation Luz Palmetto."

"Eggs are always good."

I proposed an anonymous letter.

"You know Spanish?" Snakey asked.

"Just food and the dirty stuff."

"Great," Snakey said. "'Dear *Pendejo Cabrón: Chinga* yourself and get out of town before noon tomorrow or we'll bash you with our enormous *tamales*. Your friends, the Valley Lords.' Great, Will."

We hooted. I was starting to feel better, knowing we would do something.

"I have it!" Snakey said. "White rats."

Brush said, "Huh?"

Snakey cupped his hands around his mouth, making it a tube he spoke through. "Modess," he said, ". . . because."

I stared at him. "What?"

"A product I have tested in my special labs. Absorbency. Adhesion. Turn the car around. To Rexall, men."

"Closed."

"The grocery store, then."

We sped back to Martha. Snakey refused to give us any clues. "Keep it running," he said as he jumped out the back door. He disappeared into the grocery store, then came back out with a blue box wrapped in cellophane.

"Tampax?" Brush read. "They let you just go in and buy those things?"

Snakey pointed toward Acacia Street. "The Dairy Maid."

At the drive-in he ordered a cup of warm water, tipping the carhop a penny. "Keep-o el change-o," he said. She sneered at him and we drove back to the country.

The Seabury place had been a family citrus operation before most of the land was sold to big growers. Miz Seabury still lived there, alone unless a migrant helper stayed in the fruit shed. She kept a small business in truck and hand-pick cotton. We walked across a cabbage field to get to the shed, a cinder block and corrugated tin structure that rose ramshackle in the moonlight.

Snakey unwrapped the box, slid a tampon from the cardboard tube and held it by the string. Brush and I watched. I had never seen one; my mother was discreet, and I had seen only a large blue box beneath the bathroom sink, in loopy script above a picture of a carnation the words "Modess . . . because."

The single flower looked wilted and sad. Because my discovery coincided with my father's death and my curiosity about what my mother did for so long behind the closed bathroom door, I had decided, at six, that the thick white pads were something ladies used when they wept, put them over their eyes, maybe, the "because" the word that indicated unspeakable grief.

Snakey dipped the tampon in the water, then swung it by the string, spattering us with drops. He aimed at the shed and let fly, flung it hard against the wall where it stuck in a wet, gorged, satisfying splat.

"Whoo-boy," Brush said. "Let me."

"Brilliant," I said. Against the gray block wall, the tampon looked like a fat white rat, obscene tail dangling. We took turns flinging them until Snakey said, "Wait. Cut your finger." He held out his pocketknife.

"What do you want to cut mine for?" Brush said. "Cut your own damn finger."

"Cut mine," I said. I took the knife and drew blood from my middle finger, then let it soak into the wet white cotton. I threw it against the wall.

"Ooo-eee!" Brush yelled.

When all the tampons were gone we stood back to look at our work. The side of the shed looked profane, infested, and I felt that we had sent the perfect message of gore, of shame, of violence and blemished purity. As we walked back to the car, I could hardly stop turning around to get a new look at it, to see it fresh, to see what it meant, to be glad and horrified; the fruit shed looked the way he made me feel.

Andrés was still at our house when Brush dropped me off. I heard music, and I went to stand by the front window to look in. Evelyn-Patsy sat at his feet, my mother behind her chair, leaning on folded arms, watching him play. I waited outside until the music ended.

The house still smelled of their odd dinner. My mother smiled at me. "You missed a lovely time, Will."

"I cried," said Evelyn-Patsy, pleased.

"Yeah, well," I said. I looked at him, gave a wave that was half salute, half dismissal.

"Oh, you cut yourself," my mother said. "Look at your hand!"

I held up my hand. "Car door."

"You'd better put something on it."

Andrés came forward to shake my hand, but I held it higher to show the cut. "Sorry."

My mother beamed. "I'll just show you to the door, Andrés." She said something to him in Spanish, then turned to me, smiling. "You put something on that hand, now, hear?"

"Yes, ma'am." I stood aside as they walked to the door, then I went to the kitchen to make a sandwich.

She came to stand in the doorway. "It's nice to see you getting along with Andrés."

I slathered mustard onto Wonder bread. "I don't guess he'll be around here much longer, anyway."

"Why, of course he will. He was just telling me how much he likes it here."

I shrugged. I put a piece of ham on the bread and clapped the sides together, then leaned back against the counter and bit into the sandwich.

"He lost his father early, too, Will. He told me he knows how you must feel about, oh, things. I was telling him about your trip tomorrow and he even said he'd like to come along."

I swallowed too soon, felt the bread lodge at the back of my throat.

"It would really be nice," she said. "I think he could be a friend to you."

My voice felt choked. "I've already got friends." I went to the refrigerator and took a big swallow of milk from the carton.

My mother handed me a glass. "Well, it won't hurt for him to come along. He'll be here for lunch tomorrow. I told him you-all leave around one."

I smashed my fist into the sandwich. "You can't do that. You can't just goddamn invite somebody on somebody else's hunt!"

"I'm afraid it's done. And mind your talk."

"This is crazy! He can't come. Brush . . ." I thought about what Brush would do, what he would want me to do. "You have to tell him he can't come!"

"You tell him," my mother said. "You tell him when he gets here. *You* tell him you don't want him on your hunting trip. You tell him why!"

I picked up the smashed sandwich and threw it in the sink. "I bet he doesn't even have a gun."

"I told him he could borrow Daddy's."

"Not the Parker Brothers?"

She shook out a dish towel and folded it, hung it on the towel bar. "That one in the case," she said. "You don't use it."

Until this time I had been happy just to unzip the fleece-lined case, to run my hand along the burled stock. "I would," I said. "I clean it all the time." I hated the way my voice sounded. I wanted to run get the gun from the closet and show it to her, an article of proof, so she would see that she was wrong, and when she saw the gun—polished, clean, well-oiled—realize what she was doing, stop doing it, and things could settle back the same as before.

"Well, done is done," she said. She turned, flicked off the kitchen light.

"I'm not going," I said. "I'm flat not going."

"That's your choice." She left the kitchen.

I went to bed wishing it had been a dream. I wanted to call off the trip, but my friends would go without me. I thought of sneaking off, spending the night with Brush, and I was almost out the window when I began to picture my mother tracking us down at the milo field where we hunted. The more I thought about what she had done, the angrier I became, the further from a solution. As I drifted off to sleep, occasionally an idea brushed past me, just below the surface, like the whir of Holden's wings behind my ear, but when I opened my eyes and tried to catch it, to remember harder, it flew away.

The Valley air was hot and wet, thick as the cotton lint that flocked the power lines, when Brush and Snakey arrived at one o'clock. I came out from behind the garage where I had hidden from my mother's lunch. When the Green Latrine pulled up beside me, I said, "He's coming with us."

Brush cut the engine. "Not the guy?"

My mother and Andrés approached the car, my mother following. Andrés wore my father's shell vest, the clay-colored fabric jutting from the shoulders as though it remembered my father's shape. The vest seemed to swallow Andrés, his deltoids skinny in the ample armholes. For one stupid second I thought I might cry. I took the Parker Brothers from him and put it in the trunk beside my Remington.

We got into the back seat and my mother leaned in the window. "You make the introductions, Will." She smiled at Brush and Snakey. "You boys have a good time. I'll fix you-all a big dove supper."

"Yes ma'am," they said. They tried to look busy in the front seat—Brush checking the gearshift position, Snakey patting his vest for shells—and I knew that, because of her ability to shame me, she had shamed them, too.

Our hunting place was a milo field owned by Brush's uncle. Bounded by mesquite, it provided the camouflage we thought we needed, though we knew the birds were trusting and would fly over anything. The canal was close by for the water they sought on their afternoon and evening flights, and the land was posted, so we weren't likely to meet other hunters.

The first few miles passed in silence, with Brush saying only, "Hotter than hell in a bucket." When it hit us that Andrés couldn't understand us, we loosened up.

"A wet with a gun," Brush said. "Terrific."

"Every boy's dream come true," Snakey said.

"He's Pancho Villa," I said. "Santa-fucking-Anna."
Andrés grinned at us.

"He thinks we're cute," I said. I grinned back at him.

"Just keep your eye on him," Brush said. "He's your baby."

"It's not like it's my fault."

"Same as."

When we got to the field Brush opened the trunk. We took out our guns and shells. Snakey handed around bottles of home brew. He gave me two, so I handed the extra bottle to Andrés. "*Gracias,*" he said. "*Frío.*"

I knew he meant the bottle was cold from the cooler, but I pretended I didn't understand.

We found places near the mesquite and sat, waiting for the first flyover. Andrés raised his bottle. "*Las alas blancas.*"

We knew he meant to toast the hunt, but we didn't drink with him.

"To white rats!" Brush said, and we laughed, the three of us, and drank. We made the motions of our secret handshake. I ended mine by flipping Andrés the finger.

"What a dope," I said.

We sat around in silence until a javelina shoat crashed out of the stubble at the edge of the field, surprising us.

"Oh, man," Snakey yelled. "Oh, *chinga!* Where's his mama?"

We jumped up, ready to shoot or run if the mother came squalling out of the thicket; javelinas just farrowed were a dangerous thing in the chaparral around the Valley. Andrés took aim.

"Don't," I shouted at him, but he fired a shot that I couldn't believe was anything but lucky, and the shoat fell.

"Damn," Brush said in the silence after the Parker Brothers' report.

We looked around, expecting a full-grown javelina to charge, but the pale stubble was still as the heavy air. Andrés nodded vigorously, grinned, then went to get the shoat. He brought it back, holding it by the hind legs, and offered it to me.

"No shoot, you idiot." I made flying motions. "Shoot whitewing."

"*Sí,*" he said. "*Las alas blancas.*" He gave me an encouraging smile. He extended the shoat.

I shook my head.

"Cook," he said. He rubbed his belly. "*Sabroso.*"

"Sit down," I said. "Just sit the hell down." Hot, sweating, miserable, I sat down beside a clump of huisache. My stomach gnawed at me because I'd missed lunch. Andrés sat a few yards away. Snakey passed more beer.

About three o'clock we saw the first flyover, six or seven birds, white-bellied, wing tips black as beetles against the blanched sky. "Here they come," Snakey whispered. We raised our barrels. I heard the clap from Brush's shotgun, a thinner pop from Snakey's. I squeezed the Remington's trigger, hit one.

Beside me, Andrés sat, gun across his knees. "White wing," he said when the birds wheeled and flew off.

"Why didn't he shoot?" Brush asked.

"Who the hell knows," I said.

Andrés smiled. "*Las alas blancas.* White wings."

"Right, Speedy Gonzales. Whitewing."

"*Pequeños.* Little."

"You bet, leetle. Next time shoot. Shoot the leetle white-wing."

We passed the afternoon drinking beer, trying to stay in the mesquite shade. I ridiculed Andrés, tricked him with words he didn't know, called him names. Brush and Snakey moved away. From time to time they laughed at something I said, but for the most part they left us alone.

All that wickedly hot afternoon we sat, me beside him, my insults thick as the swarms of midges around us, rising with the mercury, with our blood alcohol, until his very smell ignited me; the way he grinned and shambled for approval, his clothes, my father's vest, grew inside me until I felt strong and foul with my own sweat. I reeked with anger and I was happy in it and I

knew I was going to hit him. I stood up. "Watch this," I called
to Brush and Snakey. "Call him an asshole and he smiles. He
likes it. Call him anything. He's a goddamn puppet."

I turned to Andrés, and he stood up. "Hey there, asshole," I
said. "Whitewing?"

"*Las alas blancas,*" he agreed. "Shoot whitewing, *¿sí?*"

I took a step toward him. "Punch wetbacks. *Sí.*"

He held his hands palms up, puzzled. He looked at the sky.
"Come on, Will," Snakey said. "Lay off. It's hot."

"You don't want to do this, man," Brush said.

I ignored them, moving toward Andrés, watching his eyes.
"I'm doing it."

Brush yelled at me. "Cut it, Will!"

In that wild state where reason finally left me completely, I
held Andrés to blame when the thing I wanted least of all to
happen just then happened, when a flock of doves appeared over
the field, a host of black-tipped wings, white flash of underbelly, a hundred, maybe, more together than I had ever seen.
Snakey said, "Goddamn," broke the .410's action, loaded,
aimed. Brush picked up his Winchester, shouldered the butt.
I went for mine. "This is it," I called to Andrés. "Now you
shoot!"

He didn't move, but stood watching as the birds flew in,
eyes moving from the flock to me, the flock to me. I raised the
barrel, aimed. "Now! Shoot whitewing, dammit."

"Shut the hell up, Will," Brush said. "It doesn't matter."
Andrés didn't move.

I yelled at him. "You stupid idiot!" I crossed the distance between us and punched him in the solar plexus. His belly was
hard, but he caved in, guarding. I turned away, brought the
stock to my shoulder, raised the barrel toward the sky. "Shoot!"

I didn't hear him coming; smelled him first, beer and dirt,
sweat rancorous as mine. He stood at my right shoulder,
breathing hard, gripped my barrel with his left, swung his
right, slammed his fist into my jaw. I felt my neck wrench, lost
balance, recovered, tasted blood. Andrés drew back, spat.

I stood stock-still, my jaw inflamed and swelling, my vision scintillating whorls of sparks and blind spots, trying to focus on the flock, hold the shotgun rigid, aiming at the center; fired, broke action, loaded, fired again, again, again, felt the power that held the barrel upward and away from him, felt it buckle, give, then hold; shot and shot and shot.

We all shot, Brush, Snakey, Andrés, me; firing and reloading as the whitewing fell or swooped or scattered, and for those moments nothing mattered but explosion and recoil, aim and trigger. The doves were gone and still we fired; wild, like boys with firecrackers, until our shells were spent and pale-red cylinders on the dirt around us, our fingers stiff and crabbed, the nitrate smell of powder acrid clouds around our legs. The silence in the late afternoon resounded like the cessation of the chirr of locusts, the loudest silence.

We retrieved the birds. I walked upfield beside Andrés. His shoulders seemed to sag, and his face had gone blank and empty, nothing in it of what had happened. He didn't look at me, but fixed his gaze along the furrows, looking for felled birds. From across the field I heard the sound of Brush and Snakey arguing over which of them had shot a clutch of doves, an argument that I imagine has found a thousand subjects over the years they spent together in the Valley, but maintains its one unchanging form.

We sat around the cooler, opened beers. Brush raised his bottle, then speechless, lowered it.

"To the dumbest hunt we've ever gone on," Snakey said.

I nodded, tired, dumbstruck still. We drank. The sun looked huge and full, descending, slanting light across the milo stubble. Brush and Snakey began to clean the doves, removing each plump, grain-fed breast. Down and feathers filled the air as the pile of discarded bodies grew.

I looked again at Andrés. Moisture beaded the brown glass of his bottle, sweat runneled the dirt on his face. His head, held low, seemed to bob in an odd way, and I realized that he was laughing.

I tipped my bottle toward him. "What's the matter?"

"*Ratas blancas,*" he said. He wagged his finger at us, smiling, his teeth white and square in the dust-filled orange light. "No, no, no, *hombres.*" Again he smiled. "White rats."

"Whoo-boy," Brush said. Snakey shrugged, smirking.

Something about it—the way he sat, hunkered down in his bullfighter pants and borrowed vest, the pile of stiffening doves at his feet; the way he wagged his finger, chiding us the way old Mingo might, the way a father would; maybe just his dogged self—struck me funny. Then something about that struck me as sad, and I felt my shoulders shaking in a way I couldn't stop. Even though it seared my jaw and racked my head, awooze with beer and blood and sun, even though it made me feel as if a box of shot had spilled, was loose and skittering behind my eyes, I couldn't stop. I wasn't laughing and I wasn't crying, but I couldn't stop not doing either. I looked at Brush and Snakey to see if they were watching, but they were working at the doves and I could hardly see their faces through the feathers rising in the air.

HUEVOS

THE year my brother finally carried out the threat he'd often made, we lived in La Feria, another citrus town that banked the Rio Grande; Ben, our mother, and the Cameron-called-Punk that I was then. Our father, the silent West Virginian with the scissor-legged stride, who smelled of bourbon and Bull Durham and sometimes brought us the banderilla-toothpicks from his cafe meals, had left us several towns and years before, angling up the keel of coastal Texas toward Corpus and the offshore rigs while we moved up the border towns from Brownsville to McAllen. Our rented house was cinder block and cypress, shagged with oleander and palmetto, painted a sulphur yellow that bled and blistered in the heat and never quite concealed the black spray-painted "¡CHINGA!" on its southern side.

Ben was nearly eighteen. He had a night job working suction at the gin yard. For nine hours, sometimes ten, he stood in the big twelve-bale trailers, calf-deep in humid mounds of bolls and careless-weed, iron-rust leaves and field debris, snaking a thirty-foot vacuum pipe through stem-spiked gnarls of dirty machine-pick. Then he slept most of the day. Around four o'clock, when the sun seared the blocks on his side of the house, slicing hot stripes through the jalousies, he'd wake up, and I'd hear him pacing, lighting cigarettes, flicking lizards from the window screen with hot match tips. When I heard the clank of belt buckle that meant he was putting on his jeans, I'd turn off the television, uncap two bottles of cold Coca-Cola, and knock on his door. We'd laze around on the bed, and if he was in a good mood, he'd talk about Donna Tomlinson. I'd admire the crops of hickeys she left on his neck, and between swigs of Coke, if he wasn't looking, I'd press my cold, wet mouth into my skinny biceps to see what it felt like. I was thirteen, and when I wasn't tipped back in a kitchen chair watching cartoon reruns, I spent my time checking for sudden spurts of chest hair and thinking about the things Ben and Donna Tomlinson did to each other in the grapefruit grove behind the TexSun packing shed.

Ben's friend Jimmy Jenkins was with us one long Sunday afternoon toward the end of August. Our mother was out of town for the weekend, and we didn't expect her back until late, not until it was time for her to start her night shift at the Reno. Ben told me earlier that she and Quinn McAllister had roared off down the Matamoros shortcut in his big white Cadillac, talking about how Quinn would buy up beach property at South Padre and set her up in a real business and she'd never have to wait tables at a dump like the Reno again. Ben said it was just more big talk, more promises; what they really did on their trips was lounge around the Matamoros cantinas and swill tequila and act like they owned the King Ranch. He'd hitched a ride on a lettuce truck once, to spy on them, he said, but I didn't believe him. When Jimmy came, we sprawled in front of the oscillating fan and tried to think of something to do. Ben said there were two rules: it had to be something you could go to jail for if you got caught, and you couldn't get caught.

When I made the first suggestion, Ben flapped the back of my neck with a rolled-up *Hot Rod* magazine. "Every dickhead in the Valley climbs the water tower, Punk."

I rubbed my neck and looked at Jimmy to see if he had noticed. "So?" I said; it was my favorite word that summer and for many before it. If you said the word just right, with a sullen lift to your chin, making it two syllables with falling inflection, clipping it short at the end, it was the perfect all-purpose comeback, I thought. It started off with toughness, moved through nonchalance, gathered speed at wounded dignity, then soared toward disdain. That I had used the word many times on my brother, and mostly to no effect, in no way dimmed its shine or my hope that one day I would say it in just the right way to wound him to the quick. It would be then, by my reckoning, that we would be even.

"And my name, dickhead-Ben," I added for further weight and for the sting of correction that he hated, "is Cameron." I spelled it out for him, elongating the letters in a dim-witted slur.

Ben and I waged a war, its battleground my name. In the off-and-on years before he went to Corpus, our father had called me Punk, the way he said it giving us to know that I was his favorite. After he left, our mother stopped using the nickname. She began to call me Cameron with a determination that sometimes seemed to border on vengeance. If she slipped, she would correct herself. "I picked you-all's names without any help from him," she would say, jabbing her forefinger with its bright nail polish in a red indictment northeast toward Corpus Christi, her expression the familiar one she wore when speaking of our father, a harsh look that sometimes scared me but that even in its harshness, even after his seven-year absence, maintained its quality of hurt disbelief, "and I'll goddamn well use 'em."

She swore often. Too often, I thought; even when she talked to us, her sons, and I would feel myself flinch when she said something I didn't think a mother ought to say. But she never apologized for her language, only for using my nickname. Ben continued to call me Punk. He might have done this to flout our mother, or to show me that our father, in leaving, had passed along to him the power to define me. It was a name I'd once liked, but I'd grown to hate it, especially the way he said

140

it with an edge that let me know he was putting me in my place: four years back and always behind—younger, smaller, weaker—and I wore it unwillingly. The few times I forced him to call me Cameron, by stubbornness or pouting, I felt as though I'd stripped him of something.

"Nobody's goin' to climb it," Jimmy said, antsy, his eyes on a point somewhere between me and Ben. "They fenced it off after those little wets fell off. *Chingado,* what a mess." Jimmy laughed too hard, his big body shaking the bed and causing the springs to squeal beneath his weight.

Ben looked out the window, waiting for Jimmy to quiet down. "They got a guard dog, too."

I asked what kind.

"Who the hell cares what kind, Punk? A guard dog. D-o-g."

Jimmy elbowed Ben. "Alpo-butt Cameron cares. Remember the salvage yard?"

Ben hooted. "Doberman got himself a chunk of the stringiest *pollo* in the Valley." He reared back and flailed his legs in an imitation of the way I'd run before the dog got me. In his many performances of the incident, Ben never told how I'd nearly broken the four-minute mile across the piles of auto parts and junk, how I'd leaped six feet up onto the chain-link while he and Jimmy did an over-easy bail from their perch on the fence top, scrambling in the dust to put distance between themselves and the fence. His favorite part was that I'd screamed like an old lady: "Benny, help! It's got me, Ben!" He never tired of squinching up his voice to mimic what I'd yelled.

I shook one of his magazines open to the centerfold and pretended to study it. "Be quiet, Ben." I curled my lip in my Elvis-sneer.

When Ben stopped laughing, Jimmy said, "There's always Mexico. If you got the itch."

I decided to try out an expression I'd been saving. "Hey, we could roll on over and ream Nuevo Progreso a new one." I didn't know what it meant, just that the phrase sounded dangerous and good; ugly and powerful, tough.

Ben had narrowed his eyes. "Hot-Shot wants himself a case of turista." He flicked me under the ear with his callused middle finger. "Or maybe the crabs. You want the crabs, Punkie? You'll itch plenty. Itch and shit and bawl for your mama."

For revenge I peered at the centerfold and tried to imagine Donna Tomlinson naked, but the model was tall, blonde, and high-breasted, nothing like dark, low-slung, liquid-hipped Donna. Jimmy got up and went to the record player and put on Ben's Kingston Trio record. He swiveled his stout rear end in a dance that looked something like a hula, snapping his fingers to the clicking Spanish of "Coplas." Ben scrunched down against the headboard and lit another Winston. He blew a perfect smoke ring, jabbed the air with his finger to break the circle, then made his threat. "I'm going to split."

"Sure you will," Jimmy said, but he stopped his portly gyrations.

"I'm thinking navy."

Jimmy cut the record player's volume and looked uneasily at Ben. A bland boy who seemed to come into himself only with my brother, Jimmy took his threats as seriously as I did, though we had different ways of trying to get Ben off the subject. "Flyweight like you could never pass."

"Right," I said. "Those navy guys will take a look at your neck and think you've got a rare blood disease. Or you got attacked by giant leeches."

I started laughing and I couldn't stop, about giant leeches and about the navy doctors inspecting Ben's hickeys, scratching their doctor heads. The vision of it cracked me up. I had the crazy idea that the harder I laughed, the closer Ben would come to seeing the picture, too, and then he would laugh and forget about the navy and we could go back to being what I wanted us to be, what someone looking in, not knowing us, would think we were: two brothers in a late-summer room trying to think of a way to kill time before school started, before the daily exercises progressed to lessons, then to units, semesters, a cycle of the ordinary that left no chance for breakaway. If it meant Ben would be distracted from his talk of leaving, I wanted to laugh until September.

He shot me a look that meant I'd crossed the line. He'd take a razzing from Jimmy sometimes—Jimmy pumped him up, never laughed at him, never cut too close—but not from me. He plunked his cigarette into a bottle filled with ash-flecked sludge and peeling filters. "You watch me, Punk. Class of '63 has seen the last of Ben LaPlante."

"Come on, Ben. I just thought it was a funny idea." I tried to explain about the doctors poking at his neck, but he didn't laugh. He threw a magazine against the wall. The bright pages fluttered wildly before the magazine slipped behind the chest of drawers.

"Big seniors. Big deal. Bunch of tight-assed Holy Joes."

Jimmy shrugged and looked out the window; Ben was constricting into one of his moods; surly, violent, exciting. I knew he would do something, and when he did, we would go along, to watch, to marvel, glad not to be the objects of his rage. The Ben who walked the halls of our high school alone and quiet, closed, was just the shadow of the Ben who punched holes in walls and egged bracero trucks, heaved rotting melons from the overpass at semitrailers hauling tangerines and avocados, shouting, wild. He hated the smart-ass sons of growers and big landowners, he said. He hated their '57 Chevys and their Vettes, their white chinos, their girls, the patio parties in their big tile-roofed stucco houses on Acacia Drive, the way they looked at him. "Lower than a Meskin," he said. He hated the way we lived, what we were, and he blamed our mother.

His moods were always worse when she was gone, when she wasn't around to tease him out of his sourness, to come up behind him and squeeze him and tickle him with her hard bright nails and call him pet names—her Big Ben—until he reddened even beneath his sallow tan and I had to look away, embarrassed for them both, for Ben because he couldn't resist, like the luna moths that fluttered stupidly around the smudge pots when a norther blew in, their pale wings blacked with carbon, and for her, because she didn't see how he felt about her.

I went to the window and fiddled with the jalousie crank, trying to flash out the semaphore alphabet I learned in Scouts. I made it to G before Ben said, "Cut it out, Punk."

"No lie?" Jimmy lifted his sneakered foot and began to scratch thoughtfully at a red patch on his ankle. "Navy?"

Ben stretched. He seemed to relax, and I decided Jimmy's question had deflected the mood. He smiled. "Why the hell not?"

I'm sure Jimmy meant to turn things back toward normal, toward what any Texas boy would consider a good reason, but he said the wrong thing. "Your mama will have a cow, that's why not."

"You bet," Ben said. "A cow. She'll have a whole damn herd. Miss Crystal LaPlante." He spat the syllables of her waitress-badge name. "Edna Christine Schlegel from San Benito. They never even got married!"

I looked at Jimmy. As far as I knew, this was the first time he'd heard Ben talk about our mother; though he was busy examining the hair on his legs, I imagined I saw a rise of color to his wide forehead. "That wasn't her fault," I said. "And the Reno thought Crystal sounded better."

Ben said, "Bull. She can't help anything."

"Stop it. She's just Mama." I had been cuffed before for calling her Mama; Ben said it sounded drippy. "She's just Mom."

He slammed his elbow backward into the warped veneer of the headboard. "Then she should act like it!"

"Don't!" I had started across the room toward him. "Just shut up!" I grabbed a Coke bottle to hit him with, but when I got close enough he reached out and gripped my arm.

"Hey," he said, grinning at Jimmy, who was watching us. "A wild man! Cool it, Punk. Okay?"

He loosened his grip a little. I held still, the bottle raised. "Cameron," he said, dropping his guard, testing.

I jerked away, but the conciliatory use of my name was enough to make me sit down on the chair beside the bed.

In the few conversations we had about our mother, Ben always seemed to circle like a boxer—feinting, dancing away, jabbing again—around what he had to have known was the idea of her I insisted on maintaining, an idea he must have had once, too, but lost. And what he wanted me to do, I think, was join him in the void where he was bantam king of everything. But I was stubborn: we were fine, a mother and two sons, a little house, backslid, maybe, but a house, two jobs and school. If you tried hard enough, it could look just fine. If you remembered not to hear the late-night knocks, the whispering, the bumps and rustlings that were only the noises houses made at night, if, by the time the sun came up, you were asleep, and the footsteps on the back porch were oleander branches in the wind.

We were quiet for a while, listening to the wind slash the razor-fronds of cocopomosa against Ben's screen. Outside in the hackberry a flock of chacalacs startled the air with their buzz-saw calls. In the still intervals when the birds calmed and the wind let up, I imagined I could hear the faint pop of the red capsule-blooms of the firecracker bushes near the street. Ben rolled off the bed and rummaged in his drawer for a T-shirt. As he pulled it over his head, I noticed the corrugated stretch of his belly muscles. Though he lived on one meal a day and Coke and beer and Winstons, he was in great shape, taut and wiry. I decided that when I was old enough I'd hire on at the gin yard and see if the same thing happened to me.

"Chow, boys," he said. "Let's hit the Beer Meskin's. Then I got a plan."

"We're supposed to fix that macaroni. The note said."

Ben's tone was mocking. "'The note said.'"

We cut across the arroyo that separated our house from one of the McAllister groves and threaded our way through the orange trees and through the colonia until we came up on the back street by Tonio Garza's ramshackle restaurant. We called him "the Beer Meskin" because he sold beer to anyone who asked for it. Many nights that summer when I hung around the gin yard, Ben would call down from the suction for me to go to the Meskin's. He liked to get a buzz on, he said; it was the only way he could stand the dust and lint and noise.

I came back empty-handed the first time he sent me, but then I got the hang of it. You had to go around to the kitchen door and scratch at the punch-sprung screen. You stood in the dark dirty alley a long time, hot steam from the masa pots and the rangy smells of cabrito and menudo washing over you, scratching and scratching. When the shadowed, screen-grid face of Tonio Garza appeared, neck rolls rimed with sweat-salt and billowing out over his tight wet collar, you showed him your money. That was the signal for him to fling up his hands and swear, to bang pans and hurl cutlery and bully half-plucked chickens. If it was a slow night and he had time for a real per-formance, he'd menace you with his boning knife, jabbing at the screen. In Spanish thick and clumped as his refried beans he cursed you, all gringos, all gringo forebears from time out of mind. But if you stood your ground and held your money where he could keep an eye on it, he would relent in an elabo-rate show of tribute and surrender, lay down his knife and cup his palm crotch-high, as though hefting two enormous turkey eggs. "*Ay, huevos!*" he'd say, meaning you had the real stuff, the *cojones,* and he'd disappear into the jumble of his meat locker and emerge with two six-packs of cold Pearl. In the front part of the restaurant where contact-paper-covered tables teetered on random linoleum, the Meskin would pretend he'd never seen you before in his life.

We sat around eating chicken tacos, trying to ignore Tonio Garza's pachuco grandson Polo and his gang, who swaggered around the jukebox practicing their knife holds. Jimmy and I were still eating when Ben tipped back in his chair. Jimmy pointed to the leftovers on Ben's plate. "You going to eat that?"

Ben slid the plate toward Jimmy. He lit a cigarette and looked out the front window at a truck going by on Valencia. "Hot and loose, man."

Jimmy eyed the mashed pintos. "Mine were pretty lumpy."

"Not them, buttbreath. Me."

I slathered goat-butter on a flour tortilla, rolled it up and pretended to smoke it like a Groucho-cigar. I waggled my eyebrows. "You going to see Donna? Is that the plan?"

"Maybe. Maybe not."

"You'll see her, LaPlante," Jimmy said. He examined Ben's neck. "Your leech bites are fadin' out." He raised his forearm to his mouth and covered it with greasy smooches. "Oh, Ben, you studly thang. Oh, do it to me, Ben."

Ben grinned. "Hey, man, I can take it or leave it."

"Sure you can." Jimmy wiped his arm with a napkin. He looked at me like we were all three in on something, and I think he meant to let Ben know that what he now knew about our mother was not a big deal, that we were like a club that he was happy to be in. "Runs in the family, right?"

Ben banged forward in his chair and gripped Jimmy's arm above the elbow. I saw his knuckles whiten, the tendons rigid. "Say what you mean, Jenkins."

Polo and his gang, watching our table, edged closer, their hands near the back pockets of their black pants. I kicked Ben's leg under the table. "Stop it," I said. "Look."

He paid no attention to the pachucos. Jimmy looked, dumbfounded, at Ben's hold on his arm, then he looked at me. Across the bland, simple features of his face passed a look of vague understanding that it hurt me to look at. "Nothing, man. I don't mean anything."

"Who? Who can't take it or leave it?"

"He doesn't mean us, Ben."

Jimmy looked at me, then back at Ben. "Nobody, okay? Nobody. I was just gassin'."

Ben released his grip and sat silent, glaring. Polo relaxed his shoulders and turned back to the jukebox, his gang following. Ben reached for his wallet. "Go round back and get some brew, Punk." He flipped a five across the table.

"I don't see why I always have to do it."

His tone was exasperated. "Just do it."

I picked up the five and walked out the front door and around back.

We walked along the weed-grown railroad tracks behind the gin yard to a broken-axled flatcar where we sat to drink the beer and wait for full dark. Ben said his plan involved some timing, and it would only work in the dark.

"Any women in it?" Jimmy asked.

Ben drained his beer, then pitched the bottle against the tin siding of a trailer barn. He uncapped another. "Hell, no."

Jimmy smirked, nudging him. "Count me in, then."

Ben ignored him, shrugged. He lay back on the flatcar's oily slats, his fingers drumming on the bottle he held upright on his belt buckle. I stood up and jumped from the car, my sneakers crunching in the shell-strewn caliche of the track bed. Dizzy and weak-kneed from the beer, I tried to tightrope the rail but tripped and scrabbled on bits of limestone chat. I wanted to go home.

It was past ten when he slipped under the gin yard fence and jimmied the lock on the engine house. He came out carrying three axes.

"Is this the plan?" I asked. The axes, glinting in the light from the bulb over the gate, looked hard and sinister, weapons too dangerous for the small scene of destruction I imagined he had planned. "We have that machete at home."

"Machete won't do it," he said. He threw the gin yard padlock at a pile of scrap iron.

"Do what? What are we going to do? Quinn and Mama will be coming home. We don't have time for anything."

He looked at me. "You trust me, kemosabe, *sí?*"

"*Sí,*" I said. "I guess so."

He led us through the stands of scrub mesquite that edged the newly dusted bean fields south of town. The benzene-stench of parathion rose with every scuff of silt our sneakers made, hung cloudlike to our clothes, stung our eyes until they streamed. We passed the tumbledown houses of bracero families where packs of yellow dogs roiled growling out of gape-doored car hulks, then slunk back. The closer we came to the border, to the old Military Highway that was the shortcut to Brownsville and Matamoros, the more desolate the land-scape became, until it seemed that Ben and Jimmy and I and the coyotes yelping from the brush-fringed levee were the only living creatures on the earth.

At the place where the road curved around a bend in the river, the Army Corps of Engineers had planted lines of royal palms. With their stark trunks and dark topknots, they looked like a tunnel of tall, wild-haired ghosts. When I was younger, I wanted to ride standing up in a truckbed with a hoe handle outstretched to tap each of the close-set trees in turn, like play-ing a giant vertical xylophone or running a stick along the bars of an enormous prison.

When we reached the first tree in the line, Ben stopped. He braced his legs and ground his heels into the soft dirt, then hefted his axe and thwacked it into the palm. The fibrous wood gave easily but held the blade. He jerked it loose and swung again. He turned, axe slung back, when he became aware of Jimmy and me staring at him. "What did you-all think we were going to do with axes? Cruise Main and bash some wets?"

Shards of palm wood scattered with another blow, splinters flecking his arms. I stood back and watched him chop until the blade wedged into heartwood. "You'd better stop," I said. "It's going to fall."

He laughed. "This and sixteen more. One for every year."

Jimmy looked down the line. "You can't cut that many, man. It's a quarter mile."

"Like hell. Candles on a cake." He hacked again. "Close your eyes and make a wish." With a splintering twist the tree thumped across the blacktop in a rustle of fronds, its ragged stump-finger pointing upward into the night. He walked to the next tree.

"I hope you're satisfied!" I yelled. "You just blocked Quinn and Mama's way home!"

Again he laughed. "Now you get the picture, Punk." He poised the axe alongside the trunk. "Chop, men. It's easy."

Jimmy shook his head. "Yeah, but stupid." He dropped his axe and started across the field toward town. "You're crazy, LaPlante."

"Chickenshit!" Ben yelled after him but Jimmy didn't turn around.

I kicked the fallen tree. "Ben, let's go home. We can roll this in the ditch and just go home. Nobody even has to know."

"The whole town knows," he yelled. "The whole Valley."

"They can't," I said. "Jimmy won't say anything." I pointed across the plowed furrows. "See, he's not even half across the first field."

He raised his axe above his head and tomahawked the palm. "I'm not talking about *this*. It's her. You know it, too, Punk, but you won't admit it. You think if you pretend hard enough it won't be true. But it is."

"Isn't," I said, but it seemed suddenly that the old habit of rejoinder was all that remained of our contention, and there was no strength left in it. "It isn't!"

I picked up a clod of dirt and threw it at him. "Why can't *you* pretend?"

When I was ten and we were living in Mission, Ben had wrestled my jeans off, then tied me, yelling and ashamed, to a live oak in our front yard. Cars went by up on the highway, but none stopped, no one in them seemed to notice me, and finally I'd realized that no one could see me there in the drooping undershorts that had been Ben's, but still I fought against the knots that held my hands behind me. While I was struggling, something came to me like a great, bright picture, not like a dream with people in it but more a sense of things moving around me and beyond me, with myself outside even as I was at center, and I'd seen that what was happening—the cars, my nakedness, his laughter at me, the very air that lay heavily

over me, the highway, the house, the tree—was somehow bigger than I was, and that this was, unexplainably, both terrible
and sweet. When I'd stopped yelling and fighting, Ben had
come to untie me. I wanted that picture now, that sense, whatever it had been, but in the dark along the road, the fallen tree
across the blacktop, in the hard line of Ben's back as the clod
I'd thrown shattered into dust against his T-shirt, I couldn't
find it.

"Don't talk about it!" I yelled. "There *is* no it. You're just
mad and mean and crazy!"

He turned to look at me, and when he spoke, his voice was
gentle. "She sells it, buddy."

I stared at him. He worked the axe free.

"Chop with me," he said. "Cameron."

I didn't move.

"Chicken," he called over his shoulder, hefting the axe,
walking away. "You can't."

Mad and shaking, sick at my stomach, I walked down the
line and found a tree. "You think you know everything!"

He laughed, and in that moment I hated him. "Chop, Punk."

I didn't want to, but I chopped, and with each blow I
wanted to throw the axe and run away, or shake him and yell
that cutting down some stupid trees wouldn't make any difference. But I chopped. It was the only thing I knew to do, the
only thing he wanted from me. I chopped because he knew I
would. Harder, then, so he would know how mad he made
me, how much he scared me, how much I loved him. So that
in the fierceness of my chopping he would see these things and
the sight of them would prove him wrong, preserve us. When
my tree fell across the road, I threw the axe in the ditch and sat
beside the stump.

"Sit down and cry," he called.

"I'm not."

"Then chop," he said. "You're doing fine."

Muscles taut beneath his sweat-soaked shirt, spikes of hair
flashing across his eyes like the dark tossed tops of palms, my

brother chopped. I watched him; sweating, crazed, alive, then on fire with light when the headlights he had known would come careened around the bend, their beam cutting an arc across the pale row of palm trunks laid out like shrouded corpses. I heard the squeal of the Cadillac's tires, the tinny static of the Matamoros radio station, then yelling. In the swirling, bug-spangled glare Ben faced the car. The door flew open and Quinn jumped out. His tap-heeled boots struck the pavement like ball-peen hammers as he ran heavily toward the felled palms. When he saw Ben, he stopped.

"You better come out here, Crystal."

Her voice rose above the radio's mariachi blare. "Hold your goddamn horses, Quinn. I can't get these straps on right."

"It's your boy. The oldest."

"Quinn, you ass. It's probably some damn Meskin."

The car door opened and she climbed out, smoothing her dress over her hips. She tottered toward the trunks, wobbling in her backless heels, the outsize bows of her dress straps fluttering like blackbirds on a shaken branch. Ben stood tense and silent as she came closer, her back to the headlights, squinting into the darkness.

"Put on your glasses, Crystal," Quinn said.

"I don't have to. It's just some pachuco troublemaker." But she moved closer, peering. "Ben? That you, honey?"

He answered her—he couldn't not—and the one word seemed torn out of him. I felt my stomach buck and loosen with the sound of it. "What?"

She started toward him, shouting, her high heels pecking at the blacktop. "You little bastard!"

Though she was still too far away to strike him, she raised her fist. "Don't you know you could have killed us?"

As she ran toward him, one of her shoulder straps loosened, then came untied. One breast swung free, pale and heavy, before she faltered, clutching herself. I looked away, at Ben, who didn't look at me, whose eyes, in a look of awful triumph, never veered from hers.

He turned away and pinwheeled the axe over his head, then took the fallen trunks like a high-school hurdler. As he vaulted past me I caught his caustic smell: Pearl and Winstons, sweat, the soap-and-semen smell of corn tortillas, fading parathion, dust. I heard the rasp of breath, the catch in it when the soft soles of his sneakers hit the clear, unbroken stretch of road, running, running.

Quinn and my mother came up behind me. "Come on with us, boy," Quinn said, "we'll double back around Mercedes." I felt his hand on my shoulder and I shook it off. "I'll walk."

But I ran. Out of the headlight beam and into the dark, across the field. Gasping, shambling over furrows, I chased him. I wanted Ben, a piece of him, something more than half-remembered scent and anger; a scrap of shirt wrenched from his back, half-moon shreds of ragged skin beneath my nails, blood; Ben. My brain ran faster than my legs. I stumbled, falling headlong into the dirt. Silt and parathion seared my lungs and choked me. Dizzied, face-down, coughing, I grew bigger, stronger, older, swift enough to overtake him, tackle, wrestle him to the ground, tear him limb from limb for leaving; hit him, hit him, hit him: remember me, remember *me:* come back.

But even then I had known he wouldn't, and even then I had known I would turn around and ride back into town in the front seat between them, my mother trying to comfort me with the promise of his return. Quinn offered me a shot of his Wild Turkey—"It'll give you some stiffenin', boy"—the same Wild Turkey he would smell of every day after five o'clock for the nearly thirty years he would be my mother's husband. They would buy beach property at Padre and would prosper beyond Ben's wildest dreams of '57 Chevys and white chinos, and each time I returned from the University of Texas, it would seem that Quinn and my mother had grown so sedate there was no difference between the two of them and any other aging Anglo couple in the Valley. When Ben returned years later, haggard, road-worn, old himself, and I walked him around the property to show him the groves and canning plants we owned, the Buick dealership, when he saw our mother in her linen dresses and Italian shoes, he would see.

That this never happened, that the trace of the one thing that did—the amber burn of Quinn's bourbon at the back of my throat—is all I remember of the rest of that night, did not dim the brightness of the vision I guarded carefully, for years, until with time and distance, for lack of use, the light went out of it when one day I remembered that for months I had forgotten to keep watch for him.

On that night, on my knees, I watched him go, watched him run until he was a small, pale dot of T-shirt, then stood to hold him, running, with my eyes, until that dot stopped wavering, became a fixed and present point, a light beyond the distant, flat horizon, a constant star, its ghost.

WHAT THE THUNDER SAID

I T was winter when I first saw Call Lucas, though I'd seen
him, sure, before. Ours was more a sudden notice, like a
secret thought grown big, then bigger, till you blurt it out and
nearly jump inside your skin to hear it said. He was milking Boss, his flat man-rump on a T-bar stool, knees higher,
spraddle-legged, shouldered into Boss's flank, arm hoist round
her leg to hobble her, neck craned sideways, looking up at
nothing, at the pigeons in the rafters, then at me, at me, at
Mackie Spoon, eighteen, come in to gather eggs. His wife had
a hen that roosted in the barn, and I'd gone out to find the nest.

What we did was wrong, though there can be a way of turning something, seeing how what happens after can add up to
make it right. It was milking time, five-thirty, warm inside
from cattle, from the little things that live in hay to make it
give its own green breathing heat. The sun was tabby orange
through the slats, dust and motes around me like I'd walked
into a spangled halo, bars of orange slid across me smooth and
light as water. I smelled the warm grass smell of hay not cured
and dust and cattle, linseed oil and harness leather, swallows'
nests of mud and straw and feathers, mice, the foam of milk
from Call's pail when he set it down and milk lapped into the
dirt as he came toward me, the smell of unwashed work when

he got closer, myself in my wool coat with wet snow melting on the shoulders where it fell upon me from the eaves, myself under my dress; and we lay down in all of it, in a way that felt like all the world was gathered into one sweet skin, and though you know it's wrong, down deep, in bone and blood and muscle, you want the one thing your head tells you you're not supposed to want, and in that wanting, in that knowing it's wrong, there is a stillness at the center, calm and full and sly, that comes from knowing you will do it anyway, and you tell your head to cease its thinking, to let the bone and blood and muscle have their way; glad, for what you're doing seems the holiest of human acts. And in that time when everything's afight within you, you are whole as you will ever be, and how I knew the first went gladly out of Eden.

Call was quiet after, gave out one shiver, gathered up his pail and eased back through the stanchion bars to turn Boss out, looked back at me as though he knew me to the center yet had never seen me in his life before, and in his eyes there was a blue-eyed look of staring too long toward the sun, as though they hurt him.

I lived on the place in a little side house. I'd come up in answer to an ad to help Missus in the house. My people lived across the Oklahoma line, but I had had enough of home and of the church I had grown up in. I knew there could be something more. I knew a man could love a woman better than he loved his belt, his Bible, and the way his mouth fit round the word "abomination," that copperheads and bull snakes were a proof of nothing, that tongues of flame would not consume me if I kissed a boy whose mouth had tasted sweet and clean as broomstraw. I had my own idea of things, and so I left.

Call's was not a rich farm, mostly wheat, alfalfa, flax. He'd been hurt by the dust storms, but not as much as some. The farm was bottomland, sandy loam along the Ninnescah, and willow brakes and cottonwoods and sand plum trees had kept the damage down. Still, you could see it in the scoured look of things.

Missus was a tiny woman, bones frail as a squab's, her hair fine blonde, like chick fluff, and she wore dresses in a baby shade of blue. She was sickly, and the Hannah Circle doted on her, bringing covered dishes, cakes and pies to tempt her. They were in the kitchen with her when I got back with the eggs, twelve whites, six brown, two banty.

"Put them on the drainboard, Mackie," Missus told me. "You can wash them later."

"Try some of this peach pie, Lila," one of the ladies offered her.

"Oh, thank you, no," she said. "Maybe after while." I heard her sigh. "Right now I'm not too pert."

The Hannahs clucked around her while I stood at the sink and scalded dishes I'd let sit after supper. I felt my neck go as pink as the spots of rouge on Missus's cheeks. I'd been there four weeks then.

One of the ladies asked after her health. "Poorly," Missus said, "and tired. But I'll bear up."

"Call's so good to hire you help," another said.

"Yes," said Missus. "There's so much work, and we weren't blessed with children."

They started in on female trouble, and I tried to close my ears. I dried the dishes in a hurry, wanting to get out because I knew Call would be bringing in the house milk and I didn't want the warm new smell of it to rise into that kitchen where I stood, my head gone giddy as it ever went at any spirit hoodoo, everybody watching.

Things just went along. I worked in the house and around the yard and with the chickens. I took portions of what I cooked and ate alone at my own place, so the three of us sitting together at the table didn't happen. It was all the bumping into each other. I'd be at the sink and he'd bring in the milk to skim and there we'd be, working, breathing, so close we could smell the things we both remembered, but neither of us would speak. Neither of us acted like the other was alive, but in that ignoring there was more than if we'd tried to talk.

I made up my own world, the one I knew could be, pretending we were married, that I was the wife and he the husband, that I ran the house and saw to things in such a way that didn't need reminding. When we met each other in the barn, I stopped all my pretending and just let be, then afterwards went back to the silent way it was. I came to feel a power over Missus, that I was strong and she was weak and this was only right. I took to slamming things—her teacup at her place, a pair of scissors she had asked for—pretending accident, my slamming, and she would take it with a narrowing of eyes, but say just, "Lightly, Mackie, lightly."

This went on about a year, the three of us moving around, bumping into each other, not talking much, but busy and working, like a boxhive full of bees, until the idea of what was going on became an almost buzzing in my ears.

Then two things happened. Call took Missus to the doctor in Belle Plaine and when they came back she went to bed and didn't get up anymore. To care for her, I moved into the spare room. We put a bell beside her bed so she could call for me. She took this fine, but with her small mouth tightened, and it seemed her belly swelled as though her tumor fed itself on what it knew of me. But until the night in March when Boss had trouble calving and Call yelled out for me to come, I think she just suspected.

Boss bawled and bellowed like the earth was heaving, and we worked by lantern light to turn her calf, me kneading at her hardened belly, Call naked to the waist, his arm full up inside her, wrenching till I felt a give and shifting, slid his arm out red and warm and steaming, and we saw the baby crown. Then, above our breathing, we heard another sound, Missus's bell, but close outside, and when we looked around we saw her in her pale blue nightgown, coming through the doorway toward us in the cold, ringing, calling in a whisper. She cried that she'd forgotten something, cried because she couldn't think of what it was, and then we all three knew she knew, but none of us would say it, and so things went along with Call and me inside the house like man and wife, with Missus as our child.

"I got some broth down her," I'd tell him. "She fussed, but took it."

"She never did eat much," he'd say, and this was how we talked about her, nothing deeper, and we never talked about ourselves and what we were doing or the names we'd have to bear, but my heart sang at the way things worked out, because the second thing that happened was that I was pregnant.

It had happened one winter night the second year when I'd gone to bathe. I'd heated water at the house and carried a ewer out to my place. I lit the lamp and stood at the table washing. I heard him outside, and in my young pride and what I'd learned about desire, I'd figured out that the sight of me could stir him, so I didn't move to cover myself, only turned a bit because we still had never seen each other without clothes. When he came in, I helped him take off his things and washed him until the water went cool.

At first I just ignored the signs that even as Missus lay there I was incubating something of my own. My feet grew sore and swollen waiting on her, and I lost my breakfast soon as I could get it down, but I tried to be kind, and stopped the slamming ways. I didn't tell Call about what I was carrying, but planned to wait for it to grow big enough for him to notice and when she died do the right thing and marry me and just go on. For in that quiet grief-struck house I was happy, and the days could not be long enough. I saw the rightness of the world in everything. When the brood sow farrowed twenty piglets, I knew that number meant my age. If I gathered thirty-seven eggs, it stood for Call's. In April, lightning hit the walnut tree and forked it to the roots, and I knew this meant she would go within a month.

The Hannahs were all over us then, bringing things. More than one looked askance at me, but I kept my eyes down so they couldn't say a word against me for want of charity. "That Mackie Spoon's not missing any meals," one said, but they didn't say more because Call was known to be an upright man.

One asked me, "Where will you go when Lila passes?"

"Don't know," I said. But I knew.

"You might find a place over at the Costin farm," another said. "Bitty Costin's half worn out with all those children."

Another suggested the cafe out on the highway.

"I'll worry about it when the time comes," I said.

"Call looks bad," one said, but I said nothing.

"Feed him, Mackie," they told me. "That's all you can do."

One night in early May I sat beside her bed, sponging her with lemon water. She was wracked, her body meager as an empty grain sack, her skin the color of wet ash, gray-blue and drowned. She asked if I would put the pillow on her face, her nose and mouth, if I would hold it there. "Please, Mackie."

It was the only thing she wanted, the last thing left in her to want. For her, I wanted to, but for everything I'd wanted that I'd taken from her, I couldn't. "I can't," I said.

"A kindness. Please."

I cried into my hands, "I can't," and she cried with me, petting me and saying, "Child, I know."

Call went on about his work all through this time, but I could hear him pounding on the anvil in the toolshed late at night, I saw the blisters on his palms, the axe marks gouged like splintered wounds out on the granary floor. He stayed out of her room all that month, and though I understood it, though I didn't love him any less, I hated him a little.

I was in the kitchen after the service, after all the mourners had gone, wrapping food in dish towels and covering bowls with dinner plates when I heard a sound coming through the open windows from the barn, the way the wind would sound before the dust began to blow. I ran outside with my apron still around my middle, across the yard and toward the sound. I looked inside the barn. He was on his knees beside the hay, and I knew he'd maybe started out to pray but ended up just howling. I saw her pale blue nightgown and I saw that he was stuffing it with hay then tearing at it, stuffing it again and moaning and I watched and listened till I couldn't stand it any longer and I turned and ran with my hands over my ears and the hard weight of the baby like a stone inside me. I ran inside the house and slammed the door and cried, for me, for her, for him, for anyone who ever wanted something that was gone.

In the morning when I got up he was asleep on the floor beside her bed. I went around the kitchen quiet, fixing his breakfast. I went outside. The day was fine and beautiful. Swallows flew in and out of the barn with wisps of straw to build new nests. Off in the timber I heard the bawling of a calf. Cottonwoods were sending off their seedling puffs to gather on the clothesline wires like batting. I went to turn the chickens out, feeling wifely and washed clean as the bedding I had hung upon the line. In the air I felt a message for me that Lila was happier, and I began to feel happy for myself. I knew I could make Call happy, too, and I began to sing the "Do Lord" song—*oh, do remember me*—and I began to feel remembered in all the turning world, and when I came to the part about the home in gloryland that outshines the sun, the sun itself rose over the barn and glinted off the roof until it looked as red as flame. I took this as a sign that the world had turned itself to right again, all wrongs forgiven, and when the rooster crowed it was the trumpet blowing in the Year of Jubilee.

When I went back to the house, the door was locked. I knew better than to try the front because it was sealed shut always, since the dust storms. My suitcase was on the step. On top of it was a square white envelope, no writing on it or inside it, not my name, just five smooth twenty-dollar bills.

I've worked at every cafe from Blackwell to the Waco Wego at least once, some more. I didn't marry. I didn't tell a soul what really happened. I told my son his father was a boy I'd loved who'd moved away before he knew, and only I see Call's straight chin in my son's son. I waited thirty years for Call to speak to me, to say he knew me. I stopped the world with waiting, not to start again until he walked through the door of whatever place I worked and told me, "Mackie Spoon, I'm sorry," for I believed that day would come.

I waited for it, and in the turning of a hundred seasons I saw only Call come begging. Winters moved through springs and summers, and I waited. Sand plums fell, their ripeness gone to bruise, so he could see the shame in waste. Leaves blew from their bare and reaching branches just to show him that the wrong he'd done me was a grievous one. Frost was to remind him of a harsher cold; ice, the sharp, cracked color of his heart. But I, I would forgive him. All he had to do was ask. This moment I could see in rain, and we would then be whole again and new, and he would melt with gladness at the way I had forgiven him.

I saw him many times, caught glimpses of his truck, of him, but only once in thirty years did he look back at me, last summer when Costin's old place caught heat and burned and everybody gathered there. The barn was still burning, but the house had gone. People shone flashlights over the ash pile, but there was nothing left to see but charred wood and one lone teapot on a blackened stove. Across the ashes that had been the house, against the blaze that was the barn, stood Call. I thought I'd gone past fleshly things, but deep inside me something moved at seeing his remembered mouth. He looked at me across the burned-out house, full-face, the fire behind him hot and whipping in the wind, the flames so bright they made his eyes a shadow I could not see into, and I knew the day had come.

There is a way a summer storm will come up from the west, from mountains I have never seen but know are there, a sudden way that, seeing the dark cloud tower, you can almost think the walls of dust have come again until you feel the wind is sharp and clean and you catch the smell of coming-closer rain.

In the storm head rolling high and heavy over us, rising like a warning, there was something of a waiting, of a watching of the goings-on on earth, something in the clouds of wrong that will not be forgotten, and I waited for the lightning to appear, for the flash of reckoning that would scorch Call for what he'd done.

But on the last night I was to see him, I saw instead the message of the fool I was on earth to try to fit the signs of heaven toward the purpose of my will, and when the lightning flashed upon his eyes I saw, instead, my own, by awful trick of light, the hard and high and mighty vision of my own.

I felt my bones grow laden at the sight, with years, and with the sudden want of mercy and the very ground to hold me so I wouldn't fall, and I called out to him, "I'm sorry."

What was in him I can never know, but what was in him made him turn away.

I didn't think. I ran into the rubble and the ashes and I grabbed the teapot. The handle seared my skin but I held on and ran toward him as he walked away. The sound my throat made was a noise like none I'd ever heard—a terrible dark language or another tongue—that wouldn't cease until I threw the teapot at him, hard. It struck him in the back, a clank, a rattle hollow as a far-off clap of thunder. He stopped, stood still, began to burn, then caught himself and kept on walking into rain that came in short, quick gusts and then began to fall like rain, like only rain.

JOB'S DAUGHTERS

UNCLE had a hired hand named Larry Perkey. He came to help one year at shearing time, parking a '55 Plymouth the color of canned plums on a cedar knoll behind the house. He just stayed on, sleeping in the barn loft in summer, in a corner of the farmhouse basement in winter. He had dropped out of high school the year before, not because he wasn't smart, but because he didn't see the use of it. His mother lived alone, five miles away in the town of Renfro. He liked being outside and working with his hands, and he liked Uncle and Dotty, who had no children of their own, but who, in the summer and at holidays, filled their ample prairie house, with its wide lawns and catalpa groves, with all the nieces and nephews it could hold.

He was small, bandy-legged and muscular, with a slow smile and hair the color of ripe wheat. Often he had to "think on" things. Though he preferred the company of the boy cousins nearer his age, he suffered our group of girls benevolently, as an old dog sometimes will a litter of kittens. We called him by his last name, which was the customary form of teenage address for that time, the early sixties. We tried our fledgling wiles on him as often as we could, without appearing "forward," and we dedicated our best efforts toward the pursuit of his brown-eyed regard.

★ ★ ★

When the news from California reached our card table in the back bedroom at Dotty's Christmas dinner, my cousins and I were startled out of what had been a pleasant feud over which of us would spoon a helping of candied yams onto Perkey's plate. From the farmhouse dining room where the grown-ups sat around the big table, we'd heard our preacher uncle going on about our many blessings—love and home and family; the usual—but except to know the prayer was turning out to be a whopper, we didn't really hear what he was saying. It wasn't until Dotty came in to see if we had enough to eat that the news hit us.

Ardith, plump, oldest of us by three months, gave up her grip on the yam server to Barrie, smaller, stronger. Ardith's mouth fell open. "No!"

Barrie dropped the server and yams splattered across Dotty's crocheted tablecloth. "I don't believe it!"

"Daddy is a minister of the gospel," Ardith said. "He wouldn't lie."

Kath dabbed at the yams with her napkin, but her big hands only mashed them further into the cloth. "Nobody said he lied, Ardith."

When Perkey picked up the yam spoon and served himself, Barrie flashed a sassy look at Ardith. I made myself busy mixing cranberry sauce into a clump of stuffing and stole looks at Perkey. He seemed to pay no attention to our squabble, or to the news.

"It's just that it's so awful," Ardith said.

The news was not about the Kennedys or Cuba or Vietnam, for those far-off goings-on did not concern us. When trouble came to Renfro, Kansas, it showed itself in shapes more towering and immediate—black and simple as storm. This trouble had a name that, in our family, was as sharp as the face of sin itself, and it concerned our Uncle Hal, who had moved, after World War II, to California, and had married a woman no one had met. For these offenses, he was considered our black sheep. We cousins had seen a picture of Uncle Hal, taken in 1947 when some of the Kansas aunts and uncles went to California. In the photograph, Hal stands rakishly in front of Cliff House, grinning at the visitors. In their boxy skirts and chunk-heeled shoes, looking ill at ease, young, the aunts smile shyly back. My father, meaning to be funny, had written along the picture's border "How Okies Look to Natives!" I didn't understand his caption—which was which?—but my cousins told me that the Kansas people, naturally, stood for the natives.

Hal and his wife had four children, the oldest being Maura. We had never met her, but Dotty had told us about her: she was blonde and beautiful, an angel at the piano, and when her mother took to bed after the fourth baby came, Maura had taken over—shopping, cooking, tending to the younger boys. She had tried, Dotty said, to make things easy for her mother, but it had been too much, and Hal had had enough. There were other things, too, Dotty said, but they were grown-up things. There was to be a divorce, the first in the family, and in March he would return to Kansas with the children.

Barrie tasted her green-grape Jell-O. "I heard there's a lot of that out there." She shook her head. "You know . . . broken homes."

Kath, sitting low in Dotty's rickety sewing chair, scooted closer, bumping the table. She picked up her knife and fork and began to saw at her turkey drumstick. "I guess they're just a different kind of people than we are here."

I watched Perkey butter a slice of bread. He was a long time at the task, careful to leave no trace of butter on the knife that he placed quietly on the plate. I remembered that his mother was divorced.

My glasses had slipped down my nose, and I pushed them back up. "It's really sad," I said. "But I think it happens everywhere. To lots of people."

When my cousins looked at me, I realized that once again I'd gone against the grain of Renfro reasoning. For these offenses

I was usually forgiven—I was their cousin, after all, and it wasn't really my fault that I didn't live in Renfro—but these lapses made me feel I'd gone outside the ken, when what I'd wanted most, at thirteen, was in.

"Well, of course, it does, Jean-Ellen," Ardith said. "But only to people who . . . you know . . . trashy people." When she looked at Perkey for approval and found him paying attention only to his plate, I saw her expression shift, as though she'd just remembered, and she lowered her glance.

We didn't talk again about the news, that Christmas dinner, until the end of the day when Dotty told us everything had been decided. In March, which would be Easter vacation, Hal and the children would come to Renfro, where he and the boys would stay with Ardith's parents. We were to come out to the farm to give Maura the company of girls her own age. She was takings things hard, Dotty said, and we were to help her feel welcome in the family.

On Palm Sunday, the day before she was to arrive, we walked through the catalpa grove, scuffing our feet among the fallen heart-shaped leaves.

"What do you want to bet she's got long fingernails?" Kath said, her own bitten to the quick, knuckles swollen from her habit of cracking them.

Ardith said, "Daddy says they have weird churches in California. He said he didn't know what-all . . . Holy Rollers, Nectarines."

"Don't you mean Nazarenes?"

Ardith stiffened. "I mean Nectarine, Jean-Ellen. Just because you've got your nose in some book all the time doesn't mean you know everything. Daddy says it's every bit as much a sin to worship books as it is a graven image. And he said Nectarine." Her tone softened, and she bent to pick up a dried catalpa pod. "It's probably because of all the oranges they grow out there."

"She's probably allowed to wear makeup," Barrie fretted. "And she must be real tanned. I bet she's allowed to go out with boys."

An oldest child like Maura, with five brothers I would have happily ushered off the face of the earth, I was suspicious of her devotion to hers. "Saint Maura," I said.

Ardith fixed me with a look. "You shouldn't be talking about her like that." Kath and Barrie nodded.

Barrie, Kath, and Ardith lived in town. They went to Renfro Junior High together and reported Perkey sightings to each other, and to me when I came for family dinners. They attended Paradise Baptist together, where Uncle Ed filled the pulpit upstairs and where in the basement were held the meetings of Job's Daughters, a Masonic society for young ladies. Having worked through the Chairs—Faith, Hope, and Charity—my cousins were ready to be installed as Junior Worthy Advisors.

Much of our time the previous summer had been taken up by talk of a "color scheme" for their Installation ceremony, then a year away. They couldn't agree. Kath wanted red—they hooted her: too flashy, mannish, really. Barrie liked peach—too common. Ardith wanted lavender—old ladyish. They settled on seafoam green. Their formal gowns would be the traditional bride-white, but they would have a seafoam green cake, napkins, ribbons, and rosebud mints. I was asked to take care of the guest book, for which service I would receive a seafoam green corsage. Each cousin took me aside to suggest that I might want to buy something new to wear for the Installation, and that perhaps this something should be a little dressier than my plaid cotton jumpers. I might also want to have my bangs trimmed and think about leaving my glasses in the church kitchen.

City-dweller (we lived in a section of Wichita called the North End, as urban as a stockyard town could get), lawyer's-daughter, bookworm, lone Presbyterian among the Buxton Baptists, I was, nevertheless, by birthright eligible to be a Job's Daughter (you had to be related to a Master Mason). But, as they told me, "It's just that you live so far away. You couldn't come to meetings." They hoped I understood. I did: in goodness, pomp, devotion, lady-tact—not to mention fashion—they had gone beyond me.

"You should be thinking of ways to make her feel welcome," Ardith told me.

"What about baking her a cake?"

"Too late," Kath said.

Barrie nodded. "Dotty never bakes at night. It's bad luck."

Ardith shook her head sadly. "Oh, I just feel so *sorry* for her."

Ardith's double-edged remark set just the right tone, and I learned that we could gossip all we wanted as long as we did it in the name of pity. Lying on the beds in the upstairs room that Dotty said was to be our "dormitory" for the week, we pitied broken homes, boy-crazy California girls, wives who didn't fulfill their duties, anyone who didn't subscribe to Renfro rules, and with each fresh outpouring of pity—guided most often by Ardith, who knew exactly where to draw the fine line where one sin left off and another began—I betrayed my true opinions; worse, knew I was betraying them and toward what end. But in that warm upstairs room with my cousins lolling companionably close, I felt, for the first time, one of them.

Far into the night, we suffered sweetly from our own compassion, sadly shaking our heads, pitying our cousin, until at last the talk turned toward Perkey, sleeping two scant floors beneath us: what kind of girl would he like best, what kind of kisser might he be, would he be the same kind of fool as other boys for California girls? At midnight we staged a pajama-run across the frozen ground to the barn and back, shrieking and giggling just loud enough (we hoped) for Perkey to hear us as we hit the back porch door that led to the basement where his radio played a soft, slow "Hey, Paul," and we went to sleep after pledging to be what Ardith called "good influences" on Maura.

★ ★ ★

Our cousin's hair was blonde, but it was pallid, almost silver, and it lay thinly over what Dotty said were "Walter's ears." Walter was our grandfather, famous for his right-angle Scots ears. Still, she was delicately boned, smaller than Barrie. Her skin was pale, and she had, unlike the rest of us, the capacity to blush.

"She's flat as a pancake," Barrie whispered when the four of us had time alone in the big farmhouse bathroom.

"Look who's talking," Kath said. She cast a smirk at Barrie's chest.

Barrie sniffed. "And nobody has hair that color. It's Miss Clairol."

"Girls," said Ardith, womanly, "she's our cousin."

Kath sat on the tub rim. "Then why won't she talk to us? She just sits there like an old white mouse."

"Maybe she's shy," I offered. Having too often felt the sting of exclusion, I felt called upon to defend Maura. Also, I reasoned, if I spoke up for her this time, maybe someone would be moved to speak up for me when I was the subject of discussion, which I imagined was fairly often.

Barrie opened the medicine cabinet and took out a can of Barbasol. She squirted an arc onto the mirror and stood so the white puff of shaving cream framed her face. "Look, you guys. Me. A blonde."

"You'll have to clean that up," Ardith said.

Kath leaned back against the tile and crossed her arms over her chest. "She thinks we're hicks."

Barrie aimed the Barbasol nozzle at her. "We are not!"

"Nobody said we were." I was glad to include myself in the company of the maligned, as the charge was one they often leveled at me. "That's ridiculous."

When Barrie turned to watch the Barbasol liquefying on the mirror, Kath dropped the bomb. "Perkey likes her."

I felt the shock in my stomach, which seemed to rise into my chest, then fall.

Barrie whirled. "He does not!"

"I saw them out by his car," Kath said. "Sitting on the bumper."

Ardith slumped onto the tub rim beside Kath. "He let her sit on his chrome?"

"You didn't either see that." Barrie had narrowed her eyes at Kath.

Kath shrugged. "She was wearing his pea coat. She only brought that flimsy sweater." She picked up a bobby pin from the floor, then flipped it at Barrie. "Stop glaring at me. I'm just telling you what I saw."

"Girls," said Ardith, "stop it. We're almost Junior Worthy Advisors. We should be ashamed. We're acting like we're jealous."

"That's about half stupid," said Kath. She began to pull at her fingers, popping her knuckles in a sound that filled the quiet room.

Barrie tore off a length of toilet paper and began dabbing at the mirror. I opened a drawer in Dotty's linen chest and looked at the combs and brushes, the tubes of salve. I picked up a bottle of Mercurochrome, opened it to get a whiff of the sharp red tincture that clung to the glass wand the way I knew it would, the way I now knew I had not been the only one who had attached a hope—secret, personal, specific—to the flirting we did with Perkey. I replaced the medicine cap and shut the drawer.

We were quiet in the bathroom. The furnace kicked on, a sudden gust of hot air that set the towels stirring and made rise all the old-house mildew spores. Almost immediately, the room overheated. To break the silence, I said "My God, it's hot in here!"

Ardith gasped.

"Don't say that, Jean-Ellen," Kath said.

"What? That it's hot in here?" My glasses had fogged up, and I took them off to wipe them with my shirttail. The room looked steamy and vague.

"You know what we mean."

I put my glasses back on. "The Catholics say it all the time."

"That should tell you something, shouldn't it?"

Ardith stood. "I think we'd better pray."

"Because I said God?"

With my Renfro relations I was always afraid I would do something awful, break some rule I didn't know about, so they would have to pray for me. Many dinner plates had cooled and palms gone sweaty while Uncle Ed prayed his earnest, hopeful prayers for the members of his congregation, his family, or the benighted citizens of Renfro. Long prayers were offered up for the improved understanding of a mysterious person Uncle Ed referred to as the Man-on-the-Street. It was this Man-on-the-Street—most often living in a big city like Wichita, which Uncle Ed said was the underbelly of Babylon—who was responsible for the election of governors and presidents, for whom Uncle Ed also prayed, his prayers longer and more fervent when a Democrat held office. Though he prayed for all, he went easier on Republicans, and he laid off Eisenhower completely, the presumption being that this good Kansan already had his own hotline. Except for the Man-on-the-Street, all those Uncle Ed prayed for he mentioned by name—first, middle and last—and this was the bad part. Though I knew Uncle Ed was a good, kind man, I couldn't shake the notion that a giant yardstick might one day reach down and thwack him across his clasped knuckles for carrying tales to God, who, I imagined—if He even thought about it—didn't care much for tattletales. On this point, I wasn't really sure; the Bible offered conflicting evidence.

Worse, though, than Uncle Ed's naming of names, was the embarrassing practice I encountered summer Sundays in the basement of Paradise: the circle prayer. I had a parrot-memory for Psalms, once winning a cast-plaster replica of the Dürer hands for memorizing ninety-five of them, but I was terrified by the free-fall of out-loud group praying. On the chance that somewhere, next to the giant yardstick, maybe, there was a list of circle prayer abstainers, I always joined in, but my words seemed to jerk and lurch in spurts, rattling like gravel in a hubcap on a bumpy race toward the finish line, Amen.

Ardith, like her father, was a champion pray-er. "No," she said, "not because you said it, even though you shouldn't have. I just want to pray for all of us. So we'll do better. So we'll remember that we're Christians."

Barrie bent to straighten a ridge in the chenille rug. "In the bathroom?"

"Let's just do it," Kath said. "I'm about to roast."

We hooked ourselves up and Ardith took a deep breath. "Dear Lord, forgive us. We know You know everything and You can look into our hearts and know what's in them. Help us to forget our baser natures . . ." She sent a hard hand-squeeze around the circle. ". . . And let us welcome our poor cousin into our hearts. We just want You to know we're going to show her Your love and we wait upon You to bestow upon us Your loving kindness. Amen."

"That sure was a lot of upons," I said. It was my habit to leaven with what I thought of as a snappy, well-timed phrase any holy proceedings, thereby breaking the spell of seriousness and offering relief, I hoped, to all.

No one laughed. Barrie and Kath took their turns at the toilet while Ardith fluffed her bubble cut with a rattail comb. Sanctified and quiet, we left the bathroom and went back to Maura.

It was a long week, unlike any we had ever spent with Uncle and Dotty, unlike any we were ever to spend again. Easter was early, in March, which in our part of the country is the starkest time. It had snowed, but the wind scoured the drifts with dust and grit. Day after day, the sky was overcast. Perkey had to break the ice in the stock tanks several times, and he snapped at Kath when she asked if he would let it freeze over so we could walk on it. Dotty found a mackintosh for Maura and we took her outside to show her the farm.

None of the places we had spent so many hours in seemed to interest her. Not the rafters of the open shed we called the manger, where we staged countless nativities, once lowering

Barrie, a slip-clad angel, from a rope (we gave it up because Barrie insisted on playing Gabriel as Mary Martin); not the toolshed where, before we'd outgrown it, we had played out our more profane dramas, the ancient game we had called "Naked City." She wouldn't try the rope swing suspended from the bale winch, but kept her hands in her pockets and shivered while we swung back and forth to demonstrate how much fun it was. Had been. All our pastimes—our Kansas lives—when we saw them through her eyes, seemed leached of color and took on the drabness of the weather. Even the land-scape—our beautiful summer farm—looked suddenly mean and sparse. We told her that the gopher holes in the sand draw were rattlesnake dens. That the coyote prints around the pond were wolf tracks. But nothing impressed her. She glanced only briefly at everything we pointed out, and eventually we stopped trying.

She seemed happiest in the barn, wrapped in an army blan-ket that Perkey had given her, petting Queenie, Uncle's blind Australian shepherd, chewing on a hank of the pale hair that hung in front of her ear until it formed a dark, wet point. She smiled at Perkey when he came by on one errand or another, and now and then he would stop and sit beside her on a hay bale. They talked quietly, their heads close. What they talked about, we didn't know; divorce, we imagined, as they fell silent if we came around. At other times, the whirring of pigeons in the loft and the bleatings of the ewes with their new lambs covered the sound of their voices. She called him Larry, and one time we saw her pat his hand.

"We've tried so hard," Ardith said. "Nothing we do seems to matter. She doesn't seem to like anything we do."

"She likes *him* enough." Barrie jiggled the lid of Dotty's roasting pan so it would fit better. It was Friday afternoon and we were boiling eggs for the hunt on Sunday. "They've been out there almost an hour."

"Looks to me like he likes her back." Kath shook her head. "It's those little mouse ways."

"Yeow," I said. I had been trying to perfect the twist Renfro put on "Yeah," and I was pleased to hear that I had almost mastered it.

"Boy-howdy, you'll never catch me acting like that." Kath plunked herself into a kitchen chair and we laughed at the idea of a Kath demure.

"Boys don't really like that, anyway," Ardith said. "I read this article. It said they want a girl who's bubbly and vindictive."

"Don't you mean vivacious?"

"Jean-Ellen and her big words," said Ardith.

"Same difference," Kath said.

"Vivacious means lively," I said. "Like Brenda Lee."

"Sandra Dee."

"Debbie Reynolds."

"Annette."

"The Tasmanian Devil," I said.

Ardith shot me a look. "They want someone who isn't silly. Someone serious and good." She turned down the gas beneath the roasting pan. "It helps if you're a good cook."

Barrie smoothed one of the tucks in her blouse. "They like it if you flirt with them. Tease a little."

Ardith sighed. "I don't know what he sees in her." She lifted the pan lid and a cloud of steam filled the kitchen, fogging the windows. "What do you suppose they talk about out there?"

"Mice," Kath said, and we all laughed.

"Sheep," said Barrie, giggling.

Ardith clamped down the pan lid. "Us."

We fell silent, the only noise in the room the diminishing rattle of eggs in the bottom of the pan. Dotty, coming through the back porch door, stared at us, then laughed. "Why, you girls look as though you've seen a ghost!"

That night as we decorated eggs, the kitchen smelled of vinegar and sulphur. Uncle and Dotty had gone to town and Perkey was visiting his mother. We sat at the table gluing rickrack and sequins onto a batch of purple eggs. Maura's were prettiest, and we all told her so.

"Do all the boys out there ride skateboards?" Barrie asked. The craze had just reached Renfro.

"In Auburn, they do," she answered. "But we live out in the toolies."

"The what-ies?"

"Toolies. It's like the country, but not like here."

"The sticks," I said. Everyone looked at me.

When the eggs were done, we went to the basement for the baskets Dotty kept for the egg hunt. Perkey's corner was curtained off by blankets nailed into the joists. When Kath walked over and parted them, Maura's eyes went wide.

"Don't do that," Ardith warned, but we all crowded around Kath, peering into the shadows. A single bed was pushed against the wall beside a chest of drawers. When our eyes became accustomed to the darkness, we could make out a lamp and a clock radio. By the bed was a stack of magazines.

"I bet he's got some dirty ones."

"Barrie Kay Buxton!"

"Well, what? Do you think he does?"

From the corner of the room came a noise—Queenie's tail wagging against the pile of clothes she slept on—but we hadn't known she was there. We screamed and ran, clutching the baskets. Thumping up the stairs, knowing what we'd seen and heard but unable to stop the scramble, we got the giggles, and we returned to the kitchen out of breath.

Ardith recovered first. "Well, if that wasn't a sign to us, I've never seen one!"

"I thought old Kath was going to trample me!"

"My heart was going a mile a minute!"

Even Maura, for the first time, was laughing. "Oh, kid," she said, clutching my arm, "I almost *wet!*"

Her eyes went wide, then crinkled, and the color rose from her neck and spread across her face until it reached the tips of her ears, which looked in that moment elfin, and I knew that whatever I had thought of her before, whatever I had thought we were to each other, I now loved her. As though in that rise

of blood I saw that we were cousins, more; that we were shar-
ers of the silly heart that giggled inappropriately, that felt
things too close to the skin and needed to cover them up with
whatever it took—shyness, silence, stupid jokes, the living-in
of books—that needed the affirmation of another silly heart.

"Me, too," I said, though I hadn't felt the slightest tug in
that nether direction. I squeezed her arm. "Oh, kid, me too!"

The rest of the house was chilly, the rooms hollow-sounding
without light and family. We decided to make cocoa in the
warm kitchen and tell stories.

"There was this girl once," Barrie began, "not in our
school, but another one. She wore her hair in this terrible beehive. She was a really hoody girl. She ratted it and sprayed it
and ratted it and sprayed it and she never washed it. Not for
months. Well, one day this boy behind her is taking a test or
something and looks down on his paper and there's this thing
crawling on it, just this *thing*, and he looks around and a whole
bunch of things are crawling around on the girl's shoulders and
down the back of her blouse and they're coming in and out of
her beehive and he looks really close and it's a cockroach!"

"Ick."

Maura giggled. "Oh, kid, that makes my head itch."

Ardith mixed cocoa and sugar in a saucepan. "Well, I heard
about this girl who went to the drive-in movie with her
boyfriend. He wasn't really her boyfriend because she didn't
know him all that well, but anyway, they started making out."
She looked at me. "This was in Wichita, not here. Anyway, I
don't know if she let him touch her anywhere . . . probably
. . . but they were making out for this long, long time, and
she notices she has to go to the bathroom. She doesn't want to
tell him about it because she's too embarrassed to tell him in
the middle of making out, so she holds it. But it gets worse and
worse, and she gets even more embarrassed because she knows
if she gets out of the car now, she'll have to walk all doubled
over, so she holds it even more until pretty soon she just ex-
plodes all over the place."

"Come on, Ardith."

"No, it really happened. Her bladder burst wide open and she died right there in his arms."

I waited for Maura to look at me, then I rolled my eyes for her benefit. "How romantic."

She smiled back at me. "It's just sickening."

Ardith went to put the milk back into the refrigerator. "Stir that before it scorches, you guys. I can't do everything around here."

Maura picked up the spoon and stirred the cocoa. "That happened in California, too," she said. "Except I heard the girl's bra was unhooked and her parents found out."

Barrie shuddered.

"That's terrible." I shook my head.

"Tell the one about the hook hand, Kath," Barrie said. She stuck her finger into the cocoa, then licked it. She smiled at Maura. "This one is really awful."

Maura stopped stirring. "Is this the one where the boy finds the bloody hook stuck in the car door?"

"How do you know about it? It happened right here." Ardith took the spoon from Maura and continued stirring.

"Something like that happened near Auburn, too." Maura shivered, rubbing her arms. "It was just horrible."

We poured cups full of cocoa, then pulled chairs into a circle in the middle of the room. Kath began the story. By the time she had finished, we were clumped together, knees touching, clutching at each other and shrieking for the thrill of it. When Queenie scratched at the back porch door, we jumped. She slunk in and lay beneath the table. From time to time she sat up, alert, hackles raised, her milky eyes opaque pools.

"She hears something."

"Don't say that. You're giving me the creeps."

"No, I mean it. Shh."

"It's just the wind."

"That's no wind I ever heard."

"Quit it, Kath. I mean it."

"It's outside."

"Stop!"

"Get down," Kath whispered. "Get the lights."

By this time, all of us could hear the noise, a ferocious snarling that came from the direction of the barn. We crouched. Kath crawled over and flicked off the kitchen light. In the darkness, the noise seemed louder, closer. Queenie shook and whimpered. Maura slipped her arm around the dog. I put my hand on Queenie's head and tried to pet her.

"It's just a possum," Ardith said.

"Possum, my foot," Kath said.

"I hate it," Barrie said. "It's scaring me to death."

Kath left the circle and went to the window over the sink. We followed; it seemed better to stay together. Huddled over the sink, we peered out. For a minute I heard nothing, then I saw against the white foundation of the sheep barn an animal dragging something along the ground. The noise began again, yelping and growling, as five or six other dark forms rushed the first one.

"Coyotes," Kath said. "A pack!"

"They've got a lamb."

"Let Queenie out."

"They'd kill her."

"Think of rabies!"

"Don't open that door!"

"They wouldn't act this way unless there was something wrong with them."

"They must be starving."

The noise was suddenly louder.

"They're coming!"

"Get away from the window!"

We crouched in the dark kitchen. If we had terrified ourselves with the hook hand story, we were now hysterical. Even Kath was crying. Ardith, her face a round white moon, said, "I think we'd better pray."

179

Maura caught at my arm. Her look was quizzical, nearly comic, as though she didn't believe what she had heard, but I could only nod to her that it was all right.

There was a thump against the side of the garage, and I screamed. Ardith and Barrie grasped my hands, and Ardith began to pray.

"O Father, hear us. We know You can do anything. It was You who calmed the stormy sea. Stop the coyotes now, we pray, and keep them from us. We just pray that You will hear us and in Your infinite mercy just reach down here and just . . ."

Queenie jumped to her feet, barking.

"It's not working!"

"Shh."

We quieted, listening. The only sounds from outside were the wind and the banging of a wooden paddock gate. Ardith raised her eyes to the ceiling, but before she could speak, the noise began again, a surge of snapping and growling from the area between the house and the garage.

"Harder," Ardith screamed. "Everybody!"

We bowed our heads.

"Wait, you guys." Maura took her hands from the grips of Ardith and Kath. She laughed, a nervous, quaking giggle. "You're not really serious, are you?"

We looked at her.

"I mean, whoever heard of yoties coming inside a house?"

"What?"

"Coyotes. Whatever you call them. They're all over in California. They can't get us in here. Besides, they're more afraid of us than . . ."

The front door screen, blown open, slammed against the clapboards of the porch. Barrie screamed.

"Do you believe in God?" Ardith asked.

Maura looked around the circle. "Me?"

"Do you believe in God?"

"Well, sure, but what does that have to do with anything?"

"Do you believe He can do anything?"

"I guess so, but . . ."

"If He wanted to, He could just pick up this house right now and throw it down, right?"

"Yes, but . . ."

"You know tornadoes?" Barrie asked, her eyes narrowed. "Who do you think makes those?"

"Be quiet, Barrie," Ardith said. "Where do you go to church, Maura?" She didn't wait for an answer. "Have you accepted Christ as your personal savior?"

"I only said animals can't open doors."

"Well, have you?"

Tears welled in Maura's eyes, lucent in the darkness of the kitchen.

Ardith lowered her head and grasped our hands. "Dear Lord, Your ways are mysterious. Your wonders to perform. We see how You have brought us all together and set the coyotes outside the door. As a test for us. So we can witness to Maura. She hasn't come to accept You into her heart. Forgive her. Enter her heart tonight and take away the coyotes as surely as You rolled away the stone . . ." She faltered, panicky, looking up at us. "Help me out, you guys, or it won't work!"

Barrie's voice rose faint and breathy, apologizing for being afraid, and I saw that she was as shy with God as I was, as uncertain of her place. She prayed for help, and love, then help again, in Jesus' name, Amen.

The noise of the fight was still close and loud as Kath took her turn. I looked at Maura. She had turned away and sat clasping her knees. I couldn't see her face.

"Dear Lord," Kath prayed, "help Maura to see that with You all things are possible. Help her see how simple things can be if she would only believe. Deliver us. Amen."

Then it was my turn. I hated what we were doing, but I was afraid. I looked across the circle at Maura's back, which seemed to quiver as though she were cold. I knew she was right about coyotes not being able to get us, but in that moment, with the snarling pack outside and the confusing power of everything inside, I believed that anything was possible. And she must have doubts herself, I reasoned, or she wouldn't still be sitting with us.

"Jean-Ellen, go!" screamed Ardith. "Don't break the chain!"

Maura turned around to watch me, and I saw the look I'd seen her give to Perkey in the barn—hope and fear and sweetness, the belief that something in another person could save her. I knew we were bullying her with our prayers, but where was God? What if this was what He wanted? What if He had set the whole thing up? A test, like Ardith said. Suddenly, as I heard scrabbling in the bushes outside the back porch door, I knew that it was not a test for all of us, but for me alone, for all the times I'd prayed and hadn't meant the words I'd said. Think how He had tested Abraham, with Isaac on the altar. I was the weak link in the chain, the hinge in the door I knocked upon, the crack in the written-on wall that could send the whole house into rubble. *Mene mene tekel upharsin.* If I didn't pray now, I would be weighed in the balance and found wanting. This was the balance and the test.

But there was Maura's face, her angry, frightened, hopeful, holy face, looking at me. I could make the whole thing stop, turn on the lights or make a joke, and save her from it. I tried to think of verses that would help me do what was right. *For inasmuch as ye do this unto* . . . but the words were scrambled and mixed up.

"Hurry!" Ardith urged.

But if I had the power to make it stop, then so had Maura. What could we do if she simply stamped her foot and went upstairs? It was her fault she was weak, not mine. And maybe her weakness was part of the test; God was sometimes tricky.

We heard growling outside and Barrie screamed, "Jean-Ellen!"

I shut my eyes. "In Christ there is no east or west." The words of the hymn were first to enter my mind, though even as they spilled from my mouth I knew they sounded stupid. Not knowing what I would say next, I went on. I tried a Psalm, and in that measured, easy cadence hit my stride. From then on I was gone. Words rolled from me unstoppable as waves crashing over Pharaoh's army as I called upon the Sunday morning flannel-board pantheon: David, Daniel, Solomon; Jacob the beloved; Shadrach, Meshach and Abednego; Zacchaeus in the tree, Naomi, Ruth and Sarah, Lazarus from the Dead. Names and words and stories fed upon themselves and carried me beyond myself until there was a tension in the kitchen, a holy shock, a tighter grip of hands as the words poured forth. Brazen, I dared to offer up my cousin's name and ask forgiveness for it, to speak for the mind and soul and heart of someone else. I dared open my eyes to watch the shut-tight faces of my cousins, Maura's look of horror at me, and still went on.

"The lame shall walk," I said. "*Selah.* So be it.

"The blind shall see. Dead children rise. *Selah.*

"In Christ, coyotes open doors."

But even as I prayed, I began to wonder at myself and power, if the will behind the words was my own, not God's at all, and I felt suddenly confused, alone, and even though the words I said flowed on, beneath them ran a current: *Stop me if this isn't right. Maybe You're not really there and only in my head, our heads, only what we made You. Send me a sign. Tell me if You're really there, or else this all means nothing and we're empty and alone and mean and foolish.*

"All things are possible," a hymn title rolled toward me, "only believe."

"Stop it!" Maura screamed. "I'll say whatever you want, but stop it! I believe!" She covered her face with her hands and sat with her back to us, her narrow shoulders shaking. "Oh, God," she cried, "I hate you all."

"I think they're gone," Barrie said into the stillness in the kitchen. "I don't hear anything."

Ardith squeezed my hand. "You did it," she said. "You really did it." She tried to gather me into a teary hug, but I couldn't hug her back.

"Someone's on the back porch," Kath said. "Listen."

The door opened and we saw Perkey, the collar of his pea coat turned up. Maura rose, and it seemed she simply walked into him. While she leaned into his chest, the cold wind swirling through the open door, he held her with his still-gloved hands. We got up from the floor. Kath and Ardith tried to tell him what had happened, but he held his hand up for them to be quiet and kept his gaze on the top of Maura's head.

For a while the story passed into our canon, its focus changing with each teller. That summer at the Installation ceremony, Ardith told it as a miracle; how scared we'd been, how hard we prayed, how one of us at last forsook her outland pride to pray like there was no tomorrow, how Perkey standing at the door was like an answer, like Jesus in the nick of time. What she didn't mention, what none of us could mention, was the way he held our cousin until she was calm, then took her with him to the basement and gave her his bed, telling Uncle that he would sleep in the barn for the next few nights to watch for more coyotes, and that he never looked at us in quite the same way again.

On Sunday after the egg hunt, Maura left. Uncle Hal put her on the train to California, to her mother. Hal and the boys stayed here, where they gradually became a part of the holidays and dinners that mark the passing of our lives, and in the end, except for a touch of the faraway that seemed to cling to them, it was as though they never left.

The four of us are all still living here. Ardith and her husband have six children. She is devoted to them, but sometimes wonders why they don't appreciate the things she does for them. Kath didn't marry, and leads a capable, no-nonsense life. She directs the band at Renfro High School, the new building from which you can see, if you stand at a second story window and look east across the wheat fields bordered in Osage orange, Uncle and Dotty's empty house, now weathered to the color of dirty wool, between the two catalpas still left standing. Barrie quit school to marry a boy who later ran away, and she has brought up a boy and a girl with a tenderness and sense no one, least of all Barrie herself, would have thought possible. It is from Barrie that I continually learn that wisdom hasn't a thing to do with education.

I went away to school, and after that moved even farther. I had to move away to see the place I came from, to see how I fit into it and to learn there was a way to fit into it without becoming everything about it that I hated. I had to go away to learn that distance, in itself, does not confer superiority, or even change, that certain things, like love and home and family, are bred in the heart and not the head. But I had to go away and scorn the place I'd left, so I could later come back, knowing it for what it was, and love it, finally, in the way I'd loved it first, when it was beautiful and good, before I saw it, then love it even more for knowing what was lost.

Several years after that Easter, Perkey joined the army. In a prayer around the dinner table—we now sat in the dining room—we heard about what happened. His death was instantaneous, the letter to his mother said, and painless. Uncle Ed, who couldn't know that in a few years he himself would take a long time dying, offered up our gratitude that Perkey never knew what hit him. He prayed that Lawrence Milford Perkey had gone on to find his home in God. We raised our heads to silence, and for once I couldn't think of a funny thing to say.

This wordlessness would still be with me twenty years later, when Barrie and I went as chaperones for our daughters on the band trip Kath organized to march in the Inaugural Parade in Washington, D.C. Though it was winter, the days were fine and warm, and we tried to take in all the sights and monuments. The girls walked ahead of us down the pathway toward the last memorial. Their legs looked impossibly long in the denim skirts they wore, and their hair was done in loose, full styles we could have only dreamed of. They looked taller, stronger, more self-assured than I remembered any of us having been.

Near the bottom of one section, Barrie found a small, known name among the others.

I had to force myself to look, and when I did, though I didn't move, my body buckled with the stricken hope that was my first true prayer. I ached for there to be a heaven that would shock the prophets, an ample heaven where all that mattered was the calling—in terror, desolation, pain, in anger, grief, the memory of love, even at the final moment—of a Name, and that would be enough; a heaven into which the only ticket was a heart that once loved something good, however small, enough to fill itself, and it would be in that one full moment when the heart was known beyond all acts that it would be remembered, taken up to live forever; where everything is known, and risen hearts forgive the living for what they can't yet know; where one, the least of these or greatest, one of the thousands of his named or nameless would be there to welcome Uncle Ed into their number, thank him for his trouble even though it wasn't needed, clasp his hand and love him, saying, "Ed, you didn't know."

Though the air was bright and rarefied, the sunlight crisp, a chill seemed to rise from the riven ground.

Kath pointed out his name to our daughters. "He was from our town."

The girls stood uneasily. They were ready to move on, but seemed to know we needed something. They shook their heads and said that it was really sad.

Barrie linked her arm with mine. "He had the kindest eyes."

"Yes," I said. "He did."

We started on, and as we walked along I saw the way our shadows fit into the space between the path and wall.

We didn't see Maura again for many years after that Easter, and when we did, it was in that middle time when it seemed the world had come apart, shifted, and was just beginning to fit itself together again. We were what Dotty, if she'd been alive, would have called "young mothers," when Maura came back for her father's funeral. She was still pale blonde and small, and her face had become serene and pretty. She had twin sons the same age as my daughter, who had just begun to toddle. She kept them with her through the service. Ardith, when the four of us went to the church basement to leave our children in the nursery, remarked that she didn't think such young ones should be exposed to death and funerals, but Kath, helping with Ardith's newborn, just shrugged, and we let her comment pass.

On the nursery door, I saw a Bible verse lettered onto a sheet of construction paper: We shall not all sleep, but we shall all be changed. The verse was meant as a hectic sort of joke about all the diapers, but it struck me, and I couldn't stop thinking about the prayer circle. I asked if anyone else still thought about it.

Ardith slipped a diaper bag onto a hook. "Oh, don't be silly. That was in another life."

Kath laughed. "Jean-Ellen is the only one who'd remember such a thing."

Barrie squeezed my arm as I bent to put my daughter in a playpen. She whispered, "Who on earth did we think we were?"

I sat beside Maura at the dinner in the fellowship hall, and we talked about our children, but she seemed cool and distant. The time was never right to tell her what I wanted to say. When we said good-bye, I realized I didn't know her well enough to ask her to forgive me for that night in March. There was no funny, heartfelt way to say that I had loved her, no words to tell her that although her sacrifice—whatever it had meant to her and whatever unsaid things had lain behind it— had ransomed me for that one moment, I had been glad to see her standing there with Perkey, safe from us.

DAUGHTER OF THE MOON

THERE were two grandmothers, a tall one called Big Nana and a short one called Pye Tee. These were not their real names, of course, but what the children called them. No one could remember how the women had come by these names, but to all those gathered in the house on Locust Street in the pretty town of Enid, Oklahoma, this hardly seemed to matter. Everyone (except the children's father Stuart) was much too busy and distracted to remember that there had been a time when the grandmothers had been called by other names: Marjorie (the tall one), Lillian (the short), or Mother (both). They had become Big Nana and Pye Tee, and this was how they called each other and themselves.

Lean and brisk, Big Nana was Stuart's mother. It was she who made the children clean their plates, wash behind their ears. She saw to homework being done, piano lessons practiced, while short Pye Tee, whose plump body and thick glasses sometimes made the children think of happy, dreamy cartoon frogs, did nothing much—to Big Nana's way of thinking—except make it hard to forget the reason they were all together in the house.

Pye Tee's daughter, the children's mother, had been killed one evening on her way home from the grocery story where she had gone to buy what she hoped would be the last box of paper diapers for baby Roy and a rawhide chew shaped like a bone for Bert, who would become a dog but was then a pup, brand-new and cutting teeth on the legs of her dining room table. She had dallied just long enough to savor the store air that seemed rarefied and quiet compared to the noisy, dog-and-children, dirty-dishes air of the house on Locust Street, air she loved but sometimes needed, well, a breather from. Long enough to choose two packages of gum (sugarless) for Elizabeth and Melly, to pore over the magazine racks where she selected a book of colonial house plans, and long enough to put her Toyota wagon in the way of the pickup truck that careened through the red signal light, its driver Raymond Jolly—emphysemic, drunk—singing at the top of his dilapidated lungs (which continued to draw breath at a correctional facility in the Panhandle) a song that could have been his anthem, "Bad Moon Rising." Big Nana and Pye Tee had come to help Stuart and the children get their lives, as Big Nana put it, "back on track."

Six months had passed and things inside the house on Locust Street were not going well at all. It seemed the center that had held them all together had driven off into the night, never to return, and no one knew how to get it back. Stuart didn't even try. He spent his hours—when he wasn't at his job in the accounting department at the Santa Fe office—in the attic reading western novels. "Shoot-em-ups," Big Nana called these books. What she didn't know was that her son, father of the children, husband of Joy Ellen (dead), didn't read the books. He read one word, over and over. Sometimes it was "renegade," sometimes it was "stampede," it all depended on which word his eyes fell upon after he had eased himself into the Father's Day hammock he'd strung up between the attic rafters. "Roughshod" or "desert," the word didn't matter to Stuart, who searched among the letters and the way they fit together for an answer to what had happened in his house. From below him rose the voices of his family—Pye Tee coaxing Roy to climb down from the piano, Elizabeth and Melly squabbling over a Barbie shoe, Big Nana stepping in to mediate—but Stuart, studying his word, lying in his hammock, only closed his eyes to wait for the spaces of quiet that would surely come.

Bert the dog had grown into a hound of huge proportions, a hound of temperament so abject that he spent his days (when he wasn't slinking through the house transporting clothing he'd rescued from the hamper) in waiting at the windows. For Stuart to come home from the Santa Fe office, for Elizabeth and Melly to come home from school, for anyone who went anywhere to come back. His large head pressed against the panes, he smeared Big Nana's fresh-washed glass with his devotion, hope, and drool. His vigils filled Big Nana with rue for the day he had come into the house.

"That animal makes work," she said. She squirted Windex for what seemed like the hundredth time that week. "Look at this."

"He's crying," Melly offered. Bert was afflicted with a condition that caused his eyes to water almost constantly. Melly slipped her arm around Bert's neck, addressing his mattered eyes. "Is Bertie crying?"

The window glass squeaked beneath Big Nana's cloth. "Dogs don't cry."

"I read," said Pye Tee from the couch where she sat hemming a school dress for Elizabeth, "that they do." She held her needle above the cloth. "The article said that they . . ."

"They slobber," Big Nana said. "They chew on shoes. Piano legs." She cast a look at Bert, his ears pricked up, head cocked as though he knew he was the subject of the talk. "But they don't cry."

Pye Tee resumed sewing. "They do," she said, but she made her voice low enough so no one heard; it was important that the grandmothers get along.

But Bert's offenses were the least of all the troubles in the house on Locust Street; there were the children. Roy, now almost three, was everywhere at once, and more than the grandmothers together could keep an eye on. If Pye Tee left him in the sandbox for a minute, thinking he would go on running his plastic trucks along the roads and hills, Big Nana would look out the kitchen window to see him climbing the honeysuckle vine that grew around the power pole. If Pye Tee spread a blanket in the shade of the black walnut tree so he could play at picnic, Big Nana, weeding tomatoes in the garden, would catch him on the ladder Stuart had left propped by the garage roof.

"He's just a terror," Big Nana said one evening as the grownups sat in the den. Stuart looked at a television show while Pye Tee read a magazine. Big Nana shuffled her solitaire deck. "Every time I turn around, he's into something. He needs a leash."

Stuart shifted his gaze from the television set, but Pye Tee was first to speak. "I don't know . . . a leash?"

"We didn't use one with the girls," Stuart said.

"He's just too much," Big Nana went on. "Why, you'd have had a heart attack if you'd caught him where I caught him this afternoon." She laid out rows for her game. "A heart attack."

"He was in his bed," Pye Tee said. "I closed the door. I just ran to the basement for a minute."

"The top shelf of the cedar closet, Stuart. With all those hangers. He could have lost an eye."

"I don't know," Stuart said. "You could only use it when you took him places, right? A leash wouldn't stop him from climbing."

"I think," said Pye Tee quietly, "he's trying to find her. Climbing. Maybe he thinks he can climb up to where she's gone."

"Fiddlesticks," said Big Nana. "He's adventuresome, that's all. I'm sure he can barely remember her. In another few months, he'll have forgotten entirely." She turned up the ten of hearts, which started her on a satisfying run, the cards falling into order all the way down to the two. "He's adventuresome, that's all."

Pye Tee shifted on the couch, started to disagree, but changed her mind and held her peace.

If Stuart moved around the house as though stunned, Bert made messes and Roy was into everything, all that could be lived with. It was the little girls, Elizabeth and Melly, who pushed the trouble to its limit. Elizabeth went to third grade and Melly went to first, so the grandmothers saw them only during the time they were home, but it was when they were home that the trouble started. They quarreled. Neither ever started it, and neither ever finished it, but it seemed that half the day was spent in one uproar after another. Melly pulled Elizabeth's hair. This was because Elizabeth had hit her. Which was because Melly used Elizabeth's crayons which she hadn't asked to borrow. Because the last time Elizabeth said no. Because Melly had broken Forest Green. And so on.

"You girls," said Big Nana, exasperated, "ought to be ashamed!" She had been trying to fry chicken for supper, and the girls had brought their squabble to her. She was tired of trying to reason with them, and tired of hearing their reasons. Her ears hurt from their shrill voices; she had begun to wonder if she wasn't too old for all this. She decided to try shaming them. "You should love each other!"

Elizabeth and Melly, one's fingers in the other's hair, the other's hand clamped around one's wrist, stared at her. Ashamed? They were not ashamed. They were simply fighting, which had nothing at all to do with shame or love, and everything to do with, well, fighting.

But Big Nana, frazzled, seeing she had their attention, went on. "Shame on you," she said. "What do you think your mother would say about the way you treat each other?"

Pye Tee, in the dining room setting the table, didn't like what she was hearing. She set down the clutch of knives and forks and went into the kitchen. "Melly, Elizabeth," she said, "let Big Nana alone while she's fixing supper. Come in here and let Pye Tee tell you a story." She put her hands on their shoulders and led them from the kitchen.

The girls went with Pye Tee into the den and sat beside her on the couch, while in the kitchen Big Nana picked up the mixer and began to mash into the potatoes her opinion of Pye Tee's stories.

"When your mother was a little girl," Pye Tee began, "she had a friend named Rhonda Bean, and law, how they did quarrel . . ."

Pye Tee loved nothing better than to tell a story, whether it was real or made up. She could make herself laugh at the pranks she made her story people pull, and she loved the dear lump that sometimes rose into her throat when she got to a sad part that made it hard to go on talking for a minute or so. She told Elizabeth and Melly about the time their mother had a fight with Rhonda Bean. A famous fight, she told them, though neither fighter could remember how it started. All that mattered in the middle of it was, of course, that they were fighting. Well, they got so mad they started digging holes all over the yard. To bury each other. Pye Tee made up mad-things for the girls to say to each other, and she added details which, if they weren't precisely true, added flavor to her tale. She put in a crow that flew into the mulberry tree to perch above the girls, cawing loudly, as though to scold them. She made Rhonda Bean turn up an arrowhead in her shovel, and how jealous that had made Joy Ellen. By and by, things got so bad that Joy Ellen and Rhonda Bean began throwing dirt clods at each other, hollering and acting like wild animals, until the next thing they knew, they were laughing and they couldn't have said why. But it didn't matter, the fight was over. Until the next one.

Pye Tee felt Elizabeth and Melly relaxing into her sides, felt their quiet breathing. Roy, who had started out hanging on the back of the couch, kicking at the upholstery to pester his sisters, had fallen asleep on the afghan he'd pulled down. The smells of frying chicken and hot bread drifted into the den, and Pye Tee felt better than she had for quite a while, until Elizabeth, running her hand along the cushion Pye Tee sat on, said, "What's this wet?"

Pye Tee felt it, too, and she lifted herself a bit, then sat back down. "Oh, dear," she said.

"Did you pee?" asked Melly.

Pye Tee felt her dress. "Why, I must have. How embarrassing. How silly."

"I did that once," Melly confided. "At kindergarten."

Elizabeth, the oldest, did not admit to any such experience, but said, nevertheless, what she knew to be the right thing. "We won't tell, Pye. Don't worry." She patted Pye Tee's hand. Melly nodded gravely.

When Big Nana called them to supper, Pye Tee told the girls to say she would be a little late. She went for a cloth to clean the cushion and to change her dress, wondering how she'd come to lose control of herself.

Later, when the children were in bed, Stuart and Big Nana came into the den where Pye Tee sat on the towel she'd placed over the damp spot. She wondered if the girls had told.

Stuart, looking sheepish, began the speech they'd come to give her. "Pye Tee," he said. "Pye Tee . . ." He fidgeted with the pocket of his shirt as though to draw out matches, cigarettes, though he'd stopped smoking years before. "We think it would be better if you didn't talk so much to the children about . . ." Pye Tee felt an odd sensation in her throat, as though she'd swallowed a sponge, as he went on, "their mother. We think it upsets them."

Big Nana broke in. "Elizabeth is up there crying, Pye, and Melly has too many questions. It's hard on them."

"But they love the stories," Pye Tee said. "I think they make them feel she's still part of their lives."

"That's just the point," said Big Nana. "In the long run, it only makes it harder for them. Why, when I lost Gilson, I just kept right on going. There's nothing you can do, so why not keep right on? It's best that way."

Pye Tee straightened a bit. "You seem to forget, Big Nana, that I'm no stranger to this, either." She crossed her arms over her chest. "And I think . . ."

Big Nana moved closer to pat Pye Tee's knee. "No one is saying you shouldn't grieve," she said gently. "It's just that we think it's best for the children not to hear so much about her. Best, really, not to dwell on things."

At this moment, Pye Tee felt something happen in her heart. Something that had never happened before—not when she'd lost her husband Parker, not even when she'd learned the unholy name of Raymond Jolly. Pye Tee was a forgiving woman, a woman who believed the world turned in a way she couldn't fathom, and that everything that happened—good or bad—had its place in all the turning. She believed that bitterness of heart was nothing more than selfishness. But now, at hearing Big Nana's words, her heart had hardened. Hardened suddenly, as though it had always been waiting to happen. She knew it wasn't good to feel this way. She knew Stuart grieved for his wife with every breath, and she knew that Big Nana, for all her high-handedness, had only the children's feelings in mind. But she couldn't get her heart to come unstuck, to soften. Not now, when things felt suddenly unjust and wrong and new, not now. Later, maybe, when her pulse slowed, when she didn't feel so . . . so hot. Maybe when they were gone, not standing over her, looking at her. When she'd had time to think.

Big Nana, taking her silence as agreement, repeated their new resolve. "So we're agreed, then. No more stories." Again she patted Pye Tee's knee. "For them. And really, Pye Tee, for her."

Big Nana sat then, and turned the talk toward other things. Pye Tee could only nod, or mumble a response, and after Big Nana went upstairs to bed, Pye Tee sat for a long time in the dark, still nodding, this time at the strange and powerful *something* she knew was coming as a result of her hardened heart. Something bad.

Pye Tee had never been a drinking woman. Parker had liked a beer now and then, but Pye Tee couldn't stand the taste, preferring a sip of the dark red wine he sometimes drank with his meal on a Sunday evening. This, probably, was why it was a jug of wine she bought in her first act on the way toward the something that was going to happen. She felt strangely naughty, naughty and gleeful—almost foxy, she thought—as she poured herself a glass. She went into the den to join Stuart and Big Nana. She ignored their questioning looks and began to sip, paging through a booklet of crochet patterns.

The first glass made her feel good, the second better, and she let the crochet booklet fall from her lap. She couldn't read it anyway, the directions seemed suddenly silly, the words blurred, and besides, they hardly mattered, did they? What mattered was the crocheted thing you had when you were done—a baby cap, a bed jacket, a doily. How simple and ridiculous; she had been a fool not to understand this before. She giggled on her way to the kitchen for her third glass: wasn't "doily" the silliest of words? She must have said this aloud, but she wasn't sure; Big Nana eyed her in a way that made her think she had.

As she drank her third glass, Pye Tee brought her hand to her cheek and found her skin flushed and warm. She found she had become the wisest of women. Her legs felt firm and heavy, planted so solidly on the floor they couldn't possibly be moved, like a temple dog, she thought, a library lion. In a voice that sounded faraway, she said, "I do believe I am." The others looked at her, then away, and Pye Tee set herself to thinking: was it Brer Fox who was so tricky, or was that Brer Rabbit? She giggled; she couldn't remember. Her second act, though she had no more control over it than she'd had over her trip to buy the wine, no more control than she'd had the first time she'd done it, was to wet the couch.

The next morning Pye Tee, whose swollen head told her to sleep a little longer at the same time it told her to get up, came downstairs to a squabble that made her ears ring. In the kitchen, Big Nana was confronting Elizabeth, indignant, and Melly, crying. Roy stood on his high stool, banging a spoon against a pot, while Bert cowered by the back door, trying to make himself look small. Stuart, behind his paper, tried to make the word "amalgamated" make sense.

"Maybe it was orange juice," Big Nana suggested. "You took a glass of juice in the den and it spilled on the couch. You couldn't get it all cleaned up."

Elizabeth shook her head. "We didn't do it."

Melly wiped her nose on her sleeve.

"Roy was bone-dry this morning when he got up," Big Nana went on, "so I know he didn't do it. Maybe you girls played with Barbie's pool in there?"

The girls were silent except for Melly's sniffing.

"Well, if you girls didn't do it, suppose you tell Big Nana how that cushion got all wet? You don't mean to tell me *nobody* did it, do you?"

Pye Tee took a cup from the counter. "I did it."

Big Nana's eyes moved from Pye Tee to the girls, then back. "You're not trying to take the blame for them, are you?"

Pye Tee poured coffee, then opened a drawer to rummage for a packet of Cremora. "No."

"Well, then, what on earth . . . ?"

Pye Tee, her teeth aching, decided truth was best. "I wet myself."

Behind his paper, Stuart coughed, then got up to dress for work.

"You mean you . . ."

"Yes," Pye Tee said. "It was an accident."

Elizabeth and Melly stared at the grandmothers staring at each other. Roy, having finished his banging, chose the moment to make a leap for the counter. Big Nana was quick; she snatched him down, plunking him on the kitchen floor. "I see," she said, but she said no more until the girls had left for school and Roy was in the den building a block tower.

"Are you having trouble with your, uh, your bladder?"

Pye Tee stirred Cremora into her second cup of coffee. Her head was beginning to feel better. "I don't think so."

"Maybe you should try those things on television."

Pye Tee smiled. "Diapers?" She took a crust of Melly's toast and dunked it into her coffee. "Don't worry. Really. It was probably the wine. An accident. It won't happen again."

But it did, and Pye Tee gave up trying to guess when it would happen. She drank no more wine—the jug stayed in the cabinet, untouched—but still the lapses continued. She began to worry about the accidents, but when Big Nana brought up the subject of her "condition," she simply shrugged, assuring the other woman the problem would get better soon.

But it got worse.

"I put that plastic out, but it doesn't do any good," Big Nana complained to Stuart one evening when they were alone in the kitchen. She scrubbed at a rust spot on the sink. "No good at all."

"Is this normal?" Stuart asked.

"I hardly think so. She needs to see someone about it. A doctor."

"She hasn't?"

"She won't. I've talked to her, but she's, well, she's stubborn." Big Nana lowered her gaze as she said this. She had vowed long ago not to be a critical mother-in-law, and she believed this extended to her son's wife's mother.

Stuart shook his head sadly. Bert, cruising along the kitchen floor in the hope that something fine in the way of leftovers might present itself, was surprised and pleased to find himself the recipient of an ear-roughing and some words that sounded pleasant. "Good old boy, Bert," Stuart said. "Good old Bert."

Bert wagged his gratitude.

"Really, Stuart. She's getting to be as much trouble as the children and the dog. And she's a grown woman."

Stuart left off rubbing Bert's ears. "Maybe it will go away."

"She shouldn't be drinking. It worries me."

"She only did it once."

Big Nana's look was severe. "That we're aware of."

Pye Tee, upstairs, moving through the bedrooms gathering dirty clothes for the next day's laundry, didn't hear their conversation, but she too was thinking about her "condition." She turned the problem this way and that, looking at the what, why, when, where and how of which she was the who. It was the why that troubled her. She considered disease, but her good stout body, which always before had given her the right information, told her, No, this wasn't so. She asked herself if she was doing it on purpose, and answered, No, of course not. Her accidents were, well, accidents; she couldn't help them, could she? As Pye Tee thought, her mind sped right over blame—the idea that being forbidden to talk about her daughter had anything to do with what was going on—as though the idea were no more than a faded chalk mark on a street, until suddenly things seemed too difficult to think about. She was tired, and all she knew was that the lapses were a part of the something bad that was coming, something that she had to stop. And before she grew so addled she could hardly think at all. She set herself to considering one more time, until it came to her that in all the whys and hows, the only thing she had any control over was the where.

The next morning, Pye Tee took Roy with her to the garage, where she rummaged for the camping tent. She worked most of the morning to set it up beneath the black walnut tree in the back yard, wrestling with the flimsy threaded poles and maroon material. When she had finished, she stood off a ways to inspect her work. Fine, it looked, inviting; a dusky red dome, crisscross poles like spines of a great deep basket, overturned. When she saw Big Nana watching from the kitchen window, Pye Tee waved gaily. Inside the tent, the air was warm and musty. Roy crawled in beside her. "Pye Tee's house," he said. He lay down on the quilt she'd spread.

"The wigwam of Nokomis," said Pye Tee, remembering the Hiawatha poem. "Daughter of the Moon, Nokomis."

Dreamily, Roy waved his hands above his face. "Red air."

"Yes," Pye Tee agreed. She lay back beside him. The ground seemed to rise up to hold her, and in the moment just before she fell asleep, she was visited by the sense that she was holding something off.

As the days went by, the girls found their way into the tent. They brought toys, a doll's tea set, books, a box of raisins, and Pye Tee began to see how right her solution had been. She had no accidents in the tent, and no longer did she feel the hardened way that had caused her to buy the wine. She felt instead rather soft and dreamy about everything around her—the curve of Roy's cheek as he napped, the way Bert's tail would wag its messages, how Elizabeth's and Melly's voices formed a harmony when they spoke, a sister-sound—and in her dreamy, soft regard of these things, Pye Tee saw that deep inside the sweetness of these moments lay the promise that they would never come again. She understood that in the moments when she said, I will remember this, and this, and this, there came upon her all she needed to know of heaven and of love, and so she gave no thought to hardened hearts or blame, but was happy. No one fought, and Roy had nothing to climb, and if the children asked for stories, why, this was only natural. And so the days of late spring and early summer passed, and when evening came and Big Nana called them to supper, they neatened the tent and filed into the house.

"They're out there all the time," Big Nana remarked to Stuart one night in early June. The girls had been out of school for a week, and they hadn't pestered her to take them swimming. They hadn't, in fact, been underfoot at all. She had all the time in the world to cook and clean and launder while the children were outside with Pye Tee. "I don't like it, Stuart."

Stuart came to stand beside her at the window, looking out into the yard where along the tent sides he could see the play of flashlight beams. "I don't know," he said. "It looks kind of nice. And doesn't it keep them out of your hair?"

"It isn't healthy," Big Nana said. "And frankly, I'm worried about her. She isn't handling things. She wanders around like she's in a trance, and she's got them doing it too." She lowered her voice to a whisper. "And she's still having, uh, accidents, Stuart. The den is starting to smell bad."

Stuart let the kitchen curtain fall. "Does she do it out there?"

His mother fixed him with a look. "What on earth does that have to do with anything? How should I know?" She paused to collect herself, squeezing out a dishcloth. "All I know is that this isn't good. They've taken all their toys out there and even food. They hardly come in the house at all."

"Maybe it will pass." Stuart picked up his book and prepared to make his escape to the attic. His mother stopped him.

"Son, it's time you took part in this."

"A week," Stuart said. "Let's give it another week."

Big Nana began to scratch with her thumbnail at the rusted spot on the sink. "Really, Son, she's more trouble than she is help. The idea was to get things back to normal, and now they seem about as far from normal as . . . as . . ." Suddenly Big Nana felt the weight of all she'd tried to do for her son's family, how it always seemed that to the strong ones fell the burden of doing the right thing. She wasn't given to self-pity—hated it, in fact, especially in herself when it came to her in weak moments—but she now felt sorry for herself. She gripped the sink's edge and tried to stop her tears from welling up. "It's just that I try so hard."

She wiped at her eyes with the dishcloth. "And I'm so tired. I'm sorry, but it seems like everything I've tried to do, she undoes."

Stuart was unnerved. His mother's tears made his trip upstairs seem all the more important, as though something demanding and immediate required his attention there. He had to hurry away. Seeing weakness in his strong mother weakened him, moved him to both fear and pity, and the fear and pity, he knew, were not for her but for himself. If he started to cry now, he would never stop. But he made himself move toward his mother, and he stood still while she clung to him. "A week," he said. "Let's give it one more week." He felt wooden as a cigar store Indian, standing there with his mother's head resting on his chest, but it seemed he couldn't move, not even to put his book down so he could hold her with both arms.

But the children did not lose interest in the tent, not that week and not the next, and it seemed to Big Nana that Pye Tee grew even more raddle-headed. One night as they sat in the den, Big Nana had offered to make a hair appointment for her. Pye Tee had giggled, bringing her hands to her head as though she'd just remembered she possessed hair. There were other incidents, too—Pye Tee, thinking the bottle held dressing, had poured pancake syrup on a green salad—but it was a harmonica that pushed the situation to its conclusion.

One afternoon Roy ran into the kitchen, wanting Big Nana to reach down the Hohner harmonica Stuart kept on a shelf in the breakfront. Stuart let the children play with it, so Big Nana thought nothing of giving Roy the instrument. Seized by a burst of love for her grandson, Big Nana knelt to hug him, thinking how much he looked like Stuart at the same age, the sweet, unset face, the rooster-tail hair. "Do you want to play a song, Roy-baby?" she crooned. "Play your old Big Nana a little song."

Roy, in a hurry to get back to the tent, answered her with a wheeze of air drawn through the instrument, followed by a blast of blowing. He wrenched away from her and ran through the kitchen and out the back door, which banged behind him.

Big Nana stood up, dizzy from rising so quickly, hurt. She knew it was ridiculous, but she was struck by the unjustness of there being no reward for being strong. She saw, suddenly, that no matter how hard you tried to hold the center together, to make things right, others would pull at it until you got too tired to hold it any longer. Then they would go their way— drifting, dreamy, heedless—never thanking you, never knowing how much work went into what you'd done. Now Big Nana was angry, and her anger settled on Pye Tee in her ridiculous tent. Pye Tee who was heedless. Pye Tee who was more grasshopper than ant. Pye Tee who lured the children with . . . with *stories*. Why had it not occurred to her that this was what they were doing? Big Nana shook her head to clear it, then went toward the back door where it seemed a hand other than her own—a hand both stealthy and convinced of its own rightness—turned the knob, opened the door, then closed it quietly behind her.

The day was bright and still, the yard quiet except for a line of sparrows on the power line above the garden. Big Nana, crossing the grass toward the tent, thought, for some reason, of Indians walking, creeping, and she made her feet slide parallel across the grass. When she was close enough to hear, she stood still, listening.

"Her voice was like an angel's," Elizabeth was saying, "and she loved to sing to us. Her favorite song . . ."

Melly's voice broke in. "Her favorite song was 'Green-sleeves.'"

"Because it had her name in it," Elizabeth continued. "'Greensleeves was all my joy.'"

"Her second favorite song," Melly said, "was 'Sugar in the . . .'"

"'Sugar in the morning!'" Roy crowed. He blew a celebratory blast on the harmonica.

Big Nana felt as though the air had been knocked out of her, her worst suspicions confirmed. To hear those little voices reciting what they knew about their mother, what Pye Tee must have told them, was enough to break her heart. It was more than she could bear, and all the other woman's offenses—the wine, the sodden couch, the work she, Big Nana, had to do because Pye Tee couldn't rouse herself long enough to do what was best for the children—seemed to bore a hole into Big Nana's chest, a hole so wide and black and frightening she had to clutch herself to keep it from widening further, and she called out, "Elizabeth! Melly! Roy! Come out of there this instant!"

The sparrows fled, and it seemed the day held still, each dappled leaf-shadow held its place on the grass as Big Nana stood, waiting for the tent flap to be unzipped.

Pye Tee's face appeared in the opening. "What's wrong? You're scaring the children."

Big Nana looked at her, at her drifting gaze, the way she blinked like a toad in the sun, her frazzled hair clipped into Melly's blue barrettes. "No," she shouted. "You are!"

Big Nana heard the screech in her own voice, old and frail-sounding, cawing like a crow. She cleared her throat to try again, but when the words came out they sounded worse, a brittle croak, and she gave up, letting herself scream at them, "Get out! Get out!"

Pye Tee, alarmed by the other woman's mood, tried to make her face serene. "Oh, me-oh-my," she said, as though she'd forgotten the time, "it must be suppertime already. Run along, now. Pye Tee will come in a minute."

But she knew she wouldn't. She knew, as she watched the children filing toward the house, Big Nana shooing them along like chickens, that this was the *something*. She knew she had to go away, and that it would be for the best. She put out her hand to pet Bert, who, wavering between the movement toward the house and the warm red tent where all the smells were, had chosen to stay in the tent. Pye Tee sat in the stillness, petting Bert, then she got up and went into the house, taking care to avoid Big Nana and the children, whose voices she heard upstairs. From the refrigerator she took an apple and some cheese, and from the cupboard she took her jug of wine. Then she went back outside to her tent. She ate and drank, thinking of nothing in particular. When she felt she had eaten and sipped enough, she lay back on the quilt. "My name," she said, for no reason other than that it pleased her, "was Lillian." She cried for what seemed like a long, long time, and then she fell asleep.

When Stuart came home from work and supper was over, Big Nana sent the children to the front yard with jars to catch lightning bugs. Then she sat Stuart down for a talk. She had spent the afternoon choosing her words, among which were "mental health," "well-being," "for the best," and "back to normal." She had examined her heart, searched her reasons for even one that seemed unfair, untrue, not "for the best," but she couldn't find one. Everything her heart and mind could come up with told her Pye Tee had to go.

Stuart was not convinced. He wished the whole thing wasn't happening. He wanted time. He wondered how this would affect the children. Wasn't it too soon for other changes? Wasn't Big Nana making it sound worse than it was?

"You're not here all day like I am," Big Nana said, suddenly angry. "And even if you were, you wouldn't notice!"

Stuart blanched. "Still," he said, "I think we should talk to the children."

The children, meanwhile, had grown tired of running after the lightning bugs that seemed to blink just out of reach (except for Roy, who pursued them into bushes and the lower limbs of trees), and missing Pye Tee, had found their way to the red tent, one by one.

Pye Tee, bleary-eyed from wine and sleep and crying, greeted them, smiling. For each she poured a doll's teacup of wine, which each tasted solemnly and swallowed, not much liking it. The children gave the rest to Bert, who lapped it greedily and nosed them for more.

"Tell about her," Melly said. "That time she tried to fly."

"No," said Elizabeth. "Tell about the prairie dog."

Pye Tee made room in her lap for Roy. She cleared her throat and began. "She named it Martha Mary. Your grandpa had turned up a nest in the field he was cultivating. Prairie dogs burrow deep, you know, but somehow this one lone baby was left. He brought it in to your mother. Law, she loved that thing. Made a little bed out of a cotton box, carried it around. Every time that baby peeped, she'd pop something into its mouth— cookie, bread crust, even ham scraps; that baby loved creamed corn. Well, time went on and Martha Mary grew and she grew, until pretty soon she'd grown so fat she could hardly walk on her stumpy little legs. We'd made a place for her to sleep behind the stove where it was warm, but Martha Mary had a mind of her own. She wanted to sleep upstairs. Every night we'd tuck her in before we went to bed, but as soon as the house was quiet and she didn't think we'd notice, I'd hear *thump-bump, thump-bump,* and I'd know it was that little rascal sneaking out of her box and hoisting her fat little self up the stairs to your mother's room. Every morning, sure enough, there she'd be, old Martha

Mary, curled up like a cat at the foot of your mother's bed, and she'd open up one beady black eye at me as if to say, *I fooled you, I know where I belong.*"

Pye Tee sipped some wine from her teacup.

"Bert does that," Melly said. "Follow us."

Bert, hearing his name, thumped his tail against the tent wall as though giving his approval to his own behavior, to the simple rightness of how, when something went away, you tried to follow it. How, if you couldn't follow it, you waited, and only when nothing came of waiting did you begin to howl for it, to help it find you. From the place low in this throat that knew these things but couldn't say them, Bert whimpered softly.

Pye Tee petted his head. "Yes," she said. "He does."

"That old Martha Mary," Roy said. He picked up the harmonica and put it to this mouth to wheeze in and out in a song for Martha Mary, the sound of which moved Bert to give full voice to what he knew of missing something.

Melly laughed. "Bert says 'Aw-rooh.'"

"No," said Elizabeth. "'How-ooooo.'"

Roy slurped at the harmonica, and Bert, encouraged by the sounds, made his neck go long and sang out louder.

Pye Tee laughed. Her cup was empty, but she didn't stop to fill it, drinking, rather, from the jug. "How-rooh." She let her voice rise past the tent poles and the walnut leaves, beyond the moon, into the night.

"How-rooh," howled Elizabeth and Melly. They lay back, laughing. Pye Tee gathered her breath, gestured a count of three, then together they let out a long, loud howl that brought their father and Big Nana on the run to the back yard, to the door of the tent, where Stuart, finally, was stunned out of his stupefaction by the scene, by the smell of wine, by the vision of his children sprawled and howling, Pye Tee woozy, reared back, laughing while Bert bit at his tail, beside himself in a frenzy of delight and woe and fellow feeling.

And so it happened that Pye Tee was sent away from the house on Locust Street, first to a small hospital where the staff could find no evidence of any physical abnormality, then home to Tahlequah to live with her sister, where she passed her days pleasantly in sewing, gardening, and visiting with the friends who, if exasperating at times, came to be dearer to her as the years went by, and where she never, not even at the very end when most are troubled by such accidents, wet herself again.

The children stayed with their father and Big Nana in the pretty town of Enid, where they went to school, made friends and played and grew. Supervised at first by Big Nana, then after that good woman went to live at Willow Manor, by the gentle woman their father married—a woman they learned to love and to call Aunt Betsy (though their new half-brother called her "Mama")—the children wrote dutiful thank-you letters to their grandmother in Tahlequah when she sent them crocheted sweaters for Christmas and at birthdays. They went to see her every year, and they laughed gently along with her at how she could never seem to remember how big they were getting; later, even more gently at how she'd lost her memory for their names and faces.

Of the summer in the tent, the children remembered little, but long after Bert the dog and several of his faithful kin had gone to their reward, long after the children were grown and gone, they continued to marvel at how much they remembered of the girl who had become their mother—her favorite songs, a time she'd tried to fly, even a crow that had once scolded her— when all they could remember of Pye Tee, who must have told them these things, were her froggy glasses, her spiny handwriting on birthday cards, and an occasional, surprising jog of memory: the sharp, warm taste of wine, the way the air in certain places felt to them vaulted, still and hallowed. Sometimes, when the children were together, they would talk of this, but what they couldn't confess, even to each other, was how, in these places, when their throats had filled with lumps that had in them something of both loss and finding, what fine and silly comfort it had been to make a quiet noise—and this was the silly part, the part they would have laughed to confess—a noise that sounded, well, like howling. For Elizabeth, who went to live in Washington, this place had been the Library of Congress, where looking up, thunderstruck, she wondered why she thought of Pye. Melly, in St. Louis, felt it in the proscenium arches of old theaters, the dusky rise of velvet curtains. For Roy, it was the sky itself, the way sometimes he could lie on his sleeping bag on a ridge above Telluride, Colorado and look into the cloudless blue above him. He could unhitch his vision and the sky would drop, the distance between earth and heaven vanish.

Steve Harper

About the Author

A native Kansan, Janet Peery came to writing at the age of forty, having earlier held a succession of odd jobs—as a cocktail waitress at a supper club for seniors, as a scriptwriter for Bible school puppet shows, as an undercover agent investigating petty crime for a fast food franchise, and as a lifeguard at a small town pool. In addition, Peery has been a hospital respiratory technician and a speech and language therapist.

In 1992 she received her M.F.A. in fiction from Wichita State University. She's held fiction fellowships from Wichita State, Writers at Work, and the National Endowment for the Arts. Peery has taught creative writing at Sweet Briar College and Old Dominion University. She lives with her three daughters and is working on her first novel.